The Z Murders

The Z Murders

J. Jefferson Farjeon

With an Introduction
by Martin Edwards

Poisoned Pen Press

Originally published in London in 1932 by Collins

Published by Poisoned Pen Press in association with the British Library

First Edition 2015 First US Trade Paperback Edition

10 9 8 7 6 5 4 3 2 1

Library of Congress Catalog Card Number: 2015938526
ISBN: 9781464204913 Trade Paperback

Poisoned Pen Press
6962 E. First Ave., Ste. 103
Scottsdale, AZ 85251
www.poisonedpenpress.com
info@poisonedpenpress.com

Printed in the United States of America

Contents

Introduction

The serial killer mystery featuring a sequence of macabre and seemingly motiveless murders is often assumed to be a relatively recent phenomenon. Not so. Serial killer stories date back to the nineteenth century, and John Oxenham's "A Mystery of the Underground" (included in the British Library anthology *Capital Crimes*) sparked such alarm that it led to a temporary decline in the number of passengers travelling on the Tube. Decades later, during the Golden Age of Murder between the two world wars, serial killer mystery novels enjoyed a vogue. Today the most famous example is Agatha Christie's *The ABC Murders*, but four years before Christie's book appeared, J. Jefferson Farjeon produced a fast-paced and entertaining serial killer thriller with a title and concept taken from the other end of the alphabet—*The Z Murders*.

A passage shortly before the climactic scenes captures the appeal of the puzzle set in this kind of story: "There was not even any theory to work upon. The murders…occurred, apparently, at any time and at any place. They appeared to be motiveless and purposeless, and to form no settled scheme. Within thirty hours three tragedies had occurred, known already as 'The Z Murders' in thousands of homes, and countless anxious lips were voicing the questions, 'How many more?' 'Where will the next occur?' and 'Who will the next victim be?'"

The story opens with Richard Temperley's arrival back at Euston after a trip to the Lake District. It is early in the morning, and before moving on to his next destination, he takes refuge in a nearby hotel. So does an elderly and rather disagreeable fellow passenger, who had snored his way through the train journey. But within minutes the other man has snored for the last time—he has been shot dead while sleeping in an armchair. Temperley has a brief encounter with a beautiful young woman, but she promptly flees the scene. When the police arrive, Detective-Inspector James questions Temperley, and then shows him a token that has been discovered at the crime scene: "a small piece of enamelled metal. Its colour was crimson, and it was in the shape of the letter Z."

Fascinated by the woman, Temperley discovers that her name is Sylvia Wynne and that she lives in Chelsea. Instinct convinces him that, whatever she may have to hide, she is not a murderer. He goes in search of her, with the police (whose treatment of him throughout seems remarkably good-natured, in the circumstances) in hot pursuit. On after arriving at her studio, however, he discovers another crimson Z, lying on the carpet.

The villain, whoever he or she may be, is apparently some kind of "signature killer" (although that term had yet to be invented) but Sylvia's terrified refusal to tell Temperley what she knows, and her habit of disappearing from sight before he can save her from a mysterious fate, lead to further complications. We follow the pair on a bizarre cross-country chase, first by train and later by taxi, before Farjeon finally reveals the truth, and one of Golden Age fiction's most sinister culprits.

By compressing the action (of which there is plenty) into a day and a half, Farjeon makes sure that he never loses his grip on the reader's attention. The plotting is melodramatic, and the portrayal of the principal villain lurid, while there are regular cliff-hangers similar to those in the Paul Temple stories of Francis Durbridge, which enjoyed popularity from the mid-1930s onwards. But whereas Durbridge's approach to writing was strictly functional, Farjeon cared about his prose, and liked to spice his mysteries with dashes of humour and romance. Time and again, imaginative literary flourishes lift the writing out of the mundanity commonplace in thrillers of this period.

Joseph Jefferson Farjeon (1883–1955) published his first novel in 1924, and later in the 1920s created the character Detective X. Crook, who appeared in a long run of short stories. Crook is a reformed criminal who adopts a pseudonym to pursue a new career as a private detective. Farjeon soon became a prolific novelist, whose books are so numerous, and so varied in subject matter, that some of the genre's scholars have struggled to pin him down, while others have simply ignored him. Writing less than twenty years after Farjeon's death, Colin Watson, in his study of inter-war fiction *Snobbery with Violence*, referred to him merely as a critic and author of historical romances. Like his better-remembered sister Eleanor, Farjeon also wrote books for children. But his work had long been out of print prior to the reappearance in the British Library's Crime Classics series of *Mystery in White*, which promptly became an unexpected runaway best-seller.

Despite Farjeon's versatility, recurring patterns can be detected in some of his books. As one of his fervent admirers, Dorothy L. Sayers, said in her review of *The Windmill Mystery*: "When a young man sets out to hike through one of Mr. Jefferson Farjeon's stories he is certain of meeting (a) a girl and (b) a corpse." She added that, in his best books, "every word is entertaining" – high praise from a habitually stringent critic.

Sayers was equally complimentary about *Sinister Inn*: "The plot is a little fantastic, but not too much so; the writing is, as usual, lively and atmospheric; romance is lightly and dexterously mingled with the thrills; and the nice people are as genuinely nice as the nasty ones are engagingly nasty." Much the same might be said of *The Z Murders*, a classic serial killer mystery that until now has been unaccountably overlooked.

Martin Edwards
www.martinedwardsbooks.com

Chapter I

The Cold Grey Hour

Places, like people, have varying moods, and the moods of London are legion. Perhaps you know London best in a mood of restless toil and ceaseless purpose, or else in a spirit of nocturnal mirth and music. Perhaps your instinctive thought lingers in a dull and dreary street oppressed by the broodings of small happenings that never escape beyond front-doors; on the Embankment at dusk, with its gathering of human shadows; on the poverty of Mile End, the pathos of Regent Street, or the hard splendour of Park Lane's new palaces.

But there is one London which you may never or rarely have met. It is the London of the cold grey hour, and you are wise to miss it, for in its period of transition it has nothing gracious to offer you. The tail-end of a tired blackness. The gradual, grudging intrusion of a light not yet conscious of its purpose. The chill of empty spaces. The loneliness of eternity. Yesterday's newspaper slowly materialising on the pavement. Like a woman surprised before she has had a chance to shake off the night and beautify herself for the day, London gives no welcome to intruders at this hour. It pays them back heavily for having witnessed the ugly chaos of its re-creation.

Yet every day there are a few who, not from choice, flit silently through this ungracious hour, and nowhere is the hour more ungracious than at a railway station. If you really wish to test the depths of atmospheric depression, visit Platform No. 3 at Euston Station on an early autumn morning. The experience will try your faith, as it tried the faith of Richard Temperley when he alighted on that platform, 5 a.m., after a depressing all-night journey from the North.

It had been a peculiarly depressing journey. The earlier stages had not been enlivened by the murky Lancashire platforms through which they had glided. Shadows crept over the rowed-up milk-cans at Carnforth. Lancaster was reached in a moist gloaming; Preston, in drizzling night. At Preston, there had been a tedious change. Temperley had waited three hours for the Glasgow-London train—three hours at Preston Station on a damp Sunday evening!—and when the train had come in, it had been packed. It seemed to be suffering from a disease called People, the symptoms of which spotted the smoky, yellow-lit windows.

There had been one single minute of joy when, in the absence of a sleeper and damning the expense, Temperley had elevated his travelling status by transferring to a first-class compartment. It cost him seventeen shillings, but what was that? To stretch out fully from window to window, while elsewhere lolled the packed and perspiring humanity from which one had escaped—a sixpenny pillow behind one's head, a shilling rug over one's feet—yes, this was indeed sanctuary!

But then an elderly man had joined Temperley, occupying the other seat from window to window, and filling the newly-occupied space with grunts and snores. There had been a small dispute about fresh air. "That man and I are made of different chemicals," reflected Temperley. "How pleasant it would be to murder him!"

The thought recurred to Temperley a few hours later. And so the train, with its unequal distribution of passengers, sped through the night, rattling, thudding, snoring. It was the elderly man who did the snoring. He snored incessantly. And here, at last, was Euston, that doubtful Mecca, reached at five o'clock; and people at their worst were dribbling out on to the ill-lit platform. Fortunately ill-lit, if one dwelt on personal vanity! But, at this cold grey hour, who did?

"Are we here?" grunted the elderly man, coming jerkily out of a snore.

It was an idiotic question. "How can we be anywhere else?" thought Temperley. But the criticism, at this unintelligent moment of the morning, was as idiotic as the cause of it; so, quelling his sarcastic impulse, Temperley paused in his scrappy toilet to assure his fellow-traveller that they were here, and then completed the refastening of his collar round his tired neck.

The elderly man was in an equally ungracious mood. He sat up suddenly, in a sort of tousled stupor, and gazed at Temperley as though the whole of creation were his fault. Then he bent down to find his boots, and, failing to find them, demanded where they were.

"*I* haven't got them!" retorted Temperley, worn out.

"No need to be rude, is there?" snapped the other. "Ah! There's one, under your seat!"

And, darting an indignant hand forward, he seized an unyielding hot-water-pipe. "Damn!" he roared.

Richard Temperley smiled maliciously. London at 5 a.m. had entered into his soul. They should both have been in bed and fast asleep.

Leaving his companion to his woes, Temperley stepped out on to the platform. Then he paused, wondering vaguely how a temporarily homeless man could fill in the awkward hours between five and eight in the morning. His bachelor flat at St. John's Wood was let, and would not be free for another week. The interim was to be spent with a married sister at Richmond. Could he appear at Richmond before the servants were up and about?

A porter, accustomed to people in predicaments, intruded on his hesitation and suggested a stock remedy. "'Otel across the road, sir," he said. "You can get a shake-down there."

"Bit late to book a bedroom, isn't it?" frowned Temperley.

"Finish your sleep in the smoke-room, if you like," answered the porter. "They keep a fire going."

At first the idea seemed absurd. Walk into a hotel smoking-room at 5 a.m. and go to sleep in a leather arm-chair? Then the idea lost its absurdity, and became the logical answer to the problem. Why not? A couple of hours in a leather arm-chair before a fire that had purposely been kept up, then a bath at seven, and then breakfast at eight…

Someone went by, in the direction of the station exit. Went by with a rustle. Temperley raised his head. The faint light of a lamp glimmered momentarily upon a neat feminine back. The next instant, the back was gone. "Take your bag across, sir?" asked the porter.

Another figure went by. The elderly man. He had found his boots, and was using them. He seemed to be in a kind of fretful haste. The momentary peace evoked by the neat feminine back vanished irritably in the revived aura of those confounded boots and their confounded wearer!

The porter repeated his question. Temperley nodded. "Though why the devil," he growled, as the porter possessed himself of his bag, "we're not allowed to finish our night in the train beats me!"

The porter donned an expression of intense sympathy and understanding. It said, "Ah, if *I* were a Director, sir, things would be run on very different lines! More humane, like." The expression would have been worth an extra threepence if there had been any light to see it by.

They trooped along the platform in the wake of the lady with the neat back, and of the elderly man. Now they had reached the engine. For a moment, the engine seemed to tower above them like a tamed metal mammoth, incongruously passive. Now they had passed beyond the engine and the boundary of the buffers, and began groping their way across the broader, untenanted spaces of the station. By a silent office. A sleeping tobacco kiosk. A dead bookstall, full of little ghosts.

Suddenly Temperley shuddered. Then he turned his eyes inwards, and stared at himself. "I say—what's the matter with you?" he asked himself, accusingly.

Outside the station, it was pitch dark. This filled Temperley with fresh annoyance. He had expected some faint indication of cheer once the station had been shaken off, and he vaguely resented the lack of it. Surely the dawn might forget time-tables, and hurry a little for the sake of an all-night traveller!

"Jest across 'ere, sir," came the porter's voice. "You'll be quite comfortable."

"I hope you're not an optimist," answered Temperley.

The porter could not think of the right reply; so, with a wisdom all too rare, offered none.

A few seconds later the deserted road had been crossed, a dark square had been entered, the hotel door had been reached, and a sleepy night commissionaire was making it clear to the traveller that he was a perfectly acceptable proposition, if not a deliriously welcome one. The station porter had not lied about the smoking-room. "Lady gone in just before you," said the commissionaire. "You'll find a fire."

The luggage was stowed in the cloak-room. The porter was paid, and returned contentedly. "Along the passage, sir," instructed the commissionaire.

As Temperley turned to go along the passage, he became suddenly conscious of a figure in a corner of the entrance hall. It was the figure of the elderly man. He was bending down, as though tying his bootlaces.

The passage proved rather a long one. It broadened and narrowed, and committed various irregularities, but it maintained its principal purpose of leading unerringly to the smoking-room at the end of it. The big door of the smoking-room stood wide. Light flickered from the interior of the room. Firelight.

Reaching the door, Richard Temperley paused. He wondered why he paused; and often, afterwards, he revived the wonder. Was it because the faint outline of the lady was silhouetted against the firelight across the room? It was a large room, and the lady did not appear to be conscious of his presence in the doorway. Was it because the big arm-chair near the window did not look quite so inviting as the arm-chair by the fire? Was it because a cock with too much imagination crowed somewhere beyond the window? The crowing came faintly. It would not have been heard at all if the window had not been open a crack…No! Not these! These were not the reasons!

"But there's *some* reason" thought Temperley, unaccountably perplexed. "Otherwise I'd go straight to that chair by the window, and—"

Ah! Now he knew the reason! He had not received any check for his luggage! And suppose there was another commissionaire on duty when he left? Of course, that was it! Queer how minds worked! He would go back to the night commissionaire and raise the point. Then he would return, and take the chair by the window…

He turned, and began to retrace his way along the passage. Footsteps came towards him, from the other end. He recognised them instinctively. Again, that fretful haste! The two men who had shared a first-class compartment from Preston passed each other in the dimness of the corridor. One went on to the smoking-room. The other returned to the entrance hall and spoke about his luggage.

The commissionaire seemed a little hurt. The luggage? That was safe enough! There was no need for any ticket. Of course, a receipt could be made out, if required…

"All right," said Temperley. "I'm not worrying. Just wanted to make sure of the procedure, that's all."

He wondered why he had taken all this unnecessary trouble. His brain must be tired. Damn night journeys!

Oh, well, never mind. Here he was in the passage again, travelling its length for the third time, and soon he would be snoozing comfortably in an arm-chair. Which arm-chair? Not the one by the fire. The lady would be in that. The one by the window? The elderly man might be in that. In that case he'd have to find another somewhere. Now he came to think of it, he believed the room was bristling with arm-chairs! What a fuss over nothing!

Clang! The quarter-hour. A quarter-past five.

He neared the smoking-room door. As he did so, a figure appeared suddenly in the aperture. It was the lady. She was hurrying out. For an instant, as she passed him, they were within inches of each other. He caught a sense of fragrance, and also something far more interesting—a glimpse of her face. It was a beautiful face, and no less beautiful for the vague trouble in it.

Now she was gone, and Temperley was looking into the smoking-room again. This time the arm-chair by the window was occupied, and the arm-chair by the fire was empty. "Good!" thought Temperley. "I'm in luck!"

He tiptoed across to the arm-chair by the fire. He tiptoed quietly, with a ridiculous feeling that, if he made a noise, the elderly man in the arm-chair by the window would spring up and get to the better arm-chair first! The elderly man did not move, however. Already, he was asleep.

With a sigh of content, Temperley sank down in the comfortable leather. Yes, even though leather, it seemed comfortable. He was desperately tired. Why was he so tired? Why so oppressed? His health was generally proof against far more than he had been through during the past twelve hours. He had a queer sensation, however, that this night journey had been of a particularly nerve-racking kind, even though he could not discover any logical reason for the sensation. All he knew was that he wanted the light to come—wanted to get the occasion behind him—and then, when the new day dawned…

All at once he sat up. The room was pressing him down. He discovered that he was bathed in perspiration. "*Why the devil isn't that chap snoring*?" He gasped.

But something whispered the answer as he asked the question. The elderly man in the arm-chair by the window was dead.

Chapter II

The First Murder

While life had reigned, the hotel smoking-room had been a dead place. Now death had come, it suddenly grew alive. Faces materialised out of the pale light, voices exclaimed or whispered, and figures flitted restlessly.

Temperley was never quite certain how this necessary agitation had accumulated so swiftly, or how it had grown from a shapeless thing to a functioning organisation. He supposed he must have cried out on making his gruesome discovery. Yes, when harping back afterwards, he remembered finding himself at the door, calling to the commissionaire, and then turning and pointing to the arm-chair by the window with its gruesome occupant. But the memory was distorted and hazy, for through it ran the confusion of a fatigued and violently startled man, and also a queer, quite separate agitation for which at first he could not account.

Then he realised that the agitation was due to the abrupt departure of the lady from the smoking-room, and to the ominous persistence of her absence. Why was not her face here, among the rest?

The night-commissionaire's face—there it was, rising like a pale ghost above the little gleams of the official collar. A sleepy maid's face, flushed with nightmare; a callow youth's face, with a smear of boot-blacking on it; a tall man's, wagging over a once-resplendent dressing-gown; a constable's. These faces and others bobbed round the room, augmenting like mushrooms after rain. But the lady's face was not among them, and Temperley would have given five pounds to have seen it there…

"Why am I worrying?" he wondered suddenly. "What the devil does she matter to *me*?"

And now to the facial gallery came two further additions. One was elderly and grave. The second was also elderly, but had a sharper quality.

"Stand away, there!" came the constable's voice, quiet and important. During a short temporary lull before the arrival of the newcomers, the constable had stationed himself by the dead man as though to make sure that no one brought him to life again. Now he stepped aside, respectfully deferential towards those for whom he had cleared a path.

The newcomers reached the arm-chair, and stood for a few seconds regarding its limp contents. The second man transferred his gaze to the first man and raised his eyebrows. The first man, aware of the interrogation out of the corner of his eye, nodded.

"Dead," he said, laconically.

"No doubt about it, doctor," agreed the other, who had merely been awaiting the surgeon's verdict as a matter of procedure. "Shot."

Standing in the shadows, Temperley started slightly. Shot? He had heard nothing…

"Bull through the heart," replied the doctor, as he bent closer. "Well—it's a quick way to go, inspector. Some I know wouldn't mind."

"All depends on whether you're ready to go," grunted the inspector, his gaze now roaming towards the window. "As he's past helping, you won't want to move him till he's been photographed, will you?"

"That suits me," answered the surgeon. "My job's simple." The brief examination of the one individual beyond all personal interest in it concluded, and the inspector turned away. He gave a few instructions. Then: "May I have a few words with the man who was with—who found him?" he asked.

Temperley stepped forward. One's mind is over-receptive and over-sensitive at poignant moments, and Temperley's recorded three unrelated facts as he advanced. One was that a constable now stood guarding the smoking-room doorway. He seemed like a gate. Another was that the inspector-detective had an inch of white thread on his shoulder. The third was that the smear of blacking on the callow youth's cheek had grown from the shape of a small black apple to a long grey banana; but whether this were due to the oppressive heat of the room or the working of an agitated finger on fleshy canvas, Temperley did not know.

"Ah," said the inspector, subjecting him to a glance that merely appeared to be casual. "May I know your name, sir?"

"Richard Temperley," answered Temperley.

"Thank you," murmured the inspector, noting the fact on paper. "You are staying here?"

"Only for an hour or two," replied Temperley. "I'll explain that."

"Yes, please do," said the inspector. "And how about a couple of chairs? There's no need for us to be uncomfortable."

He motioned to the constable inside the room, and a space was cleared where the conversation could proceed with some semblance of privacy. Temperley found himself back in the arm-chair by the fire, while the inspector shoved another opposite him, and sat down in it.

"How would you like me to do it, inspector?" inquired Temperley, who had been thinking hard during the interim. "In my own words, or will you help me with questions? This is the first murder I've ever been present at, so you must excuse me if I'm a bit green."

"I can see you're green," responded the inspector, not unsympathetically, "or you'd be more careful of the words you use."

"What have I said?"

"You said you were present at the murder."

"Oh, I see." Temperley paused. "Well, I'll amend that, if I may. I don't know whether I was present or not." A sudden thought came to him. "No—I *couldn't* have been!" he exclaimed, impulsively. "That shot—I never heard it." He paused again. The inspector was watching him closely. "Unless—"

"Yes, Mr. Temperley. Unless?"

"Unless I was dozing," concluded Temperley, rather lamely.

"And the shot woke you up?"

"Yes."

"The noise was not recorded, however, in your waking dream."

"How do *you* know?"

"You'd have mentioned it, obviously."

"So I would. No—I heard nothing—either waking or dreaming."

"Do you deduce anything from that?"

"What do you mean?"

As Temperley asked the question and found the inspector's eyes boring into him with a sort of grave persistence, he began to realise the personality he was dealing with for the first time. This was no ordinary official. The inspector was a human being struggling through a queer and difficult world side by side with other human beings, and conscientiously carrying out his particular job. Relentless in his duty, perhaps, but sympathetic behind the relentlessness. So, at least, Temperley judged him at this moment; and, in the strange battle that was to ensue between them, he had many subsequent opportunities of testing this judgment.

Whether the judgment were right or wrong, the immediate result of it was to lighten a little the load on Temperley's mind, and to render him more natural. But he did not like the theory towards which the inspector seemed to be working—the theory that the murder had been committed before Temperley had entered the smoking-room...and before the lady had left it...

"What I mean is this," the inspector's voice broke in on his thoughts. "Some guns bite without barking."

"A silencer!" exclaimed Temperley, quickly.

The inspector noted his relief.

"Yes, this shot was probably one of the silent kind. But before I advance my theories, let me know your facts, Mr. Temperley. You said you were staying here only a few hours?"

"Yes, I've just come off the night-train from Preston."

"Five a.m.?"

"That's right."

"Glasgow train, isn't it?"

"I think so, but I only joined it at Preston."

"And—before that?"

"Windermere."

"On a holiday, eh?"

"Yes."

"I see. Well, and when your train arrived at Euston—"

"Wait a minute, inspector. We must go back to Preston."

"Oh?"

"The dead man and I shared a first-class compartment from Preston."

Fresh interest shot into the inspector's eyes at this information. "You know him, then?" he demanded.

"Merely as a snoring travelling companion," answered Temperley, and added, with a faint smile, "People who snore annoy me, inspector, but I don't shoot them."

If the inspector thought this funny, his face studiously avoided recording the fact. "Did anything that might bear upon this case occur on the journey?" he asked.

"Nothing," Temperley assured him.

"Or when you got to Euston?"

"Nothing."

"Who left the compartment first?"

"I did."

"Yes? And then?"

"He passed me while I was talking to a porter."

"Go on."

"The porter suggested I should finish my sleep here, in this room."

"Yes?"

"Apparently, he—the dead man—had the same idea. He was in the hotel entrance when I arrived. I went to the room—this room—"

"Wait! Did he precede you?"

"No."

"Why not?"

"He was tying up a boot-lace."

"Where?"

"In the entrance."

"I see. So you entered the smoking-room first?"

"Yes."

"And found it empty?"

"Damn!" thought Temperley. "Now we're coming to it! But it's ridiculous. A girl like that could never—"

"I know a lady was in the room before you," came the inspector's voice, "so you needn't be gallant."

"How do you know?" demanded Temperley, reddening slightly.

The inspector shrugged his shoulders, as though deprecating the world's lack of faith in his kind.

"You're not the first person I've spoken to," he said. "Where was this lady when you entered?"

"She was standing by the fire," murmured Temperley. "By this chair I'm now sitting on."

"In what sort of position?"

"How do you mean?"

"At ease? Strained? Agitated?"

"It was too dim to see."

"But, surely? When you drew closer?"

"I didn't draw closer."

"Why not?"

"I went back to the hall."

"Why?"

Temperley hesitated. Then he blurted out,

"This may sound a bit silly but I'm telling you the truth—"

"Nothing else is of any use to me."

"Exactly. That's why you're getting it. I went back to make an inquiry about my luggage. The night-porter will corroborate this. Also, that it was a quite unnecessary inquiry. I haven't any earthly idea why I asked it."

"What was it?"

"Just to know if I needed a check for my luggage."

"That doesn't seem so extraordinary."

"Perhaps not. But, the impulse—just at that particular moment! You see, if I'd stayed—"

He paused. But not till later did he have any knowledge of what might have happened had he stayed. And, when the knowledge came, his forehead grew damp.

"Well—if you'd stayed, Mr. Temperley," queried the inspector, after a pause.

"Perhaps I might have—prevented it!"

"How? The dead man was not in the smoking-room when you returned to the night-porter!" Temperley was silent. He felt he was saying too much. "Where *was* he?" pressed the inspector. "Still in the hotel entrance?"

"No."

"Where then?"

"We passed each other in the passage."

"Oh. Then he was in the smoking-room immediately *after* you left?"

"Yes."

"Where, also, was the lady?"

"Yes."

"What was his attitude when you passed each other in the passage?"

"Attitude? Oh—fretful—as it had always been."

"Nothing significant, then?"

"No."

"Did you speak to each other?"

"No."

"How long were you away? Talking to the night-porter?"

"About a minute. Maybe, two."

"Have you any idea of the time?"

"Yes. It was a quarter-past five."

"How do you know that?"

"A clock struck the quarter just as I returned to the smoking-room."

"I see. And, when you returned, you found only the man there? The lady had gone?"

"How do you know that?"

"I don't. It's a guess. A good one?"

"Yes—she'd gone," admitted Temperley. "Or, rather, she was going. She passed me as I went in."

"Did she say anything to you?"

"No."

"Was she agitated? Well, you needn't answer that. I can see by your expression that she *was* agitated. Forgive me for seeming personal, Mr. Temperley, but may I ask why you are so interested in this lady, if you do not know her? And that's another question you needn't answer unless you want to."

Temperley frowned, but found it impossible to feel resentful. Why *was* he so interested? The inspector was merely echoing his own question.

"I'm—I'm dashed if I have any idea," he replied, honestly. "Perhaps I just feel—that she *couldn't* have had anything to do with this frightful business. And, by the way, inspector, she wasn't *very* agitated—as far as I could judge."

"But she *was* very beautiful!" murmured the inspector, without cynicism. Temperley flushed again, and the inspector smiled almost apologetically. "I understand, Mr. Temperley. There was a time when I, like you, rebelled against the idea of coupling crime with beauty. But—facts beat us, sir. We must keep our dreams for our private moments. Well. This—disturbing lady. She went out of the room and she did not come back?"

"No."

"And you have no idea where she is?"

"None at all." That was something to be grateful for!

"Where was the dead man. When you entered the room?"

"Just where he is now."

"And just *as* he is now?"

"That I can't say."

"What did you do?"

"I went to the arm-chair by the fire—*this* arm-chair—and sat in it."

"The one she had stood by?"

"Yes."

"Did she sit in it?"

"What, when I was out of the room? How do I know?"

"Of course. You couldn't know. But, you know *you* sat in it. You dozed?"

"I think so."

"What made you wake up?"

"I've no idea. Yes, I have! I—I believe—"

"Yes?"

"I believe it was a sudden realisation of the fact that the man wasn't *snoring.*"

"I see. A shock of silence!"

"Something like that. You see, he'd snored solidly from Preston."

"Now, answer this, Mr. Temperley. It's very important. Was he snoring when you entered the room after the lady had left?"

"By Jove!" exclaimed Temperley, his heart leaping.

Yes, that *was* important! Because, if he *had* been snoring, then he must have been alive when the lady left.... He racked his memory. He tried to dispel the hateful impression of utter silence. He failed.

"I—I can't remember," he muttered.

The inspector shook his head gravely.

"I think you would have remembered, Mr. Temperley, if he *had* snored," he said.

"Well, even if he wasn't snoring, he may not have been asleep," Temperley parried.

"That's true," admitted the inspector. "But, subsequently, no snoring kept you awake?"

"No."

"There was no movement that you can recall?"

"No."

"In fact, the last time you can swear you saw him alive was when you passed him in the passage at about thirteen minutes past five?"

"Yes. That is so."

As he spoke, the clock in the distance clanged six. The chimes came in through the half-open window, and all at once the inspector looked towards the window and rose. "Now what's he up to?" wondered Temperley.

An instant later, another matter occupied his mind. His right hand, resting against the crevice between the arm and the seat of his chair, had come into contact with a small, soft object.

His heart started thumping. He darted a glance towards the inspector. The inspector had his back turned, and was poking his head out of the window. Surreptitiously, and trying unsuccessfully not to feel guilty, Temperley secured the small soft object and slipped it into his pocket. It was a lady's bag. The inspector's hand followed his head out of the window. For a moment he remained poised. Then the head and the hand were withdrawn.

"What do you make of this?" asked the inspector.

He held out a small piece of enamelled metal. Its colour was crimson, and it was in the shape of the letter Z.

Chapter III

The Contents of a Bag

The discovery of the crimson Z introduced a new note into the grim business. It suggested deliberation rather than impulse, and a murder that has been planned is doubly sinister. But Detective-Inspector James did not imply, as he continued quickly with his investigations, that he had relinquished his interest in earlier clues through the introduction of this later one, and the metal symbol failed to divert him from returning to Richard Temperley to conclude their conversation.

A fellow-creature had been done to death, and for the protection of other fellow-creatures who still enjoyed life the murderer would have to be found and brought to justice. For that purpose, no line of thought could be ignored; and if the line embarrassed an agreeable young man or cast an ugly shadow over an attractive young lady, that could not be helped. The excuse lay, huddled, in an arm-chair.

The conclusion of the conversation, however, was not illuminating. Temperley had little to add to his story, and the one item of real news he had just acquired remained hidden in his pocket.

"Then that's all you can tell me?" said the inspector, at last.

"Afraid so," replied Temperley. "I don't think I've done so badly."

"No. But there's one important thing we've forgotten."

"What's that?" asked Temperley, as his heart missed a beat. The inspector's eye was on his pocket.

"Your address," came the answer. "I'm afraid you'll be wanted at the inquest."

The answer was a relief, but it was also disturbing. Inquest? Good Lord! Was there to be no end to it all?

"My address is 22 Wellingley Grove, N.W. 3," he said, "but I won't be there for a week. It's let."

"Where will you be?"

"At my sister's, I think. She lives at Richmond—18a, Hope Avenue."

"You think?" queried the inspector, as he jotted the two addresses down.

"Make it ninety-five per cent. sure," suggested Temperley. "I'll keep the odd five for accidents. After all, I suppose unless you actually arrest me, I'm still a free man?"

"Certainly. But you'll justify your freedom by letting us know if the—five per cent. wins?"

"I'll let my sister know," smiled Temperley, "and she can pass on the news to whomever it may concern."

"That will be the coroner," Inspector James smiled back. "Thanks for your help."

"Does that mean I can go and have a bath?" exclaimed Temperley, as the inspector rose.

"If you want, you can go to Madame Tussaud's," answered the inspector, and, with a nod, he turned and walked towards a quiet little man with a camera.

Feeling like a released schoolboy, Temperley cast a final glance towards the arm-chair of death, and then hurried from the room. The constable on guard at the door had evidently received his cue, and was no longer a gate.

"Morning, sir," he said, as Temperley went by.

With difficulty Temperley refrained from the frivolity of wishing him a happy Christmas.

The fact was, Richard Temperley was suffering from reaction. Reaction from a long and tiring journey. Reaction from the shock of seeing dead a man whom he had so recently seen alive. Was that helpless, silent thing the same flesh that had irritated Temperley in the train, that had spoken, and grumbled, and snored? And would he, Richard Temperley, so full of vigour and of life, one day be as helpless and as silent?...Reaction from the strain of a long cross-examination. Reaction from the confusion of a contentedly-guilty conscience, for which a small purse was responsible. Reaction from the greater confusion set up by the owner of the purse, and of the ridiculous emotions her vision inspired.

"Richard Temperley," he said to himself, reprovingly. "You are an ass!"

Some one directed him to a swing-door. Beyond the swing-door was another door, and beyond this was a bath. As he turned on the tap and the steam rose up from the bath bottom, a sense of selfish happiness began to pervade him. What, at that moment, did anything matter beyond the warmth that would soon be around him? In the grip of perfect comfort, we are dulled to the discomfort of others. From steaming water we can think dispassionately of the Arctic. From a cool sea, the Equator is a theory. In a woman's arms, the loneliness of others has no power to chill. And so Richard Temperley, regaining his vigour beneath the rippling warmth of a hotel bath, must not be censured for his temporary inability to share in the tragedy that lay so near at hand. He was merely accumulating, in his callousness, new strength to deal with it, as you or I might have done in his place.

After the bath, he dressed thoughtfully. Already his sense of responsibility had returned to him, and his resuscitated mind was grappling with its problems. The immediate problem was the lady's bag in his pocket.

Amazed that he had not done so before, he suddenly took the bag from the pocket of his hanging coat, and opened it. Suppose, after all, it contained nothing but money? It would be of small use then to either himself or a detective!

The bag contained six objects. The first was a pound note. The second was a half-crown piece. The third was a small handkerchief. Temperley lifted it to his nose, praising the scent before he smelt it. It was Houbigant Bois Dormant, but he did not know that; all he knew was that it was good. The fourth was a tiny gold vanity-box. The fifth—his heart gave a leap—was a visiting card, bearing the words:

SYLVIA WYNNE, *Studio 4*, Tail Street, CHELSEA.

He stared at the fifth article so long that he nearly forgot the sixth, but the sixth was equally interesting. It was a Yale key.

"By Jove!" he murmured. "Her latch-key!" And then, an instant later, "How will she get in?"

He completed his dressing quickly. Of course, studios sometimes had maids, and there was no reason to suppose that Sylvia Wynne's had not. Still, the possibility that she might be shut out of her studio, and striving at that moment to get in, gave Temperley all the excuse he needed to hurry, and he was out of the bathroom by a quarter to seven.

In the corridor, he paused. Glancing along the passage to the left, he caught sight of the constable on duty at the smoking-room door. Beyond the door investigations were still being made, and a patient inspector was still plying questions. The answer to the most urgent question was in Temperley's pocket. "Sylvia Wynne, Studio 4, Tail Street, Chelsea." In a moment of strength or weakness—for the life of him he couldn't determine which!—Temperley took a step towards the constable. Then he retracted. No—he would see Sylvia Wynne herself first. And, afterwards, use his discretion.

Reaching this decision, he turned to the right, and nearly bumped into Detective-Inspector James.

"Hallo! Just off?" queried the inspector genially.

"Yes," replied Temperley, catching his breath. "That is, unless you want me?"

The inspector shook his head. More at ease, Temperley asked whether he had found out anything fresh.

"A few details, yes, but nothing really illuminating," said the inspector. "The dead man is John Amble. He lived over his shop in King's Cross. I believe we shall find he was in debt, so it doesn't look as though he was murdered for his fortune."

"Perhaps he wasn't murdered," answered Temperley, "but committed suicide on account of his misfortune?"

"If you shoot yourself, you drop the pistol," observed the inspector, rather dryly. "We haven't found any pistol. Besides—"

"Besides what?"

The inspector regarded Temperley for a moment, as though weighing him up. Then he remarked,

"John Amble was shot from the window."

"Why, then—in that case—" began Temperley, eagerly, but the inspector interrupted him.

"We can only judge the direction of the bullet," he said, "not the exact distance it travelled. The bullet may have started from outside or inside the window."

"I see," murmured Temperley.

"But even that may be cleared up later," went on the inspector, "after the bullet is extracted. Meanwhile, I've got on to the shop, and his assistant is coming along. P'r'aps he'll help. There's absolutely no clue as yet as to motive. Well—enjoy yourself at Madame Tussaud's, and give my love to W. G. Grace."

Then the inspector vanished.

"Queer fellow!" thought Temperley. "Is he really a humorist—or is he playing some game with me? I don't know much about detectives, but he was rather confidential!"

However, the "queer fellow" was now back in the smoking-room, so Temperley was free to make his exit without hinderance.

"Wonder what he was doing out here?" he wondered idly, as he went along the passage to the entrance hall. "Perhaps he'd been across to the station—or was telephoning. They were both wrong guesses.

The night commissionaire was back at his post. His face lit up as he saw Temperley. For the last quarter-of-an-hour he had felt rather out of it.

"Luggage, sir?" he asked briskly.

Temperley nodded, and felt for a good tip.

"Shot from the window, so they're saying," said the porter. "God—I'm glad *I* wasn't sitting in that there chair!"

Temperley paused. If he hadn't returned and questioned this fellow about the luggage, *he* might have sat in the fatal chair.... Yes, but...He doubled the tip. The night commissionaire thanked him very much indeed. "Call you a taxi, sir?" he asked.

A taxi was waiting outside.

"Where to?" inquired the commissionaire.

Suddenly Temperley caught his breath. In another second he would have handed the whole show away! He visualised the inspector demanding of the commissionaire: "What address did he give?" and the commissionaire responding, "Studio 4, sir, Tail Street, Chelsea," and, as he visualised the inevitable scene, he responded to an uncontrollable impulse.

"Madame Tussaud's," he said.

Two minutes after the taxi had started on its journey, however, he put his head out of the window and changed the address to Baker Street Station. The occupant of another taxi, twenty yards behind, did the same.

Chapter IV

Behind the Blue Door

Tail Street, Chelsea, is not one of London's chosen thoroughfares. It is short and insignificant, and perhaps it derives its name from the fact that it forms a dead end. Or perhaps, again, the name was inspired by the road's curly shape. But whatever theories are advanced concerning its origin, there can be no two theories concerning its atmosphere, which is one of unrelenting, brooding gloom; and possibly this explains why the four studios which comprise the road are so frequently untenanted.

No. 4 is at the end of the tail. Right round the curve. You think you have come to an end with No. 3, but proceeding beyond the final violent bend you suddenly see the deep blue door of No. 4, glowing out of the gloom to reward your enterprise. Not far off are buses and taxicabs. Vaguely, incoherently, their metallic music percolates through the intervening, interrupted space, droning of people. But here, in this spot, there are no people. There is no sense of company, saving in the incongruous, rather unexplainable promise of that deep blue door.

Richard Temperley paused abruptly when he saw the door. Dismissing the taxi at Baker Street and storing his luggage, he had reached Tail Street by a circuitous route, for although he was unconscious that his taxi had been followed he did not permit himself the dangerous assumption of security. Thus, he had zigzagged from north-west to south-west, using various conveyances, and leading shadows the devil of a dance.

Had he realised that one shadow had preceded him to Tail Street, he would have approached his doubtful goal even more gingerly than he did.

"Whew! What a hole!" he thought, confessing his surprise. "What on earth made her choose it?"

The blue door itself was certainly attractive, but there was nothing else to recommend the spot. Glancing backwards, he noticed for the first time that the curve had cut him off visually from the beginning of the road, short distance away though it was. This increased the sense of imprisonment. Yet somewhere in this prison was a delicious, disturbing creature who used Houbigant scent! "Well—here goes!" decided Temperley. "After all, I *have* found her purse, haven't I?"

He advanced to the door and pressed the bell. The ringing responded, muffled, from its source. He waited half-a-minute. Then he rang again. The bell sounded louder this time, but there was no joy in it. It seemed indignant.

The grudging light of a grey morning was filtering into the cul-de-sac. He turned and contemplated the inclement dawn. Above the curving bricks of a wall peeped the eaves of a sloping roof. There was a large window in the roof, and a crooked chimney near the window. The window was like a big inquisitive eye; in fact, the entire roof reminded Temperley of a head rising cautiously out of a large brick collar. But no face appeared at the window, and no smoke issued from the chimney. "And twenty-four hours ago," reflected Temperley, "I was waking up to the beauties of Windermere!"

It occurred to him that he was not being quite fair to Tail Street. If he had not come to it straight from the spectacle of a dead man—if he had called on a sunny afternoon instead of a chilly grey morning—if he had alighted in evening dress from a car, with a couple of tickets for a Cochran revue in his pocket—

"It would *still* be a godforsaken place!" he concluded grimly, as he pressed the bell a third time. "The sort of place that any knight worth his armour would rescue a fair lady from!"

He kept his finger on the button for ten seconds this time, and the noise the ringing now made seemed loud enough to awaken the dead. It unnerved him a little. Ten seconds is a long while to have your finger pressed against the button of a bell, as a test with your watch will prove to you. But if there were any dead about they showed no sign of waking, and the window in the roof of Studio No. 3, towards which Temperley glanced more than once, revealed no curious or indignant eyes.

"Now, what?" he wondered. He knew very well, but he had to argue himself into it.

"Sylvia Wynne is not at home," ran the argument, "and the reason is that she has no key. Nor, apparently, has she any maid. As I have the key I cannot possibly go away and ignore her predicament. I *must* do something. Now, what would a girl do on arriving home and finding that she's lost her key?"

As soon as he had asked the question, which had slipped into his thoughts and interrupted his argument without premeditation, he wished he had not done so. The answer was too startlingly obvious. The average girl would return to the spot where she had probably lost the key. Sylvia Wynne had not returned to the spot.

"Well—p'r'aps she doesn't know yet that she's lost it," he growled, striving against odds for a defence. "P'r'aps she went off to a friend's house." Another rather startling thought occurred to him here. "P'r'aps the visiting card was a *friend's* card—and this isn't her place at all! Well, in that case—let's test the key!"

Thus, by a circuitous but not unreasonable route, he reached the point he had been aiming for, and found his excuse. Bringing the purse out of his pocket, he opened it and extracted the key. It was a Yale key. The blue door had a Yale lock. The evidence was all in favour of a fit. "Still, you never know, you know," argued Temperley.

He wasn't going to be cheated of his glimpse by circumstantial evidence! There were millions of Yale keys and there were millions of Yale locks. These before him *might* not fit. Without more ado, he slipped the key in the hole. It went in easily. But would it turn? It turned. He pushed the door gently. It swung back over a width of soft blue carpet…

Upon the carpet lay a small crimson object, in the shape of a letter Z.

Chapter V

The Girl

Temperley stared at the crimson Z for a moment without comprehension. It might mean so many things that, at first sight, it meant nothing. Then the moment of astounded stupor passed, and was followed by a reaction so swift and violent that it sent a pang of definite pain through him. Whatever might be the precise significance of this ominous token, one thing was glaringly clear; it brought the menace of the hotel smoking-room direct to Studio No. 4, Tail Street, and coupled Sylvia Wynne with the mystery of John Amble's murder.

But as an accomplice or as a victim? As the question stabbed into his brain he shoved the front door wide and dashed inside. An insignificant hall, with little room for more than three hooks and a hat stand, widened out into the studio, and with the night shadows scarcely yet lifted the room looked larger to Temperley's anxious eyes than it actually was. The cushions of a settee on the left billowed unpleasantly in the dimness, giving Temperley a momentary and erroneous impression that a figure was lying upon it. Beyond the settee, dark space. On the right, an easel loomed. Its mission was art, but viewed now it looked like some instrument of torture. A small stool was by the easel, and a large chair was beyond it. The large chair had its back to Temperley, and the back was sufficiently capacious to conceal a slim form. On the point of dashing to the chair, he stopped, and received yet another shock. Some one was moving towards a window across the room. The north window was above, but the window which now arrested Temperley's attention was in the opposite wall. It was a fair-sized piece of glass, and though not the principal means of bringing daylight into the studio, it was quite big enough for a human form to pass through.

A corner of the room, on the side where the easel stood, was curtained off, and Temperley made a sudden dive for this sanctuary. As he passed beyond the curtain into the little recess it partitioned, his face brushed a dress, and he suppressed a quick gasp; but the dress swayed and yielded before his sudden pressure, and he realised that it contained no inmate. A faint perfume rose to his nostrils, the sole consolation of this unpleasant moment.

The curtain behind which he stood concealed was not opaque, but it was not sufficiently thin for his strained eyes to pierce with any distinctness. Though he brought his eyes close he could merely record a vague impression of lights and shadows. But one light, through the right side of the curtain, was fairly definite, and when a shadow entered into it and almost obliterated it, Temperley needed nothing more to tell him what was happening. The person who had been moving towards the window had now reached it, and was peering in.

There was a moment of dead silence. Then a new noise fell upon Temperley's ears. The person outside was opening the window.

A sentence flashed into Temperley's mind, darting from the cells of memory in obedience to the instant. "John Amble was shot from the window!" And, afterwards, the murderer had left his symbol upon the ground!

Now, at this moment, a similar symbol lay on a strip of blue carpet just inside the front door. And, a few feet away, was an arm-chair with a high back...

"God!" thought Temperley, his forehead suddenly streaming, and he dashed the curtain aside.

As he did so, the person who had been outside the window dropped softly on to the studio floor, and the studio floor began to swim. Temperley found himself staring at Sylvia Wynne.

She, also, was staring. But she was not staring at Temperley. She was staring right across the room, towards the little hall and the open front door, and she was so absorbed that she did not hear Temperley's movements as he drew the curtain aside. She seemed to be—and was—thinking, "Who opened that door?"

Perhaps five seconds passed statuesquely. A picture he had remembered since boyhood—it had hung in his father's hall—came queerly into Temperley's mind. Of a snake eyeing a small rabbit-like creature, and of a tiger eyeing, from tall jungle grasses, the snake. There was no similarity of psychology between the picture of the jungle and the picture in this studio, but "The Watcher Watched" could have been the title of either.... Then, all at once, the watched watcher in the studio became conscious of another presence, and turned her head. "Steady!" muttered Temperley.

She was swaying.

Before he knew it he was at her side supporting her. She made no protest, seeming to be caught in a momentary overwhelming weakness, and she permitted herself to be helped to the couch. Then, while she sank down upon it, Temperley ran quickly to the front door and closed it.

He closed the door in obedience to a blind instinct of self-preservation in which, naturally, the girl was included. For her sake, also, he picked the metal Z from the ground and slipped it into his pocket. Then he returned into the studio and, without a word, crossed to the window through which the girl had come.

He noted that the catch was defective, but he pushed the window to, even though he could not fasten it. After that, he turned once more to the girl.

She was not sitting as he had left her. She was on her feet again, her paleness replaced by a flush. In the studio she looked less tall than she had looked on the dark station platform and at the hotel, but she did not look less attractive, and her beauty was now enhanced by the background of definite menace.

"You don't wait to ask permission, do you?" she challenged suddenly, like a boxer rising from a count of nine and rushing in gamely to receive the knockout.

"I'm sorry—but I'm doing it for you," answered Temperley.

"I don't understand!"

"Of course, you don't! Nor do I! Please sit down again. You look about dead. I don't suppose I can get you anything?"

She sat down. His tone, as well as his words, had their effect. But Temperley could see that she was still very much on the defensive, and he hoped he would soon find some means of removing the doubt that still shone in her eyes.

"How did you get in here?" she demanded.

"Through the door, not the window," he smiled.

"But *how*?"

"I rang. No one came. So I used a latch-key." She stared at him. "You see, Miss Wynne, I've come to return your purse to you."

"My purse. Then—I *did* leave it—!"

Her hand went to her heart. He nodded gravely.

"In the smoking-room of the hotel—yes," he said, while his own heart grew more troubled.

This distress of hers was disturbing. Temperley had assured Inspector James that she had not seemed very upset. Would he be able to repeat that assurance now? And why should her dismay be so acute unless it arose from some definite knowledge of the tragedy from which she had fled?

"It was in the crack between the leather of your chair," he went on, watching her unhappily. "You remember," he prompted, as she made no response. "The chair by the fire."

"Yes, I remember," she murmured, with a little shudder. Then suddenly shot another question at him: "How do you know my name?"

"How do I know your address?" he responded. "The answer is the same. A visiting card."

Her eyes were wide now. "Do you mean—"

"It was in your purse." He could see that she had forgotten about the visiting card. "With the key, and one or two other things. But don't be too worried. *I* found the purse. The inspector didn't—"

"*Inspector?*"

She was on her feet in a flash, and this time her agitation was healing balm. She knew nothing about the inspector! In that case, she must know nothing about the murder! Yes, but, in that case, why on earth…

"Do you mean—something's *happened?*" Her question came faintly.

"Yes—something rather bad has happened," replied Temperley, "and that's why I thought you might like me to return your bag to you, instead of somebody else."

A look of gratitude was nipped in the bud by another of swift concern.

"But—it's nothing to do—" she began quickly, and then paused. Controlling herself, she inquired, more quietly, "Please tell me what *has* happened?"

"On one condition."

"What?"

"That you sit down again."

She obeyed, with a faint, weary smile.

"Thank you," he said. "Now, tell me, you don't *know* what's happened?"

"If I did, would I ask?" she retorted.

"But you left the room hurriedly."

"I see, you've a good memory."

"Which is trying to serve you, Miss Wynne. May I know why you left so hurriedly?"

"And may I know if this is a cross-examination?" She was fighting hard. Unreasonably, he thought. But the next moment she crumpled, and gasped, "Are *you* a detective?"

"Good Lord, no!" exclaimed Temperley. "I've no more to do with all this than I expect *you* have!" He conceded that in the hope of winning her confidence. "My name is Richard Temperley, and I'm just a man who is returning a lady her bag."

"And, at the same time, cross-examining the lady—"

"To prevent her from being cross-examined later on, perhaps, by somebody else."

"I see," she murmured, after a little pause. "The—inspector you mentioned?"

"I'm afraid so."

"Does that mean, you *think* so?"

"He wants to find you."

There was another pause. Odd, how they were moving all round the tragedy without actually touching it! Temperley found himself struggling to retain his belief in the girl's professed ignorance.

"You could have told the inspector where I was to be found," said Miss Wynne, raising her eyes from the foot of the easel at which she had been staring.

"Yes, I could."

"Why didn't you?"

"Hardly know."

"Was it so—important?"

"Inspector James seemed to think it was."

"But still you kept back my name and address?"

"Yes. And if you ask me why again, I can only tell you again that I don't know."

"Sporting instinct, perhaps?" she suggested.

"If you like," he responded, with a smile.

They were getting on much better now. For an instant, as she returned his smile, he forgot everything else, and had no quarrel with the world. The miracle of companionship is the only answer to the insistence of tragedy. But he was pulled back to tragedy at her next abrupt question.

"And, now—what *did* happen?" she asked.

"After you left?"

Confound it! Even after that friendly exchange of smiles, he was fencing again!

"Of course, after I left!"

"I hope you're ready to hear something pretty bad, Miss Wynne?"

"Quite ready."

"Well, then, here it is. Somebody was murdered."

She sat very still. To his infinite regret, he found that, at this poignant instant, he could learn nothing from her. Whatever she was feeling, she gave no sign.

"Why doesn't she even ask, 'Who?'" he thought, fretfully. "If only she'd act as one would expect her to act!"

But, since she didn't, he proceeded,

"You remember that man who entered the smoking-room a minute or two after you did? Elderly fellow. He was on the train, you know. I suppose you saw him come in?"

"Yes." Her voice was very low.

"Well—he took an arm-chair near the window."

"Yes."

"And—er—shortly after that, *you* left, you know."

"Yes."

"Just as I was going in. Do you remember passing me?"

"Yes."

Four yes's! And not an inflection in any of them. Temperley began to grow desperate. She wasn't giving him any help at all!

On the point of saying, "I thought you seemed worried," he desisted. That could come later. Better stick to the facts for the moment, and get them over.

"Well, when I entered the room the man was tucked away in his chair. I thought he was asleep. *I* took the chair by the fire—the one you'd just left, you know—and where I found your bag later on. Expect I dozed a bit myself. But all at once I opened my eyes, and I found that the old fellow was dead."

The silence that followed was the longest that had passed between them. The girl was absorbing the information she had just received. Temperley was waiting for her comment. He was determined, this time, that he would not break the silence.

At last she broke it with a question.

"How did you know he was dead?"

"Yes, the inspector asked me that," he answered. "He wasn't snoring."

He paused, to make her speak again.

"Why should he have been snoring?"

"He shouldn't have been. Nobody should. But I'd travelled from Preston with him, you see, and knew him to be a defaulter! So, when I found he wasn't snoring—" He shrugged his shoulders, and frowned. "I agree it wasn't conclusive evidence. But—dash it, I don't know! There seemed to be—something in the air."

She looked at him quickly.

"Did *you* notice it?" he exclaimed, suddenly. "Was *that* why you looked so worried when you left the room?"

"Worried?" she repeated.

"I thought you seemed so." There—it was out now!

She hesitated, then offered an exclamation that seemed, to Temperley, thinner than Indian paper.

"Didn't he worry *you* in the train when he snored?" she asked.

Temperley's soul groaned. What—hurry from the room just because…? And yet, after all, snoring can be the very devil! The poor fellow's noise had nearly sent Temperley potty, and after an all-night journey this girl's nerves might have been frayed, too, so that she found the snoring beyond her capacity to stand…Snoring!…*Snoring!*

"Tell me, *was* he snoring?" he cried.

The question came so suddenly and so exultingly that Miss Wynne gazed at Temperley almost in alarm.

"I told you—didn't I?" she answered, flustered. "That was why I left."

And then the exultation departed, and Temperley knew that John Amble had *not* been snoring when the girl had left and when he himself had entered the smoking-room.

He knew for two reasons. The first was the girl's attitude; it betrayed that she was catching at straws. The second was that, if Amble had been snoring, Temperley now realised the inevitability of his associating the fact with the girl's departure. "Hallo—*she* can't stick it, like!" Such, Temperley felt, would have been his obvious instinctive thought.

In his extremity, he plunged.

"Truth's a damn good thing," he said, and looked at her squarely.

"And I'm not speaking it?" she replied. "Thank you."

There was a pathetic lack of indignation in her tone.

The pathos beat him. Her lips were trembling slightly, and the whiteness with which she had first greeted him had returned. She looked unutterably weary. He ached to lift the pretty, tired feet and arrange them comfortably on the couch, so that she could relax into the peace and comfort she required. Well, he couldn't do that, but he could at least remove his penetrating gaze from her face, and for a few seconds spare her his scrutiny.

"He was shot from the window," he said, and, because he had turned away, he missed the sudden stiffening of her body. "At least, that's the inspector's theory, and he seemed sure of it. Of course, I was questioned pretty closely, as you can imagine. You see—you and I were the last people to see him alive—"

"Except for the person who shot him," she interposed, with unexpected shrewdness.

"By Jove—yes—apart from that person," answered Temperley, swinging round again. "Of course, *he*—"

He paused, and his eyes roamed instinctively towards the door.

"What's the matter?" she asked, with a catch in her voice.

She was like the wires between telegraph poles as viewed from a travelling train; every time her spirits began to rise, something happened to jerk them down again.

"Nothing," he replied, unconvincingly.

"Then why did you look at that door?"

"Don't know."

"A moment ago, Mr. Temperley," she observed, "you reminded me that truth was a damn good thing."

The reminder was accompanied by a little smile. The wires were going up again.

"Touché," he smiled back. "I do know."

"Then please tell me!"

He decided that it was best to. The situation was too grim altogether for evasion. He walked to the stool, pulled it in front of the settee, and sat down.

"Listen, Miss Wynne," he said, gravely. "This is a pretty bad business, and, in your own interests, I'm not going to keep anything back. After the inspector had finished asking me about myself—"

"But you convinced him you had nothing to do with it?" she interrupted, eagerly. "*You're* in no danger?"

"None at all. I imagine I've got a clean slate. But then he began asking me about you. I told him I didn't know anything about you—who you were, or what you were, or where you were."

"Even though it wasn't true—?"

"It was true, at first. But not afterwards—not after I found your bag. Luckily, I managed to evade the point after that, but he wants to find you pretty badly, that inspector does, and he strikes me as the sort of chap who generally gets his way in the end."

"You mean, you think he'll find me?"

"He'll have a jolly good try!"

"Perhaps he followed you here!"

"I thought of that possibility before I started, Miss Wynne. I haven't made my way here like a crow, straight, but like a crab, sideways! If anybody began following me, I'll bet I shook 'em off! But that fellow'll track you presently, and—well, one can see his point of view, you know. Can't one?"

"What is his point of view?"

"That you left the smoking-room rather suddenly."

"Yes—I did."

"And you didn't go back."

"No."

"Not even—for your bag!"

Again she showed her shrewdness. "But only *you* know that," she pointed out.

"Yes, and I wish I didn't!" he exclaimed, marvelling all at once at her acceptance of his allegiance. Was he being a blind fool? Another of the inspector's remarks flashed uncomfortably into his mind: "There was a time when I, like you, rebelled against the idea of coupling crime with beauty. But facts beat us, sir! We must keep our dreams for our private moments." Facts were certainly trying to beat Richard now. Again he made a sudden appeal to her for the truth. "Look here, why not go to the inspector and tell him your story, whatever it is?" he begged. "I'll go with you, if you like—and it's much better than having the story dragged out of you. *I'd* have been under a shadow if I hadn't stayed and found it. The inspector's quite a decent chap—provided one doesn't make an enemy of him. I imagine—*then*—he might be awkward!"

His eyes searched hers earnestly. She did not reply, but seemed to be considering his appeal. He endeavoured to strengthen it with another argument.

"There's a second reason why I think you should go to the police," he said. "You should go for your protection."

"My protection?"

"Yes. You see—there's one thing I've not told you yet. The reason why I looked towards your front-door just now."

"Yes, I'm waiting for that!"

"I told you that the inspector's theory is that the man was shot from the window. That is, from the direction of the window. The careful idiot wouldn't commit himself as to the exact point where the bullet started from, but he found something outside the window which suggests that the murderer must have been outside. A—very odd thing. It was in the shape of the letter Z."

The effect of this information was galvanic. She jumped up from the couch as though an electric current had suddenly passed through her body, and stood trembling. For an instant Temperley stared at her in amazement. Then he, too, was on his feet, standing before her with his hands firmly holding her arms to steady her.

"As bad as that, eh?" he muttered. "Poor child!" He felt her weight upon him as her strength began to leave her. "Well, don't forget—I'm here to help you, if I can."

He said the words to comfort her, but as he spoke them he knew they were true. Something terrible hung over her; brooded over the studio in which she lived; crept outside through the murk of Tail Street. It had been present on No. 3 Platform at Euston—hadn't Temperley sensed it even there, though he had not then associated it with this warm, frightened creature trembling against him. And it had followed her into the hotel smoking-room, and been with her ever since! Well, if she had no one else to turn to…

He felt suddenly cold. She had called upon some hidden reserve of strength, and, no longer needing his, had drawn away from him. Outwardly, she appeared calm again, or nearly so.

"You must think me an idiot," she murmured. "I haven't had any breakfast." Ridiculous explanation! "A letter Z? Well?"

"Look here, Miss Wynne, what *about* that breakfast?" he suggested. "Don't you think it's time you got it inside you?"

"Tell me the rest first."

"Perhaps there isn't any rest."

She thought for a moment, then replied, "If you say there isn't, I'll try and believe you. But if there *is*, and if you really and truly meant what you said just now about wanting to help me—"

"Of course, it's true!"

"Then it's impossible—*impossible* to help me by keeping anything back."

The earnestness of her voice would have convinced him even if the facts themselves had not. Naturally, nothing must be kept back. She must know the full extent of the menace, and must be given her chance of clearing out of the studio until the menace was removed. He wondered where she could go. Suppose she had no sanctuary? As this possibility occurred to him, an idea that was perhaps more intriguing than reasonable flashed into his mind. Why not offer her his sister's house? Winifred was a good sport. He was certain she would not object, and Miss Wynne would be safe there. No—would she? Inspector James had his sister's address! Confound Inspector James—what a well-meaning nuisance the fellow was!... Thus Richard Temperley's thoughts raced, tumbling over each other like an eager schoolboy's.

"You're right—I won't keep anything back," he said. "You ought to know everything. But, first, just one thing. What happened, exactly, when you got back here, and found you had lost your key?"

"Does that matter?" she asked, frowning.

"Very likely not," he admitted, "but it would be nice of you to humour me."

"Very well. I—just couldn't get in."

"Didn't know you'd lost your bag until that moment, eh?"

"That's right. And I—I started back for it. Then I changed my mind." She had spoken hesitatingly, but now she ran on quickly, as though to avoid being asked why she had changed her mind. "The back of this studio looks out on another road, you know—or passage, rather. I knew the window didn't latch properly, so I went round to the back and got in. You saw me do it."

"Yes," he answered. He refrained from pointing out that she had not accounted fully for her time. After all, was she under any obligation to? "How do you get round to the back?" he inquired abruptly.

"You have to go out of the street, and then round."

"Out of Tail Street?"

"Yes."

"I see. And you didn't meet anyone?"

"No. Did *you*?"

He shook his head. "But someone seems to have been here before us, just the same. No, I don't mean inside," he added quickly, in response to her fresh look of alarm. "Probably on the doorstep. When I let myself in—yes, I know it was jolly cool, but I couldn't get any reply to my ringing, and I wanted to make sure that everything was all right—" He stopped, and watched her rather anxiously. "I found something on the ground."

"What?"

"Well, it was another of those darned little letter Z's."

She took it well. He admired her tremendously at that moment. "How funny," was all she said.

"A bit odd," he agreed, grimly. "It had probably been slipped through the letter-box slit. Anyway, there it was—and here it is." He took the unsavoury object from his pocket and held it out. "And, if I may offer advice, Miss Wynne," he concluded, "you'll give this spot a wide berth for a while, because it doesn't seem any too healthy."

She did not reply. Was she listening? The momentary composure was departing again. "P'r'aps she's got nowhere else to go to?" wondered Temperley, with a fresh wave of intense sympathy.

"Here's a perfectly mad idea—if you've no better," he said. "My sister lives at 18a, Hope Avenue, Richmond—her name's Mostyn—she's an awfully good sort, and—"

No, she wasn't listening! Her eyes were on the front door once more. Temperley turned swiftly. Beyond the opaque glass of the door moved a shadowy, formless smudge.

Chapter VI

The Person on the Doorstep

To reach the front door you merely had to cross the little passage that connected it with the studio. Ordinarily it would take you three or four seconds. It took Temperley one. And in another second he had flung the door open. Thus it was that the origin of the shadowy, formless smudge had no time to evaporate, but stood staring at Temperley without any sign of delight in his sudden presence.

But neither was there any sign of discomposure. The origin of the shadowy, formless smudge was a rather ordinary-looking man, belonging perhaps to the workman class, but not in working clothes, and his face was unimaginative and expressionless. This lack of flurry or of menace momentarily disarmed Temperley, who had expected a chase or a scrap, and who was primed for either. For a few moments he regarded this innocent-looking fellow with vague surprise. Then suspicion and determination returned, and he barked out a sharp question: "What are you doing here?"

"Eh?" replied the man.

"I asked you what you were doing here!"

"Oh. I wanted to see the occupier."

"What for?"

"Are you the occupier, sir?"

The fellow spoke quite respectfully, but Temperley refused to be put off his guard.

"*I'll* ask the questions, if you don't mind," he retorted. "I'm still waiting, you know."

"Very sorry, I'm sure, sir," murmured the man. "I come here to see if I could get a job of work."

"Oh," answered Temperley, disbelieving him. "What sort of work?"

"Any kind," said the man. "Garden. Windows. Studio, ain't it?" He craned his neck slightly, as though to get a peep inside. Temperley tried to widen himself. "Want your windows kep' clean in a studio, sir. Or I could do a bit of posing."

"Are you sure you're *not*?" enquired Temperley.

"Eh?" blinked the man, and looked hurt.

"Well, there are plenty of burglars about these days," said Temperley, without contrition. "One has to be careful, you know. What made you choose this house to call at?"

The man thought for a moment. He seemed to be trying hard. He rubbed his chin, and then responded,

"Well, sir, you don't ezackly *choose*. You jest call—where you happen to be, if you take me?"

"And you happened to be here?"

"That's right."

"H'm. Well, I'm afraid there isn't any work for you."

"Very good, sir."

"And I'm also afraid you won't find any by trying to peep in," added Temperley, sharply, as the man craned his neck again.

"That's right, sir," agreed the man. "You can't see through a curtain."

Was it the man's words, or some new quality in his voice, that caused Temperley to swing round suddenly? In any case, he did so. Curtain?…What curtain? He found himself staring at a curtain. Like the door, it was blue. It had been drawn across the entrance to the studio, shutting it entirely from view. It had not been drawn when he had left the studio. Or—had it? No, of course, it had not. He had seen the front door from the studio. And so had the girl.…

Quickly he swung back to the man, but the man had disappeared.

Temperley closed the front door, fighting his anxiety, and hastened back to the studio, shoving the curtain aside as he ran. Then he got another shock. The girl, also, had disappeared.

"Well—I'm damned!" he thought. "What's that mean?"

Had she got a fright and taken cover? He called her name softly. Obtaining no response, he began to search the studio, trying first the corner he himself had hidden in. There was no sign of her. Suddenly he looked towards the little window.

"Open again!" he muttered.

Obvious, of course. The bird had flown out through the window. Well, he had advised her to give the place a wide berth, hadn't he? She had merely acted on his advice! Yes, but without a word, without so much as…

On his way to the window he stopped abruptly. A faint sound came from outside. His heart beat happily again.

"Miss Wynne!" he called, keeping his voice low. "You can come back. He's gone!"

"I'm afraid he hasn't," came the reply, as the individual under discussion emerged into view.

No longer asking Temperley's sanction, the unwelcome visitor climbed in through the window, and as Temperley watched him a wretched suspicion came into his mind. A moment later, the visitor was confirming the suspicion.

"I hope you'll forgive me for the pack of lies I told you on the doorstep just now, Mr. Temperley," he said, "but you've not been the soul of truth yourself, now, have you?"

"Who are you?" demanded Temperley.

"Name, Dutton," replied the man, brushing dust from his sleeve. "Working for Inspector James."

"And your work was to follow me?"

"Afraid so, sir. You see, sir—well, we guessed you weren't going to Madame Tussaud's."

"I see," murmured Temperley, and added abruptly, with a frown, "Pretty poor game, yours, isn't it?"

"That's how you look at it, sir," answered Dutton. "Maybe some'd say the same of yours."

"Mine?"

"Yes, sir. Not helping the police, I mean. You've led me a dance, and no error!"

He smiled amiably. If his words contained a reproach, his tone and his attitude were quite friendly. Temperley, trying to make the best of a situation quite new to him, wondered what his own tone and attitude ought to be.

"I take back what I said just now about yours being a poor game," he said. "But—perhaps, if you understood—you'd realise that I'm not really playing a bad game, either."

"Oh, I understand that, sir," nodded Dutton, "but I've got to go on with my job, just the same."

"Well—go on with it," smiled Temperley. "What's the next step?"

Dutton smiled back.

"What's yours?" he asked.

"Oh! Then the chase is to continue?"

"That depends on you, sir."

"What do you mean?" Dutton shrugged his shoulders. "That's not an answer. Let's start square, anyway. Why have you followed me?"

"Well, sir—p'r'aps the police aren't always such fools as people think. And that being so, sir—if I may offer a word of advice—it would be much simpler if we pulled together. It'll come to the same in the end."

"You think so?"

"Sure of it, sir."

"Listen, Mr. Dutton. I admit you've scored a trick. I'm not one of those who call policemen fools. But—well, p'r'aps *I'm* not such a fool, either?"

"I'm sure you're not, sir. If it was only you and me, I'd go fifty-fifty on the result. But you've forgotten the inspector. He sent me to trace Miss Wynne, through you—and he won't rest till he's found her." Dutton paused. Then he went on, in a matter-of-fact voice: "The lady's acting very queerly, you'll admit. I don't say she's anything to do with our business, but if she hasn't why doesn't she come forward and say so? There you are."

He paused again. His eyes roamed round the studio. Temperley watched him curiously, and also with a sense of irritation. Why were they both staying here? Why didn't they go? And, when they did go, would they separate?

Now Dutton was eyeing the curtained corner. He moved towards it casually.

"Have you got a warrant to search the place?" enquired Temperley.

"No," replied Dutton, continuing on his way.

Temperley saw his chance, and seized it. While Dutton proceeded towards the corner, Temperley turned and slipped quietly to the front-door. He opened it and closed it with a bang, then swiftly dropped down behind the hat-stand.

Five seconds later, Dutton came rushing by. The blue door was opened and closed a second time, on this occasion with an even louder bang.

From behind the hat-stand came a chuckle.

"Do your job, Dutton," murmured Temperley, as he emerged, "and all honour to the foe. But I've got a job, too, and by George I'm going to see it through. Evidence is all very well, but there's also such a thing as faith, isn't there?"

He tiptoed softly back to the studio, crossed to the little window, and climbed out; while not far off a conscientious policeman chased a shadow, and a girl fled from one, and the shadow itself stood under an archway, with a pallid grin upon its nightmare face.

Chapter VII

Temperley Decides

A clock was striking eight when Richard Temperley entered a small shop not a stone's throw from the Thames and demanded breakfast.

Eight o'clock! It seemed impossible! Only three hours ago his train had drawn into Euston, and he and John Amble had been snapping at each other. Now John Amble was dead, and the fact would soon be blazoned on eager posters. Three hours ago he had never seen that hotel smoking-room—a room which would remain in his memory now until he died. He had never seen Detective-Inspector James or his satellite Dutton. He had never heard of Tail Street, Chelsea. He had never met the occupant of Studio No. 4. She, also, would remain in his memory until he died! Life in all its vividness and death in all its stillness had been encountered during these three short hours…

"Breakfast, sir?" said the old woman who kept the shop. "Yes, sir, will you step upstairs?"

He went upstairs. The stairs wound round darkly, then led sharply to their reward—the star room on the first floor. It was a small room overlooking the river, and Temperley chose the table in the window. From there he could stare at the river, speckled with morning sunlight, into which intruded every now and then the black silhouette of a barge or little boat. Stare and think. And thought was what he needed, even more than breakfast. That was why he had chosen this quiet, secluded shop where there was small chance of disturbance.

"Eggs, sir?" queried the old woman.

"Yes," he answered kindly, to avoid forcing an admission from her that there was nothing else.

Yes, there was a lot to think about, and the first thing framed itself into a blunt question: "Am I being a thorough fool or not?"

Dutton had challenged him directly on the point when he had proposed co-operation. That, certainly, was the obvious course to pursue. Co-operation. Help the police. After breakfast go off to James and say, "There's something I didn't tell you, inspector, at Euston. I found that girl's bag, and also her name and address. And I went to the address. I've had a long conversation with her, and it wasn't any too satisfactory. She knew she had lost her bag, but was afraid to go back for it. She didn't tell me why she was afraid. She didn't tell me why she left the smoking-room in a hurry—at least, one explanation she attempted was an obvious lie. She didn't tell me anything. And now she's disappeared again. But I expect your man Dutton has already reported that to you?"

In his imagination, he continued with the conversation, to see where it was likely to lead: "Yes," said the imaginary inspector, "and he also reported the trick you played upon him to get rid of him."

"I had to get rid of him," replied the imaginary Temperley.

"Why?"

"I needed time to think." Thus Temperley argued with his conscience.

"And also to see whether you could find Miss Wynne again?"

"That's true. But I couldn't find her. She'd vanished into thin air."

"Why, do you suppose?"

"Fright."

"Why was she frightened?"

"Can't say."

"She didn't tell you—even though you were obviously trying to help her?"

"No."

Temperley paused in his imaginary conversation. It wasn't going too well! Still, he had to follow it to the end—to see whether he would risk turning the imagination into reality.

"Have you any idea why she didn't confide in you?"

"No."

"Perhaps that fright you mentioned just now was fright of the *police*?"

"I don't believe it!"

"Then what else could it have been?"

The imaginary conversation was interrupted by the reality of the old woman, who reappeared with two boiled eggs. "If there's anything more you're wanting, will you ring the bell?" she said.

"Yes, yes," answered Temperley.

And resumed the imaginary conversation while the old lady's footsteps grew fainter down the winding staircase.

"What else could it have been, inspector?" repeated the imaginary Temperley. "Well, assume for a moment that she *isn't* implicated."

"Well?"

"Then somebody else is!"

"Well?"

"And she may be frightened of that *somebody else*!"

"It's possible. But have you any direct evidence of this?"

"Yes, I have!" cried the imaginary Temperley, while the real Temperley felt instinctively in his waistcoat pocket for the proof. "I forgot to tell you *this*, inspector! I let myself into the studio with a key I found in her bag. On the floor of the hall I saw another of those letter Z's! It was when I mentioned this to her that she nearly fainted. Jove, the poor child was scared stiff!"

His fingers went on fumbling in his waistcoat pocket.

"And yet, even *then*, she didn't want the protection of the police!" observed the ruthless imaginary inspector.

That was a nasty one! Temperley thought about it hard, while his fingers still fumbled in his pocket.

"And why did you have to let yourself into the studio, Mr. Temperley?"

"There was no reply when I rang."

"But you say you met the girl there?"

"Yes."

"Did you let her in, afterwards?"

"No."

"How did she get in, then?"

"Through a window."

"In other words, she had to break into her own studio—she preferred this to returning to the hotel and reclaiming her key! Sounds a bit thin, sir! Well, let's look at this second letter Z you found."

And there the imaginary conversation ended. Temperley discovered that he hadn't got the second letter Z! His mind now raced on a new tack. The eggs began to cool. What had he done with it? When was the last time he had had it?

The scene came back to him. He had taken it out of his pocket to show Miss Wynne. Then they had seen the shadow outside the front door. He must have laid the Z down unconsciously when he had rushed to the door. Yet he was certain it had not been anywhere about when he had returned. This meant that the girl had taken possession of it, and had escaped with it. Was that significant—or not?

Temperley refused to think so. He was certain that the inspector would think so, however. Yes, if he went to the police with his full story, their suspicions of Miss Wynne would strengthen, and she would be fighting alone against a double danger.

"By George, she *shan't* fight alone!" exclaimed Temperley, now finally reaching the decision from which, in the strange days that followed, he refused to deviate. "I'm as certain she needs my help as I'm certain she's innocent! Good-bye, Inspector James. Au revoir, Mr. Dutton! You nearly got me, but not quite! We'll be honourable foes!"

But, he added in vindication, foes with the same object in view—bringing to justice the guilty, and clearing the innocent. Different roads to the same end, that was all.

Meanwhile, in the shop below, one of the honourable foes was solemnly purchasing four ounces of acid-drops.

Chapter VIII

The Value of a Sister

Winifred Mostyn, née Temperley, sat in her comfortable drawing-room with an unusual frown on her face.

As a rule her face was as composed as her drawing-room. She loved adventure in her secret heart, and although she was always ready to enthuse obediently over Shaw and Huxley, her favourite author was still Robert Louis Stevenson; but five years ago she had played for safety by marrying a bank manager, and the agreeable routine of a bank manager's home had entered into her soul and her expression.

She liked to do things well, and if routine had to be done, then she would do that well. The punctual breakfast at 8.30, the affectionate peck before sending Tom off to catch the 9.9, the morning round, the solitary lunch, the afternoon of mild diversions leading up to, and never interfering with, the pleasant reunion with Tom at 7.4—such details as these were rendered agreeable by her conscientious attention to them and her bright personality. Her contentment was not a pose. It was a habit. Thus the frown on her face as she sat in her drawing-room on this particular afternoon was not a frown of self-pity. It denoted that something had interfered with the routine; that law and order had been, in some sense, outraged.

The frown was to deepen as the afternoon progressed, but at the moment it was born of two causes. The first was that her brother Richard, expected that day for a week's visit, had not turned up yet—but then *he* was not a creature of routine! Still, he *might* have sent a wire, if anything had gone wrong, for even a methodical sister can be worried! And the second…

Yes, the second was very odd. Someone had telephoned to Richard, as though expecting him to be there, and had refused to give her name.

"And she knew *my* name!" reflected Winifred Mostyn, with vague indignation.

The telephone conversation, as she recalled it, had run precisely thus: "Hallo."

"Hallo."

"Is Mr—? Who am I speaking to?"

"This is Richmond 0086."

"Are you Mrs. Mostyn?"

"Yes. Who is it?"

"Could I speak to Mr. Temperley?"

"He's not arrived yet."

"Oh!"

"But I can give him a message when he comes."

"I see. You—you're expecting him."

"Yes. Who shall I say 'phoned?"

"It doesn't matter."

"But wouldn't you like me to—?"

And then the receiver had been abruptly replaced at the other end, and the conversation had concluded.

"It's certainly very odd," frowned Mrs. Mostyn, without realising how much she was secretly enjoying the oddity. "A nice voice—but why wouldn't she give her name? And how did she know mine? And—and why did she seem so—?"

So what? Frightened?

"Yes, she *did* seem frightened!" decided Winifred Mostyn, suddenly refusing to hedge. "I wonder what it was about—and whether she'll 'phone again!" Then her mind swung back to her first worry. "I *wish* Dick would come! He could tell me—unless it's the skeleton popping out of his cupboard! Well—a jolly nice-sounding skeleton!"

She glanced at the china clock. It had shepherdesses about it. Sixteen minutes to four.

"I *do* hope nothing's happened to him," she fretted. "I got the cakes especially!"

She hated feeling anxious. That was why she tried to ascribe her anxiety to the cakes. The argument against routine is that it makes one over-sensitive when the routine is disturbed. Ten minutes ticked by. In another six Jane would bring in the afternoon paper. At five minutes to four, the telephone rang again.

"Which will it be?" she wondered, as she rushed to it. "That girl again, or Dick?"

It was neither. A man's voice answered her "Hallo," and it was a voice she had never heard before.

"Hallo!" said the man's voice. "Am I speaking to Mrs. Mostyn?"

"Everybody knows me, but I don't know anybody!" she thought indignantly, as she answered aloud, "Yes. Who is it?"

"Inspector James. May I have a word with your brother, Mr. Temperley?"

"Inspector—?" Her alarm grew like a flame. "My brother isn't here—has anything happened?"

"No need for alarm, Mrs. Mostyn," came the inspector's calming voice. "He and I met this morning over a certain matter, and he told me that, if I wanted to get into touch with him, I could communicate through you. You're expecting him, I suppose?"

"I've been expecting him all day!"

"Then—he hasn't been in touch with you?"

"No. Please tell me—Inspector James, did you say?—what is all this about?"

There was a short silence, during which the inspector considered his reply.

"I think perhaps I'd better leave him to answer that, Mrs. Mostyn," he then said. "Meanwhile, please let me assure you that you have no need to worry on his account. No need whatever. I apologise for troubling you. But may I ask one more question?"

"I don't see why not—since you say I've no need to worry on his account."

"And I repeat that assurance. Has anybody called at your house to-day to see your brother?"

"Called here? No."

"Or telephoned?"

"Yes. At least—" She paused, wondering suddenly whether it was wise to give this information. But the wonder came a second too late. "Yes, someone did telephone, inspector, but—well, I rather feel as if I'm talking into a blank wall."

"I appreciate your position, Mrs. Mostyn," came the inspector's reply; how irritatingly pleasant the man was! If only he had been rude, so that one could have snubbed him, or cut him off without any conscience qualms! "Don't answer any questions you prefer not to. But if you could tell me whether it was a lady who phoned—"

"It was a lady," interrupted Winifred, "but if you ask me who she was or anything about her, I can't tell you. She rang off as soon as she heard my brother wasn't here, and that's all I know."

"Thank you," said the inspector. "Again, please accept my apologies." And he, also, rang off.

The china clock now said three minutes to four. The three minutes passed in serious but unproductive contemplation. Then the clock gave a little wheeze and tinkled four, and Jane brought in the afternoon paper.

"Don't bring in the tea till I ring," said Winifred, and opened the paper.

We like to believe ourselves sympathetic, but, in truth, Nature has designed us, perhaps necessarily, to be callous. A murder in Newcastle is of less importance than a cut finger in our own home, and therefore Winifred Mostyn was only mildly interested. All at once, however, the mildness evaporated. In the next column a name had caught her eye. It was the name of her brother!

Euston! Yes, of course! Her brother would have arrived at Euston! But how did his name—?

She read the account eagerly, with a fast beating heart. It was a carefully-worded account. Possibly, officially inspired. A man identified as John Amble had been found dead at 5.30 a.m. that morning in a hotel arm-chair. He had been shot. There seemed to be no motive for the murder, nor clue to the murderer, saving a small metal token in the form of a crimson letter Z which had been found outside the window. Among those questioned by the police were a Mr. Richard Temperley, address not given. (Winifred thanked heaven that the address opposite his name in the telephone directory was Wellingley Grove and not Hope Avenue—otherwise she might have been inundated with inquiries!) Mr. Temperley, the account made clear, had satisfied the police with his information, and had not been detained. The case was in the able hands of Detective-Inspector James…

"James!" she exclaimed. "That was the name! Of course, he wanted to speak to Richard about—*this*!"

But the other one? The girl? Winifred scanned the report, and found no mention of any girl. Temperley—John Amble—night commissionaire—Inspector James—Dr. Benson—but no reference to any girl. There was a total absence of femininity in the report, saving for a housemaid who had fainted.

A moment later, Winifred Mostyn herself nearly fainted. The telephone rang again, and the newspaper slid to the floor as she jumped from her chair.

"Really, I must get a hold on myself!" she exclaimed angrily. "I'm behaving ridiculously!"

But she could not quite steady her hand as she lifted the receiver. "Hallo!" she called.

"Hallo!" came the reply.

"Thank God!" she cried, devoutly relieved as she heard her brother's familiar voice. "How are you?"

"No need to worry about me, Winnie," replied Richard. "How are *you*? You sound upset."

"Well, I've had a bit of a shock!"

"You mean—this wretched murder business?"

"Yes. I've just read about it. Tell me, Dick, you *are* all right, aren't you?"

"Of course, I am," he answered. "What makes you think I'm not?"

"I don't know. But—well, never mind. We'll talk when you come. You ought to have rung me up before, you bad boy! Where are you now?"

"Never mind, old thing. And I'm afraid we'll have to do our talking over the telephone, because I'm not coming."

"Not *coming*?"

"Well, not just yet."

"Why not?" There was a pause. Terror suddenly leapt into Winifred's voice. "Dick! Dicky! You're—you're not—"

"If you mean, did I kill John Amble," interposed Richard, quickly, "I didn't. And nobody thinks I did. Just the same, you'll have to excuse me if I'm a bit mysterious. One day you'll have the whole story, but just at the moment I want your help more than I can say. Has anyone called on you?"

"No—"

"Or 'phoned?"

"I seem fated to answer questions and not to ask them. Yes, two people have 'phoned."

"Ah!" There was no mistaking the eagerness of that exclamation. "Who?"

"The first was a lady."

"By Jove!"

"Dick!" exclaimed his sister, admonishingly. "Are you on the edge of a scrape?"

"Yes, but it's not my scrape. Be a sport, dear, and don't ask questions. Time's precious. Was it Miss—Who was the lady who 'phoned?"

"So I'm not to be told her name?"

"Not if you don't know it."

"I don't know it. I'm not good at guessing the names of perfect strangers by their voices."

"When did she 'phone, and what did she want?"

"She 'phoned at twenty to four, and she wanted you."

"What did you tell her?"

"That you weren't here."

"Yes! Do go on!"

"You keep on interrupting. She wouldn't give me her name, but she knew mine, goodness knows how."

"P'r'aps I told her."

"Are you ill, Dick? You're becoming positively informative! When she found you weren't here she said it didn't matter, and she wouldn't leave any message. She just rang off, and left me guessing."

"Didn't say she'd ring up again?"

"No."

"Dash! Well, if she does ring up again—no, wait a minute! What about the other 'phone?"

"Yes," answered Winifred, grimly, "I think you'll want to know about that, too. The other 'phone was from Inspector James."

"The devil!" came a grunt. "Mug I was, to give him your address!"

"Yes, how many more people have you given my address to? Everybody can see me but I can't see anybody! I'm like the 'It' in Blind Man's Buff!"

"Sorry, my child! What did Inspector James want?"

"Same thing as your lady friend. You. I told him you hadn't arrived yet. Let me think, did I put it like that? Yes—I told him I'd been expecting you all day. He seemed rather surprised that you hadn't 'phoned or anything."

"Did he ask anything else?"

"Yes. He asked if anybody else had 'phoned or called. I said somebody had. I can hear, by the commotion at the other end, that you don't like that, but don't blame *me*, my dear! If these situations are bounced upon me without warning, you can't expect me to be prepared with clever answers."

"Of course, I don't blame you, Winifred. You're the best ever. I just wish—Well, what did you tell him?"

"Precious little. In other words, exactly as much as I knew. Then *he* rang off—and now here *you* are. I expect the next will be the night commissionaire, and then John Amble himself!" But the moment of levity passed almost as soon as it had dawned. "Well, Dick, what's the next step?" she asked, soberly. "Am I to know anything at all, or not?"

In the silence that followed she could almost hear her brother thinking. Before his thinking had ended a new voice broke in: "Time's up. Do you want another call?" Two more pennies were dropped in a little black metal box somewhere in London. Then Richard Temperley said: "Listen, Winnie. I know you're a sport. Do you think *I'm* one?"

Impressed by the tone of his voice, she responded,

"Best in the world, Dick—after me."

"Good enough! Well, I'm not going to tell you all you're bursting to know, because the less you know, the easier your job will be."

"My job?"

"Yes—if you'll accept it."

"What is it?"

"Perhaps, nothing at all. Perhaps just—well, standing by. But, in any case, keeping quiet about this conversation, and being ready to help me if I want help at any time."

"Really, you're distracting!" she exclaimed. "What *sort* of help?"

"Well—if my lady friend, as you call her, 'phones again, take the message, and say nothing. Or, if I 'phone, take my message, and say nothing."

"I see. A sort of a go-between?"

"Something of the kind, I expect."

"Very much of the kind, *I* expect! And the person I'm particularly to say nothing to is Inspector James?"

"You get me."

"Yes—I think I'm beginning to get you, Dick," she replied. "Well, I make no promises, but I'll do what I can, and I only hope it's in a good cause."

"You can count on that. There's just one more thing you can do right now," said Richard. "Peep out of the window, and tell me if anybody's watching the house."

"Watching the house? Good gracious! What next?" She ran to the window quickly and peered into the road. A moment later she was back at the 'phone.

"Of course, there's nobody watching the house!" she reported, almost indignantly.

"Road empty, eh?"

"There was one man in it, but he was merely reading a paper."

"H'm! Just under my height? Dark brown suit? Thinnish?"

"Yes! How on earth did you know?"

"I didn't know. I guessed. And another guess is that he's not reading that paper, but looking through a hole in it. Well, thanks, Winifred. I'm glad to find you're the same old sport as ever. If Tom wonders why I've not turned up, tell him some sudden business has made me change my plans. Anything you like. You've a fertile brain. Good-bye."

But before he replaced the receiver she detained him with a sudden question. "Dick!" she exclaimed. "You're quite *sure* she's innocent?"

"I'm rather glad you asked that," he responded, after a tiny pause, "though you'd better forget about it again, if you can. Yes—she's innocent, my dear. And if ever a girl needed a friend, by George *she* does!"

"She needs two, apparently," commented Winifred. "Well, provided I can remain on the right side of my husband and heaven, I'll try and be the second."

The conversation over, she moved towards the window again, but this time more cautiously. The thinnish man in the dark brown suit was still absorbed in his newspaper.

Chapter IX

The Second Victim

Richard replaced the receiver and left the public telephone box, glancing to right and left as he did so. Already a depressing and unaccustomed furtiveness had entered into his behaviour, and for the first time in his life he was realising the sensations of the hunted. "This is bad enough when you haven't done anything to deserve it," he told himself. "When you really have, it must be hell!"

In addition to the consolation of a clear conscience, one other factor helped to lighten his immediate mood. A practical, not a spiritual, factor. The blessed absence of Dutton.

Dutton had been a terrible difficulty, a difficulty which was not decreased by Richard's instinctive liking for the odd, annoying fellow. Descending from his contemplative breakfast in the dingy Chelsea shop, he had found the police sleuth buying acid-drops, and had even been offered one. The offer was accompanied by a solemn wink.

"No, thanks!" Richard had muttered.

"They're refreshing," Dutton had urged.

"I leave you to the refreshment," Richard had retorted.

"Don't hurry—I'm leaving, too," Dutton had smiled. "Which way are you going?"

And then had begun a ridiculous game of hide-and-seek which had wasted valuable hours.

Dutton's methods were the reverse of soothing. Sometimes he stuck close. Sometimes he pretended to lose himself. His absence was as nerve-racking as his presence, because you could never depend on it. Just when you believed you had shaken him off, you would spot him up a by-street, or find his reflection in a shop-window. He was never disturbed by discovery. He merely smiled or winked.

"You think you're winning, don't you?" Richard growled once, as they met on top of a bus.

"Bound to win, sir," he replied. "I've got the whole of the law behind me."

"If only you had the sense to see that I'm not against the law!"

"Then why not join up with the law, sir?"

"We've already discussed that."

Dutton nodded.

"And I've told you I'm choosing my own method," Richard went on.

"Different methods. Same object. Quite so, sir," agreed Dutton, and lit a cigarette.

"Do you really think that your method, at this moment, is leading anywhere?" demanded Richard. "Do you think you're going to learn anything from me while sticking to me like a leech?"

Rather to his surprise, Dutton considered the question seriously. Then he responded: "Nothing at all, sir. Good-day!" And left the bus.

Richard was not deceived. He knew he was still under observation. But, in the afternoon, one of his many ruses did actually succeed when, affecting an air of relief and confidence, he boarded a Richmond train, contrived to leave it without being observed, and returned Chelsea-wards. It was from a telephone box in Chelsea that he had just communicated with his sister, and had learned the satisfactory news that Dutton was reading a newspaper in Hope Avenue.

But the other news he had learned was less satisfactory. Sylvia Wynne had wanted to get in touch with him, and had failed. Likewise, the detective-inspector, though in his case the failure caused no tears.

"Confound that fellow Dutton!" Richard growled. "But for him, I might have made a bit of headway by now!"

Well, Dutton was off the board for the moment, and it would be folly to waste the moment. He turned towards Tail Street, deciding that the first use to which he must put his freedom was to revisit the studio. Perhaps Miss Wynne might be there, waiting for him! The mere thought added speed to his feet.

He left the telephone box at nine minutes past four. At twenty past he was in Tail Street, right round the curve of it, and facing the blue door. It was nine hours since he had first seen that door. He had spent most of the nine hours wandering fruitlessly about. How had others spent the time?

Had Richard known how two others had spent it, the frown on his face would have been considerably deeper, and would have meant rather more than, "Yes, but how am I going to get *in*?"

He no longer possessed the obliging latch-key. He had returned it, in the bag, to Miss Wynne. Would he have to repeat the performance of ringing the bell?

On the point of doing so, he changed his plan. He remembered the window at the back of the studio—the window with the defective catch. It had been open when he had left in the morning. If no one had returned, it would still be open.

"Yes, and if it *isn't* open," he reflected, "then some one *will* have returned, and it will be up to me to find out who that some one is!"

He wound his way out of the street, and steered for the narrow back alley. Now he was in the alley, walking with exaggerated stealth. Like Tail Street itself, the alley refused to go straight—possibly it was affected by the habits of the locality—and an angle hid the studio window from view. Despite his stealth, Richard rounded the angle almost at a run.... Then, abruptly, he stopped short. "Closed!" he muttered.

Yes, the window was closed, proving indisputably that somebody *had* been in the studio since his last visit. Who was that somebody? Dutton? Inspector James? Sylvia Wynne herself? Or the as yet unidentified Terror who was responsible for the activities of all three, and also of Richard Temperley?

More important: Was the somebody still in the studio? Straining, at this very moment, to discover the identity of the new intruder in the alley?

This thought induced an increase of caution, and Richard bent low as he approached the window, keeping well beneath the level of the ledge. Reaching the window, he raised his head slowly. "If anybody is watching me from inside," he reflected, grimly, "they must be getting a nasty shock at this moment!" Well, he'd had several, so it was only fair!

Now his eyes drew up to the glass. For an instant he could only see the reflection of the brick wall behind him. Then, as he advanced his eyes closer, he saw into the room. In the distance, a paper-boy was calling.

The room was empty.

Well, that did not mean that the whole place must be empty. There were a couple of rooms off the studio. Probably a small kitchen and a small bedroom. He must get in somehow, and find out whether they, also, were empty.

He examined the window. The defective latch indicated the obvious solution. In a few seconds he had profited by the defect—how many others had profited by it before him?—and had got the window open. One leg over the ledge. The other leg. Now he was inside once more!

He stood still and listened. A faint sound came from one of the little rooms off the studio. Faint and regular. He took a step towards the door, and then stopped again. He didn't like the idea of an open window behind him. Stealing back to the window, he quickly closed it. He discovered that his heart was thumping. The discovery annoyed him. "You mustn't develop nerves, my lad!" he reproved himself. "That'll never do!" He put it down to Dutton. Dutton, in spite of his amiability, would upset the nerves of a sleep-sodden toad. "It wouldn't surprise me to find the fellow sitting at the easel when I turn round," thought Richard. And turned round swiftly to disprove the unpleasant possibility.

Dutton was not sitting at the easel. The stool had no occupant. It was lying on its side.

"Who knocked that over?" frowned Richard.

The paper-boy's cry in the distance grew a little nearer.

This overturned stool was disconcerting. He had not noticed it when he had first dropped in through the window. It could not have toppled over while he had turned back to the window, could it? Perhaps the sound beyond the door had completely monopolised him. His attention had immediately been directed to the sound. Yes, but what had happened to the sound?...Ah, there it was, still! When you are staring in astonishment at an overturned stool you ignore your ears, and when you are listening to a disquieting sound you ignore your eyes....Faint and rhythmic. Like dripping....*Dripping!* "My God!" he gasped.

He was across the studio floor in a flash. He seized the door handle, and threw the door open.

Nearer still grew the paper-boy's voice. Very faintly, the words could now be heard.

"Another Murder! Another Murder!"

Richard did not hear the words. He was passing through one of those devastating revulsions that twist our contorted feelings into knots and give us an impulse towards hysterical laughter. He was staring into a little kitchen scullery, and a tap was dripping into a sink. "So *that* is what's been sending cold shivers up and down my spine, eh?" he thought. "Yes, really, Richard, you are a bit of an ass!"

A face grinned back at him, long and distorted. He shook his fist at it. It was his own face, reflected in the bright surface of a pan.

Well, that was that. The dripping was not blood, but water. Even the water, however, emphasised the fact of a recent presence, and hinted ominously at a rapid departure. A methodical person—the sort of person, for instance, who would keep the surfaces of pans so bright—would not leave a tap dripping and a stool overturned unless the departure were inspired by some special urgency.

Quickly he completed his examination of the little kitchen, after turning off the tap and terminating its unwelcome music. He found nothing else either to disturb or to comfort him. Leaving the kitchen, and closing the door, he opened the door to the other room, pausing for a moment with his fingers on the handle.

This would be her bedroom. That necessitated a little breath of reverence. Besides, you had to pause before every new thing you did, especially when you were passing through the studio. You might find another chair overturned, or a moving smudge beyond the frosted glass of the front door that could be glimpsed at the end of the little hall-passage, or a figure emerging from the curtained corner.

His eyes roamed towards the curtained corner. He had hidden there once himself. Something impressed itself vaguely on his consciousness. A small object on the ground, gleaming dully from a shadow. A handkerchief? The newsboy's voice was silent.

Richard entered the bedroom. For an instant he forgot terror and all the unsavoury things that mock at life. His gaze rested on a bed. It was smooth and neat, and a covering of blue silk lay over it. The pillow was also smooth and neat. A chair, a small dressing-table, and a small chest practically completed the furnishing of the room. Silver-mounted toilet articles lay on the dressing-table, reflected in the mirror, and looking very tidy and orderly. A blue boudoir cap hung from a knob on the mirror. "Blue is her favourite colour," Richard decided. The decision was justified by a glimpse of two blue shoes peeping from under the bed. As his figure joined the toilet articles in the mirror, he paused and questioned it.

"I say—who was the last figure reflected here?" he asked. "The one before *you*?"

The reflection stared back solemnly. It knew no more than did its origin. And mirrors themselves never reveal their secrets. If they did, their stories would put those of mere novelists to shame.

Regretfully he left the bedroom, and now his eye was again caught by the small object gleaming dully from the shadow. This time it grew into the focus of his consciousness and registered there. He walked to it suddenly, and picked it up.

It was not a handkerchief. It was a scrunched, orange envelope. "By Jove! Telegram!" he exclaimed.

He opened the envelope eagerly. There were no contents. This was disappointing, since the message might have told him much. It might have given him a clue to Miss Wynne's whereabouts....

"Yes, but is it *to* Miss Wynne?" he thought suddenly.

He flattened out the surface. "Wynne, 4 Tail Street, Chelsea." That settled the question. She had returned. She had received it.

"Well, maybe she's left the form somewhere else," he reflected. "On a table or something."

He began to look around. He went to a desk, opening drawers and poking his hand in pigeon-holes unscrupulously. There was not a sign of any pale pink form. But he made one discovery of interest. He found a packet of white telegram forms—telegrams start white, and only turn pink in transit—and on the top form was the vague indentation of recent writing.

He studied the indentation closely. He could just make out one-and-a-half words, but simple deduction turned them into two. They were

"...ribly urgent"

An open book on the settee suddenly caught his eye. Recognising its familiar appearance, he hurried to it. It was an A B C, open at page 72, and the names of Brimscombe, Brimsdown, Brinkburn, Brinklow stared up at him.

The paper-boy's voice rose again, now considerably closer.

Brinkworth, Brinscall...

"Another Murder! Another Murder!"

Brislington...

"Bristol Murder! Murder in Bristol! Another Murder! Murder in Bristol!..."

Chapter X

And How She Died

It was a memorable occasion for the paper-boy. Two murders in one day! You didn't often have such luck!

Test Matches and Cup-Ties got one sort of people. Robbed actresses and divorces got another. By elections got another. But murders got everybody, from top-hats downwards, and a couple of murders inside twenty-four hours was almost more than a starved little soul could stand. There is a limit for our capacity to register pure joy.

Thus, there was no hint of tragedy on the face of the paper-boy when, at twenty-five minutes to five on this auspicious date, an eager young man nearly toppled him over. The eager young man came running round a corner, and a collision was only averted by the paper-boy's smartness at ducking. He had learned this from intercourse with policemen.

"Paiper, sir?" piped the paper-boy.

The eager young man nodded, and snatched the extended periodical. Obviously, here was a genuine murder fan.

"Old woman, sir," volunteered the paper-boy, to save time. "Fahnd on 'er 'ead in a ditch."

The young man paid no attention to him. He had already begun to read.

"Blood orl over 'er," went on the paper-boy, disappointed. "Hupside-dahn."

The young man still paid no attention to him. The boy became resigned, and also practical. There was something the young man would have to pay to him.

"'Aven't 'ad the penny yet, sir," said the boy.

"Eh? Oh," jerked the young man.

He produced a sixpence and, while continuing to read, held it out. He appeared to think it was a penny. The paper-boy saw no reason to disillusion him, pocketed the coin, and abruptly departed.

This is what Richard Temperley was reading in the afternoon paper for which he had unconsciously paid six times its value:

"WOMAN IN DITCH
AVIATOR'S GRUESOME FIND NEAR
BRISTOL
SECOND TRAGEDY TO-DAY

"Following on the discovery of a dead man in the smoking room of a hotel at Euston this morning (reported in another column), comes a report from Charlton, near Bristol, of another gruesome tragedy suggesting foul play.

"Flying-Officer Turndike, of the Royal Air Force, training at the Filton Aerodrome which is attached to the factory of the Bristol Aeroplane Company, was passing over the village of Charlton at about one o'clock to-day when he noticed a figure below him crossing a field. He was flying low, a common occurrence in this neighbourhood owing to its proximity to the aerodrome, and he dropped lower still, with the idea, he admits, of impressing the figure beneath him with the dexterity of the Air Force.

"The figure turned out to be an old woman. She glanced upwards, paused, and remained staring into the sky. A moment later she dropped dead.

"Turndike effected a landing in an adjacent field, and then ran to the spot where the woman had fallen. He thought, at first, that she might have dropped through heart failure, but one glance at her proved that this theory was wrong. The woman had been shot.

"He immediately reported the matter, and the local police are busy searching the countryside for the mysterious individual who fired the shot, but who, up to the present, appears to have dissolved into thin air. With aviators on the spot, however, to assist in the search, an early capture is expected.

"Meanwhile, a grave question arises out of to-day's two tragedies. Are we on the verge of a new crime wave, and, if so, is Scotland Yard sufficiently alive to the position? As we have repeatedly stated in our columns..."

◇◇◇

But what had been repeatedly stated did not interest Richard Temperley.

There was no suggestion in the report that the two tragedies were definitely connected. But—*were* they connected? And, if so, by what links?

"Nonsense! Impossible!" he decided at one moment.

And then, the next, he thought of the open A B C. While the paper-boy outside the studio had called the word "Bristol," he himself had been staring at the word on an open page. Eye and ear recorded, simultaneously, the identical name, exaggerating its significance! Exaggerating? Yes, of course, exaggerating! Yet, to admit the exaggeration was also to admit a startling coincidence.

"What coincidence?" Richard demanded of himself.

"This coincidence," he replied to himself, bluntly. "Miss Wynne was at Euston when the first murder was committed. And now she has gone to Bristol!"

"How do you *know* she's gone to Bristol?" he again demanded of himself.

And again replied:

"I *don't* know! But the A B C was open at Bristol. She sent and received a telegram. She left the studio in a hurry. It's obvious she's gone to Bristol!"

The dispute continued:

"Well, suppose she has gone to Bristol?"

"Doesn't worry one, eh?"

"Yes, of course, it worries one! But—yes, look here! She telephoned to Richmond shortly before four, and this second murder was committed before *one*!"

"She could have got to Bristol by one, and could have returned to London by four. Inspector James would point that out in a twinkling, and might suggest that it would be a clever way to try and establish an alibi. Besides—how do you know she didn't telephone from Bristol?"

"Don't talk arrant nonsense! Let's get this straight! Are you suggesting that *she's* committed these murders?"

"Of course not. You know that a girl like her couldn't hurt a fly. But what's the use of arguing? You're worried about her—worried stiff—and, if you don't hurry, you'll miss the next Bristol train."

"What! Am I going to Bristol?" he challenged himself. "Am I going to do a fool thing like that?"

"Of course, you're going to Bristol," he censored himself. "You're next door to in love, aren't you, and when a fellow's in that condition he does *any* fool thing. There's a taxi. For goodness' sake, stop thinking, and call it!"

He hailed the taxi, but it did not slow up for the very good reason that its flag was down. Five unendurable minutes passed before he found a cab that was not engaged. Then followed ten minutes even more unendurable, for the cab turned out to be one of the two taxis that had gone into the Ark, and it was being driven by Noah's grandfather.

"*Can't* you get a move on?" Richard called at last, out of the window.

The driver responded by applying his brake and stopping. Then he dismounted from his seat, made an examination and discovered that he was out of petrol.

To find another taxi took another three minutes. Paddington station became an inaccessible Mecca during a long traffic blockage. But it was reached at last, and the impatient passenger leapt out.

"Oi! The fare!" cried the driver. Like paper-boys, taximen have sometimes to look after themselves.

Within thirty more seconds, Richard had paid the taximan, bought his ticket, and reached the platform from which the Bristol train departed. Now that he was free of London streets he could make his own time. Petrol does not run out, and policemen do not bar your way, on railway platforms.

But other mishaps can happen. When he reached the platform from which the Bristol train was due to leave, he found that it had just departed.

Chapter XI

Shocks

The train Richard Temperley missed by a narrow margin of twenty seconds went at 5.15. There was not another till 6.30. An hour and a quarter to wait—an hour and a quarter during which to hang on to a mad impulse and to argue with sanity!

"Fate made you miss that train," Sanity was insisting in his ear. "Accept the ruling of Fate and drop the whole business. Go to your comfortable sister in Richmond and play bridge."

"Sylvia Wynne may be on that train you've just missed," whispered Mad Impulse in his other ear. "Going to the very spot where the second murder was committed, just as she went to the first. And she rang you up before leaving—wanted to get in touch with you. What! Leave her to face things alone, after *that*?"

Then another thought occurred to him. Perhaps she had telephoned to Richmond a second time? And perhaps, this time, she *had* left a message? In that case, Fate might not have played him such a bad trick, after all! In two minutes he was in a station telephone box, speaking to his sister.

"Any news?" he asked, without preamble.

"Yes," came the prompt reply. "The canary's swallowed a pip."

"Don't rot!"

"I'm not! It's quite true."

"Of course, you're incorrigible! Is there any other news, then?"

"She hasn't 'phoned again."

"Has anybody else?"

"Only the butcher."

Richard took a breath, and started afresh. "What about the fellow by the lamp-post?" he asked.

"He went away, but now he's back again," she told him.

"Don't worry! He never went away!"

"I'm inclined to believe you. Do you want me to do anything about him?"

"Yes. Keep him there!"

"Certainly, dear. I'll hang a bit of toasted cheese outside the front door."

"I suppose you *must* be foolish?" he sighed.

"Foolish? I like that!" came the retort. "How do you *expect* me to keep him here? Go out with a rope and lassoo him to the lamp-post?"

Richard smiled.

"You're quite right, Winnie," he said. "I imagine I'm a bit potty."

"I hope you're nothing worse, Dick! Where are you telephoning from?"

"That's a leading question."

"It's meant to be."

"Sorry. Nothing doing. Love to the canary. Good-bye."

He rang off. He did not feel in the least apologetic. The less his sister knew, the better it would be for her if there were any trouble. And Richard believed there was going to be a lot of trouble. In which prediction, he did not err. Leaving the telephone box, he glanced at the clock. Twenty minutes past five. How the hands were crawling!

He went into a restaurant, and ordered tea. By slow-motion eating and drinking he managed to prolong the meal to half an hour, and afterwards he sat and smoked. Just as well, he decided, to stay in the restaurant. He was not in a mood at the moment to court publicity.

At a quarter-past six he left the restaurant and walked towards the platform from which the 6.30 Bristol train was due to start, but suddenly he changed his mind and re-visited the telephone box.

"How's the canary?" he asked, when connected once more with Richmond.

"What about a canary?" came a male response.

"Blast!" muttered Richard, and rang off hastily.

He certainly did not wish to discuss matters with his brother-in-law! Why on earth had Tom Mostyn chosen this afternoon of all afternoons to return home early? It was a wretched nuisance! If he rang up again, ten to one his brother-in-law would answer again. And if he waited—well, the train wouldn't!

Thus, a moment of facetiousness prevented Richard from learning some news that would have interested him.

He walked to the platform. The train was almost due to depart, and late-comers were hurrying to find good seats. There were plenty of good seats, as it happened, for the train was not crowded, and Richard was able to select an empty compartment. He was soon joined, however, by a stout, good-natured countryman who selected the seat opposite Richard, opened his newspaper, and became immediately social.

"'Ave ye read about second murder?" he exclaimed.

Richard frowned, and replied rather shortly,

"Yes. Gruesome, isn't it?"

He wished he had not added the "isn't it?" for this invited a continuation of the conversation, and Richard was not feeling social himself. He wished the countryman in Jericho. He wanted to think. The countryman, however, seemed to prefer conversation to reflection, and as Richard sat down in the corner seat opposite he observed that it was a sight more'n gruesome. It was *funny*!

The word "funny" was significantly emphasised.

"How do you mean, funny?" asked Richard, wondering how to choke him off without being rude.

"Well, I'm not meanin' hoomerous, lad," observed the countryman, solemnly, "but—*funny*!" Then, as Richard refused to press him further, he went on, "Do ye s'pose, now, second murder had aught to do wi' first murder?"

The countryman could hardly have asked a question more likely to force his companion's interest. Noting its effect and the sudden gleam in Richard's eye, he leaned back against the cushion in a sort of triumph.

Richard, on his side, regretted the gleam. His interest was genuine, but he was not disposed to reveal, even to a simple countryman, its extent. As casually as he could, he observed: "That's rather an odd idea of yours, isn't it?"

"Mebbe 'tis, sir," answered the countryman, "but then so was war in 1914. There's many an odd idea that turns out to be right idea."

"Quite true," agreed Richard, "but that doesn't prove every odd idea to be right. How on earth do you connect a murder committed at Euston with another murder committed at Bristol on the same day? Euston and Bristol aren't exactly next door to each other, you know."

The countryman, now definitely challenged, closed his eyes, and it seemed as though he were defeated. The guard blew his whistle. Some one was told to "Stand away there!" and disobeyed. The train began to move.

"You can go from one place to t'other, can't you?" said the countryman. His eyes were wide open again. "Same as we're doin' now?"

He goggled his eyes. He reflected the attitude of a man who has just made a good move at draughts, and all at once Richard, realising the possibilities of the game, decided to finish it. After all, two minds are better than one, even if the second mind has expanded among cabbages.

"You've evidently got something up your sleeve," smiled Richard subtly, "but I'm bothered if *I* can make out what it is!"

"Well, you see, I've bin thinkin'," replied the countryman, in the manner of one imparting an unusual fact, "and I've bin puttin' two and two together—"

"Don't you mean, one and one?"

"Eh? Oh! The murders! That's right, sir! And I come to this. First murder, she was committed, as they say, at five in the mornin'. Or thereabouts. Second murder, *she* was committed at one." He fished for a cigarette, found it, and lit it. He was a bit of a dramatist. "Well, sir," he remarked, as he threw the match away, "that's eight hours. Now, it ain't takin' *us* eight hours to go to Bristol!"

Richard nodded, and expressed his appreciation of the point. "But I still don't see the precise connection," he added.

"Train connection," the countryman pointed out.

"I mean between the two murders themselves," explained Richard, "not between the places they were committed at."

"If the murders was committed by same person, lad," asserted the countryman, doggedly, "there must be connection!"

"You're putting it the wrong way round," Richard retorted. "You've got to prove the connection before you can say that the murders *were* committed by the same person."

The countryman found this a little difficult, and he puzzled over it while they went through Ealing Broadway. Then he blinked and asked:

"Well, sir! What's *your* idea, now?"

Richard shook his head.

"I didn't say I'd got any idea," he parried. "We're discussing yours, aren't we?"

"Ay, but I thort, with smart mind like your'n, you'd hit on somethin'."

"Not a thing. I'm waiting to hear what *you've* hit on!"

Ruthlessly pressed, the countryman closed his eyes once more, sought inspiration, and reopened them. "'Ow about mad?" he asked.

"That's always a possibility," answered Richard.

"But, mind ye, not one o' them madmen ye can tell by the look of 'em. Ordin'ry person. Same as you and me might be, if one of us was mad, sittin' 'ere and torkin', and not knowin' which!" Yes, this countryman undoubtedly had ideas! Richard regarded him quizzically while the ideas ran on: "I knew a feller once, clever as politishun, 'e was, and you'd never know there was screw loose. Poured out tea fer me many a time, 'e did, and 'One lump fer you, George,' 'e'd say, 'I'm not one fer fergettin'.' And one day 'e goes out and comes back on a cow sayin' 'e's Black Prince. Back to the Battle o' Crecy, 'e was. Well, then, sir, mebbe this other one—one we're torkin' about—" He paused and looked down at his newspaper, which had slipped on to the floor of the compartment. "Mebbe this other one, now, thinks 'e's Crippen?"

He stooped, and regained the paper.

"And mebbe, if 'e does, we'll soon be readin' about *third* murder." He opened his paper.

"And mebbe, again, it isn't man at all, but *girl*!"

This apparently exhausted the countryman of his

complete stock of notions, and he buried himself behind his newspaper again to find new ones.

Richard, staring unprofitably at the newspaper screen, found himself frowning. He wondered why he was frowning.

Having nothing else to do, he set about trying to discover the reason. One frequently falls into a depressed state without being conscious of the cause, and the depression usually remains until one has unearthed the cause and proved its folly. Richard hoped, by this same process, to dispel his frown and to rid himself of a vague, disturbing sensation.

Was he annoyed with the countryman for having conversed with him about the murders? Couldn't be that. The murders were to-day's bright topics! To-morrow's would be a Government reverse, and the next day's a fire in Fleet Street. Was he annoyed with himself for having entered into the conversation and encouraged it? Couldn't be that, either. He had not committed himself in any way. How *could* one commit oneself to a simple-minded countryman?...

"Watch yourself, Richard!" he thought. "You're getting over-sensitive!"

Was he worried by the countryman's allusion to lunatics, and did he think the countryman might be one himself? Ridiculous! Was he worried by the countryman's suggestion that the murderer was a girl?...

"Might be that," he conjectured, fretfully. "Yes—might be that!"

But he knew it wasn't that. He knew it was something far more subtle, something that remained just round the corner of his eye, like an untrappable shadow. A moving shadow. Now with a vague shape. Now with no shape. Now with a shape again. A shape like a horse....

Horse? Why, on earth, a horse? Yet it was a horse! There it was, galloping absurdly through Richard's mind! A black horse. And, on the horse, a prince. A black prince...

"Eureka!" thought Richard, galvanically. "The Black Prince! And that Battle of Crecy! That's what's worrying me! How the devil does a simple countryman who can't pronounce his 'h's' know that the Black Prince fought at Crecy?"

The discovery of the cause did not, in this case, conclude the discomfort. On the contrary, the discomfort was increased, and for several stations Richard revolved the discovery in his mind, trying to ridicule it out of its assumption of significance. If only the countryman had lowered his newspaper and had continued with his conversation, Richard could have marked him now more closely and could have settled his suspicions one way or the other. Now he was anxious to get another glimpse of the face so persistently concealed behind the newspaper, and to hear once more the voice so doggedly silent. He could have learned from them whether the man who remembered history so well had truly been born among the cabbages!

But the man made no attempt to renew the conversation—perhaps he, also, had his secret anxieties and his self-doubts!—and he refused to respond to Richard's own attempts. A remark about the weather was apparently unheard. So was a request for a match. And when, making one more effort, Richard asked his invisible vis-à-vis whether he would mind having the window down a little, the only response he received was a faint snore. The newspaper was now frankly covering the countryman's head, like a tent.

"Confound the fellow!" thought Richard, angrily. "I'll bet he's got his eyes wide open, and is watching me through the print!"

He quelled a sudden impulse to snatch the paper away. That would have been too blatant a declaration of war! Later on, he thanked heaven for his restraint, for if you smell the enemy it is just as well not to let him know that you are sniffing.

The sense that he was under observation increased, growing more and more distressing. Snores from beneath the newspaper also increased, and did not lessen the distress. But presently a happier moment came. The voice of the dining-car attendant sounded from the corridor. He was announcing that seats could now be taken for the first dinner.

It was a welcome diversion, and Richard took immediate advantage of it. The newspaper stirred—apparently the sleeper behind it had his ears open as well as his eyes!—but Richard stirred first, and was in the corridor with a speed that, to an uninitiated onlooker, would have appeared almost gluttonous. "You're not going to sit at *my* table, young feller me lad!" decided Richard, grimly. "I've had as much of you to-day, Mr. Dutton, as I can stand!"

But another shock awaited him in the corridor. The smile of momentary relief with which Richard had emerged from his compartment disappeared as he came upon an elderly man with a grave face talking to a ticket official. He paused abruptly. The elderly man paused also, and turned towards him.

"Good-evening, Mr. Temperley," said Detective-Inspector James, and stood aside with a smile.

The shock of James was greater than the shock of Dutton. You had grown to expect Dutton, but you thought you had finished with James! Great as these shocks were, however, an even greater awaited him in the dining-car.

As he entered it, some one looked up from one of the little tables that lined the right-hand wall, and he found himself staring into the eyes of Sylvia Wynne.

Chapter XII

Dinner for Two

In looking back over this most amazing period of his life, Richard Temperley did not award himself a hundred marks for proficiency. He recalled many occasions when he had acted cumbrously and many moments when he had acted foolishly. Was not the entire adventure, from a sober point of view, an expression of folly? Even if it were not, even if young men were permitted by the laws of sanity to chase all over England in the cause of young ladies they had no knowledge of, Richard was not especially fitted for this sort of thing, and this was his first personal introduction into the complexities of crime and the subtleties of the police force.

"Put me against a demon bowler," he reflected, "or stick me on a tennis court, and all's serene. But Scotland Yard and Bill Sykes don't see me at my best!"

It must be remembered, too, that he was also ploughing through an emotional confusion that had nothing to do with crime or detectives, and that was centred in the mysterious attraction by which Nature catches and utilises us for her inscrutable ends.

Nevertheless, Richard did congratulate himself, and with justice, on the manner in which he handled the astounding moment when his bewildered gaze fell upon Sylvia Wynne in the dining-car. Another man might have given the moment best, thrown up his hands in helpless submission, and cried, "Kamerad!"

The thing he wanted most in all the world to happen had happened, but it had happened in the worst possible circumstances. He was being shadowed—so he had been given to believe—with the sole object of revealing to his pursuers a lady whom they were anxious to question, but whom so far they had never met. He, Richard Temperley, was their only key to the lady's identity. And here, before him, was the lady. And, only a little way behind him, were the pursuers. A single false move at this moment, not merely on his part but on the part of the lady who was assumedly unaware of her danger, the merest word of greeting or glance of recognition would be fatal.

And when your whole heart is bursting to say the word and to give the glance, it is trebly to your credit if you control yourself sufficiently to avoid them.

Richard did not control merely himself. He controlled, also, Sylvia Wynne. He saw the startled light dawning in her eye, and he realised that she could give the game away even more easily than he could. She was facing the corridor from which, at any instant, Detective James and the confounded countryman might appear, while he himself had his back turned to the corridor. Profiting by this fact, he threw the girl a look intended to warn her of her position.

It was a most difficult look to muster all in an emotional moment, and perhaps it was as well for his vanity that no mirror reflected it for him; but, however lacking in aesthetic value, its practical value was immediately demonstrated, for it produced the desired result. The girl, with an intelligence little short of his own, swiftly banished her expression of astonished recognition, and removed her eyes casually to the window.

Then Richard completed his strategy with a culminating stroke of daring subtlety. He gazed about vaguely, and, with an expressionless face, took the unoccupied seat at Sylvia Wynne's table.

"Inspector James knows I've seen him," ran the mind behind the expressionless face, as Richard sat down, "and he will know I am on my guard. Surely, the last person in the world I would select to dine with in these circumstances would be the very girl they hope me to lead them to! Just as the last person *I* ought to have suspected was an old countryman who voluntarily opened a conversation with me!"

It was an astute move, as well as a very desirable one. The question remained—would the astute detective be equally astute, and read through his bluff?

That was not the only question that remained. There was another. Could two young people who were furiously conscious of each other continue the bluff and act as perfect strangers?

While Richard strove to play his part, a voice fell upon his ears and a faint dampness grew on his forehead. He fought the dampness with all his might. "I can control my expression," he thought, desperately, "but how the deuce does one control perspiration?" He had not discovered the answer when the individual who had evoked the perspiration came by, and stopped at the table.

"This is a lucky meeting, Mr. Temperley," said Inspector James, pleasantly. "I've been trying to get into touch with you."

"Have you?" replied Richard, racking his brain to find out whether he ought to admit his knowledge of this fact or not.

"Yes. I telephoned to Richmond. Didn't your sister tell you?" Subtle fellow, this James!

"I've not been to Richmond," answered Richard.

"Oh, I see. I thought you might have been there after I 'phoned. Mrs. Mostyn said she was expecting you."

"That's right. She was. But I couldn't manage it."

"As a matter of fact," pursued the inspector, "she seemed rather anxious about you. She'd been expecting you all day, and hadn't had a word."

"And when a detective-inspector rang up," smiled Richard, praying that his forehead did not look as moist as it felt, "I don't suppose that lessened her anxiety?"

Richard, even while he suffered, could be subtle, too! By this casual remark, he identified the inspector for the benefit of his vis-à-vis.

"I'm afraid it didn't," admitted James, "but I did my best to reassure her. I hope you reassured her, also? Some one else had rung you up, you see, just before I did."

"Nice of you to be so interested, inspector. Yes—I reassured her."

"I suppose she told you about my 'phone call?"

"Well, naturally."

"Oh, then you knew I'd been trying to get in touch with you?" The inflection was that of a question, but the significance was that of a statement with a tinge of reprimand in it. The inspector's voice remained quite amiable, however, as he added, "And the other call? Did she mention that, too?"

Then Richard, deciding that he had had quite enough for the moment, and that all this needed sorting out before he could proceed any farther, applied the closure by playing another of his bold, audacious strokes. He donned a slight frown, and glanced significantly at the girl opposite him. His frown attempted to convey to the inspector, "I say—is all this really necessary before a stranger?"

The stranger did not seem to be taking any interest in the conversation. She was staring idly at the River Thames over which they were just passing. Inspector James, however, appeared to realise Richard's point, and he nodded, with a faint smile.

"We'll resume later," he said, and passed on.

"How did I come out of it?" wondered Richard. "Not too badly, I hope. I don't think I told him anything he didn't already know. After all, Dutton will have kept him pretty well posted! And Miss Wynne now knows who he is—for I'll wager her ears were wide open—while if he swallowed my implication that I disliked discussing matters before strangers, I'm something useful up!"

The necessity for caution was not yet removed, however, and Richard endured an anxious moment when he found the girl's eyes on him again. He refused to meet them. Taking up the menu he murmured to it, "Not just yet—there's another," and became quickly absorbed in the relative merits of Consommé Laitue and Crème Tomate as the "other" came along.

There may have been some among the well-dressed diners who were surprised that a very considerably less well-dressed countryman should search for a seat among them. Snobbery is not rife in a third-class dining-car, where all classes mix with the exception of the essentially first-class; but this countryman was particularly unshaven and grubby, and some social distinction still exists.

Richard himself, however, was not in the least surprised—his emotion was just acute annoyance—and it seemed quite obvious to him that the countryman should select, of the only two vacant seats left, the seat nearest his own, despite the fact that the three other occupants of the table were two highly fashionable women and a man with an eye-glass. "Room fer a small 'un?" the countryman inquired, with somewhat heavy jocularity. A frigid silence gave consent.

Well! Now what? The situation was intolerable! Fruitless minutes slipped by—minutes that were precious, and that should have been crowded with good work, both practical and spiritual. Waiters with cleverly-balanced plates appeared. The soup came and went.

In vain Richard tried to devise some plan by which he could open a conversation without inviting suspicion. Yet even if he opened the conversation, how could he steer it into productive channels? What could he say that, while conveying something to Sylvia Wynne, would convey nothing to other listening ears?

The fish appeared before the plan, and he was driven to the feeble device of passing the salt.

"Thank you," murmured Sylvia.

"And that's that!" thought Richard, impotently. "Oh, for the brain of a Poirot or Sherlock Holmes!"

Their eyes had met for an instant over the salt-cellar, and he gathered from her expression that the strain was beginning to tell on her, also. He grew more and more disgusted with himself, as the situation grew harder and harder to bear. Was nothing beyond salt to pass between them during the entire meal? Would they rise at the end of it, and separate wordlessly to their respective compartments? And would he lose her again, to resume his search in Bristol?...

And then, at last a plan came to him.

It was not much of a plan. It could not lead to any immediate intercourse. But it was a move, if only a pawn's move, in a game that was threatening to develop into a stale-mate; and a move that, despite its limitations, required the most careful handling.

It took Richard Temperley six minutes to complete the move, for he only moved a little bit at a time. The first bit was to affect interest in a cross-word puzzle in his afternoon paper. He still had by him the newspaper he had bought, for sixpence, outside Sylvia's studio. The second bit was to take his pencil from his pocket, and to jot down his inspirations. The next, apparently prompted by the approach of the waiter, was to desert the cross-word puzzle for the menu, ignoring a politeness that might have urged him to let a lady consult it first.

His pencil was still held carelessly in his hand, and the next bit of the move was to use the pencil on the menu. The pencil was well concealed behind the menu, and unless you had been actually looking over his shoulder you might have assumed that he was merely running over the items with his thumb.

The next bit was to lay down the menu, once more ignoring the polite attention of handing it across the table, and turning again to the cross-word puzzle.

The waiter drew up, and looked inquiringly at Sylvia.

"Mutton," said Richard, growing more and more careless of his manners.

The waiter, more insistent on manners, ignored the order, and handed Sylvia the menu. Richard rejoiced inwardly. This was exactly what he had hoped the waiter would do, and why he had refrained from passing the menu himself. The girl glanced at the menu. She studied it rather a long while. But her expression did not change, and all she said as she laid the menu down was: "Beef."

She gave no indication that the menu bore the pencilled addition: "When and where?"

In due course, the beef and the mutton turned up.

"Mustard?" asked Richard, his manners improving.

"Please," she replied.

He shoved the mustard over. The pencil went over with it. "Thank you," said Sylvia, politely, and suddenly stooped to regain her serviette.

The serviette, rather obligingly, had slipped from her knees, and when she picked it up she placed it carelessly on the table, over the pencil.

If men could purr like cats, Richard would have purred just then. He would have purred with delight at his knowledge that she had responded to his gesture, and that she was not wanting in coolness and ingenuity. She had now definitely joined in the game—a game for Two versus the World—and before long she would doubtless make a move herself....

Yes, but meanwhile he must not declare to all and sundry that he wanted to purr! He sobered his expression, and directed it severely towards his mutton.

Her move came with the next course.

"Ice or fruit?" inquired the waiter.

"Fruit," replied Sylvia.

"And you, sir?"

Richard stretched his hand towards the menu. The waiter had only mentioned ice and fruit, but there might be something else. There was something else, though all Richard said was: "I'll have fruit, too."

The something he did not mention ran:

"Bristol, outside station, 11, will try."

As he laid the menu down she leaned towards him.

"Sugar?" she inquired.

Their eyes met again; and when she passed the sugar, their fingers met, also. Thus, after valiant duty, the little pencil came back to him, and gave him an instant that glowed like warm sunshine through the gathering shadows. "Thank you," he said.

The countryman's voice sounded suddenly in his ear.

"Can I 'ave sugar after you?" asked the countryman.

Chapter XIII

Temperley Versus James

Mohamed went to the mountain because the mountain would not come to him. Richard Temperley went to the detective because he was quite certain that, if he did not, the detective *would* come to him, and he did not wish to betray his anxiety by attempting to avoid a meeting that was inevitable. Possibly the detective realised all this. Detectives are supposed to read your mind like a book. But, thought Richard for his consolation, detectives often have to assume knowledge they do not possess in order to acquire that knowledge from an unsuspecting dupe; and Richard determined, as he entered the detective's compartment, that he was not going to give anything away voluntarily. If James tried to find out what he knew, he would return the compliment, by trying to find out what James knew!

"Ah, Mr. Temperley!" exclaimed James, looking up. "And how have you been using your time since our meeting at Euston this morning?"

He smiled, and Richard smiled back. Richard was in a fighting mood. He was under no delusions as to the odds against him, and he certainly did not commit the fatal error of underrating his enemy, but he had just emerged successfully, he told himself, from one important skirmish, and the victory was all the more complete because the enemy knew nothing whatever about it.

There was another reason why Richard felt in a fighting mood. For half an hour he had sat opposite the Cause for which he was fighting. It had strengthened his resolve, and had made the fight doubly worth while.

"What have I been doing?" he repeated, sitting down opposite the inspector. There was nobody else in the compartment. "Sounds rather like a leading question, doesn't it?"

"It is a leading question," nodded the inspector, unabashed. "I want to know everything you care to tell me about yourself."

"Don't you mean, everything I don't care to tell you?" suggested Richard.

"Right again, sir!" replied James. "The things you don't care to tell me are the things I want to know most. Assuming, of course," he added, "that there are any things you want to hide from me? Are there?"

"That's rather like the question of the business man who said to another business man, 'Oh, before we begin, are you honest?'"

"Well, I believe you are honest."

"Hooray! I'm terribly hopeful on that point myself."

"Only, if you are, why not give me an honest description of how you've been spending your time?"

"You'd better apply to an individual named Dutton," answered Richard. "What he doesn't know about me is hardly worth knowing."

"You seem to know something about him, too," remarked the inspector, rather dryly.

"I know all I want to, thank you," retorted Richard. "Where did you pick the fellow up?"

"I hope he hasn't annoyed you?"

"Good Lord, no! His intentions have been most flattering! If I'd been a Hollywood star I couldn't have been followed more assiduously! By the way, inspector, I believe one can seek redress for being followed in Hyde Park. Can I sue Dutton for pursuing me through Oxford Street, Regent Street, Hammersmith, Tottenham Court Road and the Zoo?"

"It takes two to make a chase."

"Meaning?"

"That if Dutton had a reason for running after you, you had a reason for running away."

"Well, suppose it was just a sporting reason? Suppose I object to being run after, and decide to make my pursuer breathless?"

"And suppose we stop fencing, and see whether we can really get anywhere?" proposed Inspector James, with a slight frown. "Dutton's out of it, for the moment—"

"*Is* he?" interrupted Richard. "To go on with our supposing, suppose he *isn't*?" James raised his eyebrows. "Listen, inspector. I admit I'm green to this game. Even if—for sport—I pit myself against you, I realise that I'm up against all your organisation and experience. But I have my moments of intelligence, and I had one such moment in this train when I realised that all countrymen are not as countrified as they seem to be!"

The inspector absorbed this information silently, and suddenly Richard cursed himself. Was this one of his moments of intelligence? Had he admitted too much? "By Jove, I *am* green!" he thought. "If Dutton learns that I guessed who he was, he may guess on his side that I was putting up a bluff during dinner! Why isn't there some invention for taking words back!" When James spoke, however, he did not refer to Dutton.

"Sport," he said, reflectively. "Yes, I agree it's an excellent hobby. But does it sometimes interfere with serious business, do you think?"

"In that case, I retract the word," replied Richard, quickly. "I regard this as very serious business."

"I'm glad to hear you say that, Mr. Temperley, although I've never seriously doubted it. We're on common ground here, at any rate. It is very serious business indeed, and I'm afraid the business may grow more serious still before we've finished with it. You know, of course, why I'm travelling to Bristol?"

"To help Dutton shadow me?"

"I'm going to Bristol to investigate a second murder that has been committed to-day."

"I see."

"Do you?"

"What do you mean?"

"I'm going to trust you with some information, Mr. Temperley, that so far has not been trusted to the newspapers. I take it, you've read about this second Charlton murder?"

"Yes, of course."

"A woman dropped dead in a field."

"Yes."

"While an aviator was doing sky-tricks over her head."

"Yes."

"She was shot."

"By the aviator?"

"Only if the aviator was at Euston at 5 a.m. this morning, and I have already ascertained that he could not have been."

"You mean," said Richard, watching the inspector closely, "that your opinion is that these two murders were committed by the same person?"

"That's my opinion, just as it is your opinion."

"How do you know it's my opinion?"

"Isn't it?"

"I asked my question first."

"Then I'll answer it, because, after all, mine wasn't necessary. This journey you're taking proves that it is your opinion."

"Oh, does it?" murmured Richard. "Well, for the moment, we'll let that point go. But does your opinion rest upon my opinion?"

"Not in the least. We have arrived at the same conclusion, you and I, through quite separate channels. My opinion rests upon the information I was going to trust you with. A smart Bristol constable who arrived on the scene of the murder within a few minutes of Flying Officer Turndike's report found something in the grass a few yards away from the dead woman. Can you guess what it was?"

"Good Heavens! You don't mean it!" cried Richard Temperley, thereby proving that he guessed.

"Yes—another of those crimson Z's," nodded the inspector, gravely. "And I'm beginning to wonder, Mr. Temperley, how many more of them we are going to find before we've finished the job?"

There was a silence, while the train altered its note and flashed through Didcot. Beyond, it resumed its song of the open.

"So perhaps you can understand," resumed the inspector, "why I'm so keen to get all the assistance I can. Why Dutton has been following you, and stood so patiently outside your sister's house at Richmond. And why I, after telephoning to Richmond and gathering a few fragments of information, went to a studio in Chelsea to have a look round."

"What! Did you go to the studio, too?" exclaimed Richard.

"Just a few minutes before your own last visit."

"My own—? How do you know I went there again?"

"Because I was there during the whole time that you were. Behind a curtain in a corner. It was rather amusing to watch you doing almost the identical things I had just done myself. You got through the window in the same way, and closed it after you in the same way. You were interested, as I was, in the overturned stool. You were deceived by the dripping of a tap—only you turned it off, whereas I didn't. You examined a lady's bedroom—and took rather a long time over it."

"Well, I'm damned!" muttered Richard. "Suppose I'd found you in your funk-hole?"

"It would merely have advanced this conversation by an hour or two," answered James. "At one moment I thought you were going to find me. But you picked up a telegram envelope instead. I had thrown it down just before your arrival—in the spot where *I* had found it. And then you made another discovery that hurried you to Paddington station, where you missed the 5.15 train, and also a certain young lady who was travelling on it. Again, as I did."

He paused. Richard, drinking all this in, found the draught a little intoxicating. They had missed the 5.15 together! But so had the young lady who was supposed to be travelling on it! Was Inspector James genuine in his suggestion that he did not know the young lady had missed it, also?…

"What more do you know?" inquired Richard.

"Well, I know that you telephoned from Paddington, and I conclude that you telephoned to Richmond. I also telephoned to Richmond—"

"Oh, so *that's* how Dutton got on to it that I was on this train!"

"Dutton and I certainly had an interesting conversation. I suppose, the second time you telephoned to Richmond, your sister told you that Dutton had left the lamp-post?"

"Ah!" murmured Richard, non-committally.

Of course, Winifred had not told him. He knew that she would have done so, however, if she had answered the telephone instead of Tom.

He found himself struggling against a sensation of not too reasonable resentment. It was perfectly logical, in the circumstances, that his actions should have been so closely watched, but the fact was not soothing. Anxious to get a little of his own back, and to reinstate himself, he observed:

"Well, inspector, your Mr. Dutton's a smart fellow, I'll say that for him—but the next time he disguises himself as a half-witted countryman, tell him to avoid studious references to the Battle of Crecy."

"Yes, that rather interests me," answered Inspector James. "You see, Mr. Temperley, Dutton doesn't happen to be disguised as a countryman."

Chapter XIV

Nightmare

When you do not know what to say, the best plan is to say nothing. Richard Temperley said nothing for three minutes. And three minutes can be a long time when keen eyes are watching you from beneath iron-grey eyebrows, and when you are suffering from the shock of a mental bombshell.

During these three minutes, facts and theories and queries chased each other relentlessly through Richard's mind. He tried to resolve them into something coherent, but how could one attain coherence with those keen, watchful eyes immediately opposite? One needed to be alone, and unobserved. Then one might think! But thoughts become a mere jumble when somebody else is trying to discover what they are.

It is even doubtful how much one will gain by organising the jumble in such circumstances. A thought that is clear in one's mind may be clearly read by another mind!

At the end of the three minutes, however, Richard discovered his policy. Ultimate decisions must be delayed. For the moment, he must compromise.

"Do you admit armistices in your profession?" he began.

"What kind?" asked the inspector.

"There's only one kind, isn't there?"

"No, there are several kinds. They don't all end like the one in 1918."

"True," nodded Richard. "I suppose you mean it depends on who it's with?"

"Coupled with the particular circumstances," replied the inspector. "My profession isn't a hobby, you know. It's my duty to try and win."

"Yes, I appreciate that," said Richard. "Would your chances be decreased, do you think, if you arranged an armistice with *me*?"

"I'm afraid we're back where we started, Mr. Temperley," smiled the inspector. "I'm bound to repeat—what kind?"

Richard glanced at his watch. It said a quarter-to-eight. "Say, twelve hours and a quarter," he suggested. "Till breakfast time?"

"And what happens in those twelve and a quarter hours?" inquired the inspector, without showing any great enthusiasm.

"That's just what you mustn't inquire," retorted Richard.

"Then what must I do?"

"Why, draw off your sleuth-hounds."

"So that we can lose you?"

"That's rather a nasty one, inspector. You'd have my promise to meet you over the eggs and bacon."

"Yes, but suppose you couldn't keep the promise, Mr. Temperley?" suggested Inspector James. "I take it that, during the armistice, you'll be chasing a certain young lady. She may lead you a long way from my breakfast-table."

"Marvellous, how you think of everything! Just the same, if I *didn't* turn up, I could almost certainly report by telephone or wire."

"I don't like the 'almost.' "

"Nor do I. But it may be a sign of my good faith that I don't ignore it. Yes, it's a slight weakness in the situation that 'almost,' and you've got to work out whether it's a vital weakness or not."

"The weakness may take you into another county," remarked James, after a short pause. "As far removed from Gloucestershire as Gloucestershire is from Middlesex."

"Seems hardly likely," answered Richard, "though I won't deny the possibility."

"Well, let's forget the weakness for the moment, and look at the other side," said James. "The weakness suggests what I may lose by the armistice. What will I gain?"

Richard chose his words very carefully.

"You may gain my complete co-operation," he said.

"Depending on the result of a conversation with a certain young lady?"

"Possibly."

"And assuming that the conversation is as completely satisfactory as you expect your future co-operation to be?"

"If the conversation takes place, I am convinced that it will prove satisfactory," replied Richard, earnestly. "If I weren't, I'd have been with you from the word 'Go!'"

"Then why hasn't a certain young lady been with me from the word 'Go'?"

"That's what I want to find out. The armistice will help me."

"I see your point," murmured James, reflectively.

"Then—"

"But I may not share your optimism. If our young lady will not confide in the police, why should she confide in you unless you first convince her that you will not pass her confidence on? And if I haven't your word that you'll pass the confidence on, what *do* I gain by this armistice?"

"Your mind doesn't miss much," frowned Richard.

"I wish I could agree with you," smiled the inspector. "It misses a lot, and that's why I have to be so careful with it. And why I've got to go slow over this armistice idea of yours. Now, tell me, have I got it right? It means that you walk out of this compartment, and I lose all sight and knowledge of you till eight o'clock to-morrow morning. Then you turn up or communicate with me at some arranged place. Meanwhile, I've made no effort to watch you or follow you, and I've given instructions that nobody else shall make any effort. Is that what you mean?"

"Exactly what I mean," answered Richard.

"And, meanwhile, another murder may take place," said James. "And another little Z may be added to the collection." Richard was silent.

"How do I face my superiors, if that happens?" insisted Inspector James.

"Look here!" demanded Richard, suddenly, in return. "Do you really and truly connect Miss—this lady—"

"Miss Sylvia Wynne, of Studio 4, Tail Street, Chelsea," said James.

"Yes. Of course, you've got on to her name by now. Do you connect her with these horrible affairs as closely as all that?"

"Mr. Temperley," replied the inspector, leaning forward slightly in his seat, "it is obvious to me that Miss Wynne is closely connected with these horrible affairs, and you must know that as well as I do."

"Connected, perhaps! But not in the way you suggest!"

"I'm not suggesting anything beyond the fact that we have *got* to get in touch with her!"

"Very well! And how will you get in touch with her, excepting through me?"

"We may have other sources. But, assuming we haven't, isn't that all the more reason why we should refuse to sever our one link?"

"It won't *be* a link, if you watch me every moment!"

"You mean, you'll sit down somewhere in Bristol and do nothing, unless I agree to the armistice?"

"It would queer your pitch, wouldn't it?"

"And yours, sir. I play poker."

Richard thought furiously. Disappointment ran through him like a knife. He had believed he was winning, and now the inspector was hardening. Why on earth couldn't the fellow see things in his light...Poker? By Jove, Richard could play poker, too! And, all at once, he said,

"All right, Inspector. You talk of 'other sources.' Try them! Because, unless you *do* agree to my armistice, I'm *going* to sit down somewhere in Bristol and do nothing! Yes, and then," he added, "what will you say to your superiors if another of these murders takes place?"

Now it was Detective-Inspector James's turn to be silent, and hope rose once more in Richard's breast. He could see that this ultimatum was being seriously considered, and the knowledge proved two vital things to him. Firstly, that James had no faintest suspicion that Sylvia Wynne was on the train. Secondly, that the "other sources" referred to by the detective either did not exist, or were negligible.

"Yes, I *am* his only source!" he thought. "And he's wondering at this instant how best to use me!"

During the silence, someone passed along the corridor. It was the countryman. He paused and wagged his head at Richard, while the inspector raised his head suddenly and shot a sharp glance at him. Then the countryman stepped into the compartment for a moment; but it was only to let three impatient people precede him along the corridor.

The impatient people were the two well-dressed ladies and the superior young man with the eye-glass.

"That's a' right, lad," said the countryman as the young man with the eye-glass elbowed by him, "don't mind me! I'm only farmer!" Then, with another wink into the compartment, he, too, vanished.

"I agree to your armistice, Mr. Temperley," said the inspector. "Let's get the details fixed. I draw off my 'sleuth-hounds,' as you call them, till eight o'clock to-morrow. Then you call at Bristol police station, and we will have a chat."

"By Jove, you're a sport!" exclaimed Richard, in relief.

"If I am, it's only because I'm banking, as a practical man, on your being a sport, too," answered James, a trifle dryly. "It's arranged, then?"

"Wait a bit! Suppose I can't report at Bristol police station?"

"I'll have to risk that. It'll square up with your own risk."

"What's mine?"

"Well, you won't be followed, but our respective routes may cross each other, or even lead along the same trail. We shall leave *you* alone, but we don't guarantee to close our eyes to—interesting femininity, if we come across it during our own separate investigations. That's reasonable, isn't it?"

"Yes, I suppose so," murmured Richard, and suddenly smiled. "Life's always a risk in one form or another, however you look at it."

Inspector James smiled, too.

"Yes, and it's yet to be proved, Mr. Temperley," he said, "whether the greatest risk lies in the ugly face or the pretty one. Well, now we've settled our bargain, I'll begin on my part at once. For twelve hours from this moment, you cease to be under observation."

He rose, and left the compartment with rather disconcerting abruptness.

Richard looked after him. The conversation had terminated on a better note than he had expected. Twelve hours of freedom! Twelve hours without having to dodge Dutton! Twelve hours in which to re-establish communication with Sylvia Wynne, and find out the truth from her! It was an eternity!

All the same, Richard was taking no undue risks. At eleven o'clock that night Sylvia would meet him outside Bristol station, and until that time he would sit upon his impulses and ensure that he and she were not seen together, even accidentally, by Dutton, or by James, or by the countryman...

The countryman! Who the devil was the countryman? Richard closed his eyes, to probe this mystery further, and in the darkness of his closed lids he hit upon a solution so simple that he smiled. The countryman was just a countryman! Suspicion alone had given him a sinister interpretation. That allusion to Crecy...pooh! Nothing at all! Even the humblest of us have some scrap of knowledge, some remnant of the schoolroom, that stays by us when other knowledge has flown, and we love to trot the scrap out to create an impression. We may even subtly lead the conversation round to the scrap. The countryman's scrap was the Battle of Crecy!

The Battle of Crecy began to form in the darkness. Richard was tired, and the throb-throb of the speeding train acted as a soporific. Thus his relaxed mind became a facile battle-ground for history both past and present, for fact and fancy, for beauty and the beast. The arrows of archers merged into murderous bullets, the galloping of mail-clad horses melted into the song of the sleepers, flags became faces, and the charging steeds created a draught resembling a breeze through an open window....

The draught was wonderfully realistic. The horses, of course, were just dream illusions, but the draught seemed actually to be playing upon his face. "Am I dreaming?" he thought, fretfully. "I must wake up!" He made an effort. One of the horses descended upon him violently. "Hey, I don't like this dream!" he reflected. "I *must* wake up!" But he couldn't. The horse was upon him, and his head was facing downwards, and he was being kicked and shoved about... nearer and nearer the breeze...nearer and nearer a dim vastness that seemed the very home of wind...

Then another vision flashed abruptly into his mind. A vision of the countryman. Was this, too, fancy? He did not know. But whether it was fancy or fact, it stirred him to sudden violence, and all at once a weight that had been impelling him towards the rushing void ceased to exist.

He flung out his hand, and grasped something swaying. For an instant he swayed with it, and the rushing void swayed, also; now receding, now advancing, till it became immediately beneath him. Then Richard found that the thing he grasped was a door. The carriage door. It was open.

Dizzily, he closed it. The train, heedless of this minor incident at one small point in its length, sped on through the night. Richard's eyes, now wide open and staring, turned towards the corridor.

The young man with the eye-glass was passing by.

Chapter XV

Eleven P.M.

In a flash Richard was in the corridor. The young man with the eye-glass paused and turned his head. Then he took a step into the entrance to the nearest compartment and waited for Richard to pass him.

But Richard made no movement. He was regarding the young man intently, and the young man's eye-glass dropped from his eye in a sort of mild protest.

"I thought you were in a hurry?" the young man queried, raising the eyebrow that was no longer required to imprison the monocle.

"Aren't *you*?" challenged Richard.

Now the young man replaced the monocle, and returned the intentness of Richard's gaze. Then he smiled rather acidly, and answered: "As a matter of fact, sir, I am." And, to prove it, he left the compartment entrance in which he had been politely waiting, and continued coolly on his way.

If Richard Temperley could have been in two places at once he might have followed the young man with the eye-glass, for one of his obvious objects in leaving his compartment had been to find out who had made the attack upon him, and he was by no means certain that the monocled passenger was as innocent as he looked. But a second object had been to satisfy himself that no similar attack had been made on Sylvia Wynne and to protect her against the possibility of one; and now, in the compartment outside which he stood, he suddenly caught a glimpse of Sylvia, sitting composedly beside an elderly woman in a severe black dress.

He did not permit himself more than this one quick glimpse. Resisting temptation, he turned his head away and stared out of the corridor window into the night. The glimpse had achieved his second object, however. The lady by whom Sylvia was sitting, though uncongenial, did not look murderous, while two other people in the compartment—a clergyman and a depressed lady who might well have been such a clergyman's wife—helped to appease his immediate anxiety.

But it did not lessen the general anxiety set up by the mysterious attack upon him. Somebody (whether he wore an eye-glass or not) was on the train who did not stick at quietly opening a door beside a dozing passenger and trying to push him out on to the line; and there could be no question, in these circumstances, of leaving the vicinity of Sylvia Wynne once she had been found.

So, as the train ran through its last lap, Richard stayed where he was and smoked a cigarette.

The light of his match, reflected in the window, abruptly blotted out a dim and sinister stone quarry, and substituted his head. "Yes, and my real—not my reflected—self might have been lying in a stone quarry at this moment," pondered the owner of the head, "if those eyes had remained closed just one tiny second longer!" The match went out and the head vanished, as though frightened by the prospect.

But the head reappeared intermittently behind the fitful glow of the cigarette, travelling along with the train that left all else behind. Dim fields, dim roofs, little lights under the dim roofs, came and went. The dim fields grew fewer, and the dim roofs more. The train ran through a station. "Stapleton Road, for South Wales." Hallo! Must be nearly there! Richard glanced at his watch and found, to his surprise, that it was a quarter-to-nine. Due in a couple of minutes. He must have slept longer before his unpleasant awakening than he had imagined....And might have slept for ever!

The roofs now reigned, their victory marked by an overwhelming army of black blotches. A long, low smudge of bank, the last gasp of the unseen grass. "Lawrence Hill," the words just caught as they ran backwards. The ghosts of seven tall chimneys, presided over by the ghost of a still taller steeple. Asleep on a blacked-out hoarding, his work for the day done, "Mr. Wise, of Fry's." The tapering ends of platforms, like the station's outstretched fingers. A straggling row of porters, hoping dully for tips...Bristol...

The train stopped, and, as it stopped, Richard Temperley turned to glance once more into the compartment outside which he had stood for ten minutes. The severe woman in black was on her feet. The clergyman and his wife were fussing with their luggage. Sylvia Wynne...where was Sylvia Wynne?

"Well—*she* hasn't wasted much time!" reflected Richard, with a little frown. He would have welcomed one more reassuring glimpse of her. "Still, I dare say it's just as well."

As Sylvia herself had disappeared, so had every other familiar personality by the time Richard stepped out on to the platform. He caught one momentary glimpse of the two well-dressed ladies who had sat at the table with the young man with the eye-glass, and he dived through a small knot of people in the hope that the ladies would lead him to their dinner-companion; but somebody in the middle of the knot of people objected to the process of bisection, and by the time the objection had been over-ruled the two ladies had vanished.

"Not my best moment, this," Richard decided. "But, after all, what would I have done with old Monocle if I'd found him? Maybe it'll be better to avoid the dramatis personae until I've had my talk with Miss Wynne!"

His hand went into his breast pocket, and his fingers found comfort in the tangibility of the thin cardboard they touched. Richard had stolen a menu from the Great Western Railway Company, to ensure that nobody else stole it. It was the menu that confirmed the 11 o'clock appointment.

Eleven o'clock. And it was now, if station clocks tell the truth, ten minutes to nine. Two hours and ten minutes to burn. How could the time be burned most profitably? "I can hang round and wait," he thought, "or I can take a trip to Charlton, and see if I can pick up a few useful things there."

He compared the two alternatives.

If he went to Charlton he would almost certainly bump into the police. The police, like himself, would be trying to pick up useful things. Of course, he had Inspector James's assurance. Relying on this, he felt sure that neither the inspector nor Dutton would interfere with him. But suppose some other suspicious member of the force—a local man, say—or suppose some person from the opposite camp followed him back to Bristol afterwards? That would not be too good!

"On the other hand," he argued, "if I stick around here for a couple of hours I'm bound to attract attention—and *that* wouldn't be too good, either. Besides, I'm dashed if I've the patience to stand still and do nothing!"

The idea of a compromise occurred to him. Why not go *towards* Charlton, stop on the edge of it, and search for some voluble local gossip?

"Yes, that's the ticket!" he decided, and strolled out into the wide open space that separates Bristol station from Bath Parade.

The extent of this space rather worried him. A smaller area would have made a more definite meeting-place for the darkness of eleven o'clock. Still, he did not suppose he and Sylvia would miss each other. Hailing a taxi, he inquired of the driver:

"Do you know Charlton?"

The driver smiled rather pityingly.

"I've 'eard of it," he answered, in the tone of one who informs you that Queen Anne is dead.

"Well, what's the name of the place just before it?" went on Richard.

"D'you mean Westbury, sir?"

"Ah, Westbury! How far is Westbury?"

"About four mile, sir."

"From Charlton?"

"From 'ere."

"Then how far is it from Charlton?"

"From 'ere?"

"No, man, from Westbury! From Charlton to Westbury. Have you got that?"

"Another couple," answered the driver, slightly hurt.

"Right," said Richard. "Then drive me to Westbury—and a good tip if you're smart!...No, wait a moment!"

Not far away, somebody was standing in the shadow of a wall. The stillness of the figure impressed itself upon Richard. Ahead of him, on the road to Westbury, would be the police. Was this figure waiting to form a sort of rearguard? "You know, Richard, your mind isn't functioning properly!" he chided himself. "Surely, even to go in the *direction* of Charlton spells idiocy?" And, all at once, he chose quite another direction. "Changed my mind," he said to the driver, laconically. "Clevedon."

The driver blinked, then shrugged his shoulders. A good tip had been mentioned, and probably the best way to earn it was to refrain from obvious opinions. In a few seconds, the taxi was gliding out of the wide station yard and turning westwards towards Clevedon. Meanwhile, the figure slipped from its shadows and turned northwards, towards Charlton.

But other figures were abroad that night, and Richard's decision to avoid the north road was not due entirely to the figure he had spotted. The trip to Clevedon was in the nature of a big shake, and it was intended to shake off anybody and everybody. If you feel that bees are buzzing round your hair, you do not necessarily stop to identify them. You just want to be sure you are rid of them. Richard told himself grimly, as his car wended its way towards its absurd destination, that when he returned he would be entirely free of insects!

The driver worked for the tip he eventually got. His direction was changed several times, and, as a matter of fact, they never touched Clevedon at all. With five miles still to go they turned south, and played hide and seek with a little place called Nailsea, though Richard Temperley never knew its name. Afterwards, they looped back Bristolwards by another road, and the car was dismissed in the south of the city.

It occurred to Richard as he paid his very large fare that a word of explanation might not come amiss, and would perhaps save gossip.

"If you'd like to know," he said, "you've just taken me over some ground I've not been over for twelve years." That was true. "I was born here." That was not.

The mixture of truth and untruth, coupled with the tip, served its purpose. Sentiment binds all English people together, whatever their county. The cabman had been born in London.

Then Richard zigzagged back to the wide space outside the station, and, as he turned into it, a voice hailed him softly. "Mr. Temperley!"

It was the only voice in the world he wanted to hear, and his heart raced with gratitude.

Chapter XVI

A Strange Partnership

Even in the darkness he noticed her agitation. She had been composed in the dining-car, and had looked serene enough during that solitary glimpse he had subsequently had of her in the compartment, but now the composure and the serenity had gone, and he sensed once more the horror that had threaded through their first interview. Was this the general horror of the situation in which she appeared to be involved, or had something now happened during the past two hours to increase her fear?

"Let's get away from this spot before we talk, shall we?" he whispered, taking hold of her arm instinctively. "I've an idea it may be better."

She obeyed him without protest, and they turned their back on the station. When they had passed through one or two streets in silence, she asked: "Where are you taking me?"

Her voice was unsteady, and he patted her arm in a vague attempt to comfort her.

"I haven't any idea," he replied. "I just thought, somehow, that the station mightn't be too healthy."

"But why?" And while he sought an answer to the question, she flashed another. "Is anybody following you?"

"Don't believe so," he responded. "Is anybody following *you*?"

She looked round quickly, then shook her head.

"But somebody *has* been?" he pressed.

"I don't know."

"You think they might have been, though?"

"Yes."

"Why should they?"

"Why should they follow *you*?" she parried, with the shrewdness that never seemed wholly to desert her even in her terror.

"Well, if anybody is following me—and, you remember, I said I didn't believe anybody was—it will probably be because they know I'm interesting myself in you. You see, Miss Wynne, in a sense I'm your partner, though so far you haven't technically admitted me into the business."

"A partner generally wants to know something about the business before he asks to be admitted."

"This partner is burning to know more about the business! Meanwhile, he's banking on instinct—and the business can draw upon him to the last ounce."

She stopped suddenly. Then went on again. Her voice was still unsteady when she spoke, but not this time with fear.

"I—I simply don't understand," she said. "Why are you doing all this for me?"

"The biggest things are always the most difficult to understand," answered Richard, gravely. "I'm not going to pretend that I understand myself. Shall we give up trying, and just accept the fact? Accept the fact that I *am* doing this for you, and want to do ever so much more? Look here, Miss Wynne, if you don't need a friend I'm the worst guesser in the whole of Creation. Regard me as your friend, and see if you can't find some way of making use of me.... No, not that road. It's too wide! I like the little dark ones, don't you?"

She smiled as he led her round a corner, but the smile did not last. A tired mind was thinking desperately.

"Do you remember some advice I gave you this morning, in your studio?" asked Richard, breaking a rather long silence. "I advised you to confide in the police. Well, I still advise it."

"Even when I don't confide in you?" she replied.

"I wish you would confide in me!" he exclaimed. "But, even if you did, I believe I'd still advise you to pass the information on. You see—dash it all, aren't the police here to protect us?"

"You're showing wonderful confidence in me!"

"Of course I am! If you told me you'd killed a moth, I wouldn't believe you! But policemen don't bank on instinct, you know. They want facts. And they won't show any confidence in you unless you give them a few facts first."

"Such as?"

"How on earth do *I* know?" he retorted. "Probably an account of to-day's doings would satisfy them." For a moment, her dogged silence almost angered him. "What *have* you been doing?" he demanded.

"I can't tell you—yet," she murmured.

"Thank you for that 'yet.' I'll remind you of it later!"

"Meanwhile, what have *you* been doing?"

"Shaking off a police spy for the first part of the day—"

"Do you mean, that man who called at the studio this morning?"

"And who sent you dashing out of it? Yes, that's the fellow! His name's Dutton, and his job is to find you through me. But don't look so anxious. I've arranged a temporary truce, and we're safe—from *him*—for a few hours."

"A truce?" she repeated, puzzled.

"Yes. I'll come to that in a minute. First let me tell you what happened after I shook Dutton off. I telephoned to my sister at Richmond. It was just after you had telephoned yourself. By the way, why *did* you telephone?"

The abruptness of the question appeared to fluster her. "I—I'm not quite sure," she stammered. "I think I wanted your advice."

"Well—here I am."

"Yes, but—it mightn't be so necessary, now."

"You mean, you've *come* to Bristol?"

"Won't you go on, please?"

"All right. My sister told me about your telephone call, and I enlisted her on our side. You see, she has faith in me, just as I have in you. But the inspector also telephoned, and he isn't quite so trusting. I imagine he telephoned from your studio, because he was there a few minutes afterwards—"

She stared at him, but he hardly saw her in the darkness; he was following a sudden thought of his own.

"I say—how was it the detective didn't bump into you?" he asked. "Were you there together?"

"No," she muttered. "But—I heard someone coming, and—"

"Bolted?"

"Yes."

"For Paddington?"

"Yes."

"Tell me, Miss Wynne. Did you just miss the 5.15 for Bristol?"

"Just? No, by about ten minutes."

"Then I must have been at Paddington before you. I missed it by ten seconds. You couldn't have gone direct."

"Is that a question?"

"Please!"

"You're good at cross-examination."

"Rather—when I'm on the side of the person I'm cross-examining! What caused your delay?"

"Well, you see—when I left the studio, I hadn't quite made up my mind."

"You mean, you had to decide whether it was wise or not to take this trip to Bristol?"

"Yes. And now, please, I want you to tell *me* something. How did you know I'd gone to Bristol?"

"By a bit of simple Sherlock Holmes work. Your A B C was open at Bristol, and as I was staring at the name, a paper-boy was calling out the latest news." He paused, and felt her sudden shudder. "You know what it was, of course?" he asked, softly.

"You mean—no, tell me!" she answered.

"The second murder, Miss Wynne," he said. "The second murder that has brought Inspector James here, and that has brought you here—"

"It *didn't* bring me here!" she interposed, breathlessly. "I didn't know anything about it until I got here!" She stopped short, and began to falter. "At least—no, I didn't know—but—"

She floundered into an unhappy silence.

Longing to press her further, but deciding that she needed a few moments to recover herself, Richard tried to work out her movements in the light of this fresh information.

She had run away from the studio when Dutton had called that morning. Then there was a big blank. During that blank she had received and sent a telegram. There was no intimation regarding the contents of the telegram she had received, but the telegram she had sent had contained the words, "terribly urgent." Shortly before four, she had telephoned to him at Richmond from the studio. Assumedly in connection with the matter raised in the telegram. Assumedly, but not certainly. She had heard James arriving, and had run away from the studio a second time. She had not decided whether to go to Bristol or not. Deciding, at last, to go, she had reached Paddington Station at, say, 5.25, while he had been having tea there. Assumedly, she tucked herself away in some other spot till the 6.30 train started. Hidden herself, in fact, which might account for the fact that she had not come across a later edition of the afternoon paper containing the report of the second murder. She did not know of this second murder. Incredible as this seemed, in view of her movements, Richard accepted her assurance without question. She must, however, have made her trip to Bristol for some purpose *related* to the murder! That, also, seemed incredible, but also had to be accepted without question, since the long arm of coincidence could not stretch so far as this. Reaching Bristol, she had slipped immediately from the train, and had disappeared. She had then, Richard believed, received a shock. The shock, perhaps, of discovering the second murder. But what reason had *she* for connecting the two murders? Did *she* share the secret knowledge which Inspector James had passed on to Richard....

"Miss Wynne!" he exclaimed, abruptly. "Have you any reason to suppose that this second tragedy is connected with the first?"

Again the abruptness of his question caught her unprepared.

"What do you mean?" she asked, weakly.

"Well, I'll put it another way," he replied, trying to ignore her distress. "Do you know of anything that suggests the two murders were committed by the same hand?"

"Do—*you*?" Her words came faintly.

"Yes, I do," he answered, after a moment's rapid consideration. James had entrusted Richard with his secret in order to incite Richard's co-operation; Richard was now entrusting it to Sylvia with the same object. "Another of those crimson Z's was found near the spot where the second victim fell."

She swayed against him. He stopped, and put his arm round her to keep her from falling. Heaven and hell combined in that moment, confusing it utterly.

The moment passed. She raised the head that had lain limply against his shoulder, and her eyes bore a new light. There was appeal in the eyes, the appeal of one who felt herself beaten. "Now I am going to receive her full confidence!" he thought, in happy exultation. "Now, at last, we shall be able to work together!" Unconsciously, his arm tightened around her.

But the light suddenly changed. She was no longer appealing to him. She was afraid of him. And, a second later, he learned the reason.

"That truce!" she whispered. "You haven't told me—were there any *terms*?"

Richard gritted his teeth in his disappointment. He forgot that, but for the truce, he might not have been able to contrive this interview.

"I'm supposed to have an interview with James when it is over," he said, bluntly. "At eight o'clock to-morrow."

Her fear increased.

"To—tell him what I tell you?"

"That's his hope," Richard answered. "But all hopes aren't fulfilled, you know. It's understood—distinctly—that I use my own discretion. This isn't—spy work."

The damage had been done, however. He realised it at once. Her trust in his good faith remained, but even the faithful can stumble if over-weighted with dangerous knowledge…

"Then I'm not to know?" he asked.

She shook her head.

"Does that mean this is the end?"

She looked at him earnestly, and now some of the appeal returned.

"I don't know," she said. "It depends on whether the—partner is still willing to help me in the dark—and whether I have any right to ask him to."

"Right?" exclaimed Richard, hope returning.

Our desires are big, but we are content with little!

"Haven't I already given you the right?" he went on. "I said that you could draw on me to the last ounce."

"But now—"

"The position's unaltered, as far as I'm concerned. I meant what I said. How about testing me?"

He waited anxiously for her answer. She turned away, and stared along the black road. He would have given much to have been inside her mind at that moment—to have known the pros and the cons that were battling there. At last she turned back to him, the battle over.

"Will you come with me to Charlton?" she asked. "*Now?*"

Chapter XVII

What Happened at Midnight

If one man's meat is another man's poison, one person's murder may be another person's income. Thus tragedy and happiness interweave, forming life's queer pattern. Fall over a cliff to-morrow, and somebody will benefit from your fall—a press photographer, a gossip-monger, a little boy who had previously been rather bored with existence, or an aunt in India.

It has already been shown how the murder of John Amble brought pennies, and at least one sixpence, to a small newsvendor in London. He was merely one of hundreds of newsvendors who reaped a similar harvest. Now, in Bristol, the murder of an unknown woman was bringing unexpected affluence to taxi-drivers. They had taken journalists to Charlton, officials to Charlton, sight-seers to Charlton, and others unclassified. They had driven one wicked old man who, shedding false tears, had hoped to identify the dead woman as his wife; and they had driven his wife after him, to bring him home again. Charlton, a peaceful rural village, preferring sign-posts to petrol pumps, and inhabited mainly by hens, sheep, cattle, a white pony and an enormous pig, had become a temporary parking-ground, while its quiet greens buzzed beneath the louder buzzing of aeroplanes. There was buzzing, also, in the Carpenter's Arms, where glasses were busy and had to be re-washed an unusual number of times.

And all because, earlier in the day, a woman had walked across a gently-sloping field, and had suddenly dropped down dead.

If the woman had realised how she was going to change the quiet scene on which her eyes rested as she crossed the field, her last moment would have been illuminated by a startling vision; but, happily, such visions are spared us. We pass, merely guessing, from second to second, and only know for certain the second that embraces us.

Among the taximen who were affected by this woman's death, two stand out prominently. Each ran up a record fare, and of one we shall speak later. The other was Ted Diggs, of whom we must speak now.

It was Diggs who had driven the hopeful old man's wife after him, and who had congratulated himself subsequently on his own bachelorhood. He had also driven the father of Flying-Officer Turndike, of the Royal Air Force, to Charlton—the aviator who had seen the woman fall dead—and had been the first to learn that the officer had shown his interest in aviation at the age of three by trying to fly into a garden from a roof. Turndike's father had increased the fare by going from Charlton to Filton, where the aerodrome was, and finally back to Bristol station, very late, to catch the last night train to London. The 11.15. The train of despair, that pitched you into Paddington at twenty minutes to three in the morning.

But that was Turndike Senior's affair. Ted Diggs's own affair, after having deposited Turndike Senior at his platform and discussed the theory of Jack the Ripper's ghost with an imaginative porter, was to seek an earlier bed and to enjoy a well-earned rest. But the best-laid schemes of mice and taximen gang aft agley, and as Diggs turned out of the station yard and began wending his way homewards, he found himself unexpectedly hailed by a young man who stepped out of a narrow side-street.

"Are you engaged?" asked the young man.

"What—at this time o' night?" replied Diggs. "Yes—to a bed!"

"We want to go to Charlton," said the young man, "and it'll be worth a couple of pounds to you. Think you could postpone that bed?"

Charlton again! And a couple of pounds! And "we"! Where was the other?

Diggs strained his eyes, and found the other standing a yard or two off. A girl! H'm—did that make any difference?

"It's rather urgent," pressed the young man, in the tone of one who was anxious to make his point agreeably, but who held insistence in reserve.

"Ay, and it's also rather late," answered Diggs.

And he was also rather tired. But—a girl? Could you expect a girl to walk six or seven miles at night? *She* might be rather tired, too. And he hadn't got a nagging wife to go back to.

Diggs was not a saint. He was, however, just one point above what a sceptical world expected of him, and perhaps something in the attitude of the girl reached him through the darkness. In any case, and whatever the reason, he suddenly decided that he would take on the job, and he told his passengers to hop in. And thus began the most amazing trip of his existence. A trip less amazing, however, than that of the other Bristol taximan who, before cock-crow, ran up a record fare.

"What part of Charlton?" inquired Diggs, as the passengers got into the cab. "*You* ain't goin' sight-seeing at midnight, are you?"

Apparently the young man was not quite sure of the part. He glanced inquiringly at the girl. The girl hesitated, then murmured something.

"The Carpenter's Arms," said the young man; and added, after the girl had murmured something else, "Only stop just before we reach Charlton, will you?"

Diggs nodded. Seemed a bit mad. Still, it wasn't his business, and two pounds was two pounds at any hour of the day or night.

"Well, that's all fixed," said Richard Temperley, as they settled in their seats and the car began to move. "And what do we do when we get to the Carpenter's Arms?"

It was a long while before Sylvia replied to this question. The car slipped through the dark streets, went by a lightless cinema and over a bridge. Beneath the bridge dark water flowed, while on their left rose the slim ghosts of masts. On the morrow the sun would transform the masts into happy substance, and some of them would move over water no longer dark towards the open sea; but now they belonged to a different world, a world of eerie fancies and dark thoughts....Up a steep hill, where sleeping tram-lines were momentarily awakened by the car's headlights. Up on to a green common...

"Of course—it'll be closed," said Sylvia.

"Yes, it's a bit latish," agreed Richard, as though there had been no interim between the question and the answer, "but I suppose there'll be a bell. Do we ring it?"

"No."

"Then how do we get in? Are you expected?"

She only replied to the first question.

"I—I don't believe we shall go in," she said.

"Don't—*believe*?" he repeated, trying for her sake to remain matter of fact, and to conceal his bewilderment.

"No."

"But you're not quite certain?"

"We'll know soon."

"Right. I'm trying not to worry you, Miss Wynne, but—well, I've got to ask a question or two, haven't I?"

"You're being—wonderful."

The adjective made the inside of the taxi the chosen spot in all creation. After all, what did the outside of the taxi matter? Richard strove to remain practical through his elation, and also to put the elation in its proper place. Naturally, a girl who was receiving the kind of help he was giving would use glorified adjectives once in a while...they didn't mean anything...

"Here's another question, Miss Wynne," he said. "You're not sure whether we shall be going inside the Carpenter's Arms—but do you know where you're going to sleep to-night?"

"I'm not even sure of that," she admitted.

"Got a bag, or anything?"

"No."

"Just left London as you are, eh?"

"Didn't *you*?"

"Not even a toothbrush!" He smiled. "Aren't we a couple of derelicts?"

She smiled, and he felt that she had moved an inch closer to him. He blessed the inch. But the smile was only momentary.

"Would you find out where we are?" she whispered.

He put his head out of the window.

"Where's this, Bill Jones?" he asked.

"Westbury," answered the driver. "Jest comin' to it. And my name's Ted Diggs!"

"Thank you, Mr. Diggs," replied Richard, and brought his head in again.

"Did you hear him?" he inquired. "We're just reaching Westbury, and his name is Diggs."

This time the humour missed her. As they descended into Westbury she repeated the name under her breath, and suddenly asked: "Then we're about two miles from Charlton, aren't we?"

"Yes," he answered, and wondered how she knew. He had gained an impression that she was not familiar with the district. Then a possible solution occurred to him. She might have made this journey once before. Between nine and eleven p.m.

They ascended out of Westbury, which stood in a little dip, and wound through a curly, low-hedged lane. Westwards, the dark undulations looked gloomy and desolate. All at once, her fingers tightened on his arm. It was his first intimation that she had laid her fingers there. "Ask him to stop!" she whispered.

Richard gave the instruction, and the car came to a standstill. His companion's mind seemed also to have come to a standstill, and Richard decided that it was time for him to assist it. "Tell me, Miss Wynne," he said in a low voice. "Is there any slight danger to you if you go to the Carpenter's Arms?"

"I—don't know," she answered. "I must think for a moment."

"No, let me do the thinking for you. There's no danger to *me*, anyway, is there?"

"I don't see how there could be."

"Very well, then. Here's a suggestion. You stay here and wait in the car, while I go on and do—" He paused. "Whatever you would have done yourself. Is that possible?"

"Would you?" she faltered.

"You've no need to ask that," he said. "Just tell me what it is."

"It's really—quite simple, if you'd do it," she whispered, after a pause. "And—no, there wouldn't be any danger. It's—it's just to walk by the Carpenter's Arms—it's a little way round that bend on the right—and then come back and tell me if you meet anybody."

"That sounds distinctly simple!" he responded, in surprise.

"Only don't go in the hotel, or don't knock, or anything."

"You want me to avoid attracting any attention?"

"Yes. Go beyond the hotel. Perhaps a hundred yards."

"And suppose I do meet somebody?"

"Then come back, and tell me what they're like."

"I see. Come back and report to you what I find, or what I don't find. Right, Miss Wynne. You shall have the report in five minutes. Meanwhile, I demand one thing in return."

"What is it?"

"That you don't move from this car unless some real danger presents itself."

"I won't."

"That's a promise?"

"I won't break it."

He took her hand, gave it a reassuring squeeze, and stepped out on to the road, closing the door of the car after him. Ted Diggs, waiting patiently on his seat, turned his head.

"You're to stay here for a few minutes," Richard told him, "and to look after a very valuable lady."

Diggs grinned, and something in the grin conveyed to Richard that he had read the fellow aright. Diggs, with a responsibility, was the man to be relied on!

And now Richard left the car, and walked away from its comforting headlights into the blackness beyond.

Ahead was a dark, triangular space, with a sign-post sticking up out of the middle of it. The sign-post looked unpleasantly like an uncompleted gallows. Roads forked round the triangle to left and right. He took the right road, and walked quietly around its curve.

The curve straightened. Soon—sooner than he had expected—an unpretentious building grew out of the shadows on his left. This would be the Carpenter's Arms. But nobody was waiting outside the little hotel. Nobody stood in the porch, or lurked beneath its walls.

Having paused to satisfy himself on these points, he turned and stared along the continuation of the lane. Blank again.... No, *was* it a blank this time? Did something stir somewhere, making the hedge appear to move? By Jove! Yes...

"Steady!" thought Richard. "A man can take a stroll through a country lane without felonious intent, can't he?"

In the distance, a church clock chimed faintly midnight.

He hurried forward. The movement in the hedge ceased. Then all at once, it began again, grew, and became definitely human; and Richard found himself staring into the eyes of the countryman.

As he stared, something even more arresting began to take shape in the corner of his eye. The something was lying at the side of the road, under the hedge by which the countryman was standing.

"Looks like accident, lad," said the countryman, softly.

Richard stooped. Beside the prone body was a small, faintly glistening object. A monocle.

"God!" muttered Richard, and swung round fiercely to the countryman.

But even in that instant, the countryman had disappeared.

Diving to the hedge, Richard looked over. A shadow flitted across a field. He tried to break through the hedge, but it was thick, and by the time he had forced an opening the shadow had gone. Then the figure on the ground reverted to his mind. Yes—the man with the eye-glass must be attended to first! Was he just knocked out? Or—?

Richard swung back to him. His heart missed a beat. The man with the eye-glass had evaporated!

Chapter XVIII

The Next Move

When we are suddenly presented with a baffling problem, we attempt, if there is time, to work it out; if there is no time, however, we do not probe into the why's and the how's and the wherefore's, but confine ourselves merely to dealing with the result.

Many questions rushed through Richard Temperley's mind as he stared at the spot where, a moment or two earlier, the young man with the monocle had lain. Had the man been shamming? If so, did the countryman know he had been shamming? Were he and the countryman acting with each other or against each other? Did they constitute a joint menace, or separate menaces? Like untrappable shadows these bewildering query marks sped through Richard's brain. He did not pause over any of them, however. He merely tried to guess which of the two necessities which now comprised the whole of existence for him was the greater—the necessity of finding the countryman, or the necessity of finding the man with the monocle?

He concentrated for an instant on the man with the monocle, for the simple reason that the man with the monocle, having disappeared last, must be the nearer of the two. He went a few yards along the road, his eyes skinned, his senses alert. Then, finding nothing, his thoughts reverted abruptly to the countryman.

The man with the monocle, apparently, had dropped through the ground, but the countryman was still racing across dark fields. Or had he stopped by now, and was he stealthily watching Richard from some distant cover?

Something told Richard that the countryman had not stopped—that he *was* still running. Why would he still be running? And why should this queer instinct be insisting to Richard that he was still running? There must be a definite reason for both the fact and Richard's knowledge of the fact. Some reason…Some reason…

"Good heavens!" gasped Richard, as the reason came to him sickeningly.

The countryman had not stopped because he had divined that somewhere in the neighbourhood of Richard Temperley would be a girl in whom that countryman was interested. And he had divined right! It was because of this fellow that Sylvia had feared to venture near the Carpenter's Arms! Thus ran Richard's thoughts as he turned and, like one demented, flew back along the road.

He fought nightmare visions as he ran. A vision of an empty road. Of Sylvia gagged and bound. Of the car, with the helpless girl inside, disappearing into the black void as the countryman and the young man with the monocle had disappeared before her. Of a man lying in a ditch, and slowly coming to, and muttering, "I couldn't 'elp it, sir—'e'd 'it me on the 'ead before I could say Bristol Channel."…

Now he was out of the lane that led to the inn, and, veering leftwards, he was passing the dark triangle with the sign-post. His heart almost stopped beating as he swung round the point just beyond which he had left the car. Would it still be there? In a flash he would know heaven or hell.... "Gone!" he gasped.

But something was moving somewhere. Not frankly, but furtively. Richard saw red, and dived for it.

"Whoa! Let go!" gurgled a familiar voice.

The startled eyes of Ted Diggs stared up at him.

"What's happened?" muttered Richard, unsteadily.

"Ay, but it's my throat you've got 'old of!"

Richard let go, and repeated his question while Diggs swallowed carefully to find out whether he still could.

"Nothin's 'appened," he answered. "What's this all about?"

"If nothing's happened, where's the car?"

"Eh? Oh! The lady got anxious, sir, and it's down a lane. Seemed as if she thought she'd be safer there."

"But why aren't you with her?"

"Me?"

"She's not safer *alone*, man! You promised you wouldn't leave her—"

"'Ow can I be in two places at once?" demanded Diggs, injured. "I 'ad to be 'ere to let you know she was there, didn't I? If you'd come 'ere and found nothing, you might have thought she'd been kidnapped!"

"I *did* think she'd been kidnapped," growled Richard, "and if we don't hurry back at once, she may be."

"What's that?" blinked Diggs, in astonishment.

"Do you suppose we're doing all this for *fun*?" barked Richard. "Quick, man! Which is the way? We mustn't waste a moment!"

Diggs shook his head uncomprehendingly. It was all rather beyond him. But, obviously, as his male passenger had just pointed out, this queer couple hadn't come out on a joy-ride! Otherwise, there wouldn't be all this jumpiness, and nerviness, and neck-twisting....

"For the Lord's sake, get a *move* on!" cried Richard.

Diggs turned, and without more ado made for the lane up which he had driven the car. They certainly were a queer couple, no mistake about that. Still, having been enlisted in their service, Diggs was anxious to see the adventure safely through, and of course he didn't want them to come to any harm. Nor his taxi, either! Despite himself, some of the jumpiness and the nerviness was entering into *him*, and he now led Richard hastily to the turning beyond which the taxi ought to be.

Ought to be? Don't be silly! Where the taxi *would* be! And here was the corner, and—yes, there was the car! But, lummy, what was the car up to? It was beginning to move! "Hey, there!" shouted Diggs.

He increased his speed. Somebody, increasing faster, shot past him. It was Richard. The taxi stopped moving. A smudge loomed momentarily, then vanished. By the time Richard reached the car, it no longer bore its phantom driver.

Nor did it contain its passenger, for she had leapt out, and stood in the lane panting, white and startled.

"Quick! Get back!" ordered Richard.

"What's happened—who was it?" whispered the girl.

"Actions first, explanations afterwards," answered Richard. "In with you!" As she obeyed, Richard's hand dived out, catching Diggs on the wing.

"Oi! What's that for?" choked Diggs.

"You don't want to go after that fellow!"

"Don't I? Trying to steal my car—"

"Well, he's not stolen it, and we're going to move before he attempts any more damage."

"Ay, but—"

"D'you hear me?"

Diggs shrugged his shoulders. After all, he was only conceding a point he could never have made. There really wouldn't have been any chance at all of catching the taxi-thief.

"Very good, sir. Where are we to move to? Back 'ome?"

Richard considered for an instant. Sylvia, acting more swiftly than Diggs, was already in her seat again. He turned to consult her, then changed his mind and made the decision himself.

"No, drive on for about five miles," he said, "and don't mind if you twist about a bit. In fact, twist about all you can. Five miles. Then I'll give you fresh orders."

Five miles! And in the wrong direction! Was there a limit to a taximan's allegiance?

"You know it's after midnight?" observed Diggs, mounting to his seat.

"It doesn't matter if it's after a dozen midnights!" retorted Richard. "Now, then! Step on it!" The car entered another stage of its remarkable journey.

"Please, what's happening?" whispered Sylvia, as the car began to move.

"Dashed if I can tell you more than bits and pieces," muttered Richard. "But, first, are you all right?"

"Yes."

"You're sure? Not hurt or anything?"

"Of course not!"

"How did that fellow get into the driver's seat?"

"I don't know!"

"Do you mean—you didn't see him till he was actually there?"

"I hadn't any notion. I was staring along the road. He must have been very quiet, though—"

"Yes, and he must have sneaked round by the other side. Probably peeped in at one window while, as you say, you were staring out of the other. Peeped in—saw that you were there, and that the driver wasn't—and then hopped into the driving-seat.... Yes, but when the thing started to *move*, Miss Wynne?"

"I noticed it then, of course. But it all happened so quickly, and for a moment, you see, I thought it was our own driver, and that he was going to meet you."

"Yes, I see," murmured Richard, frowning. "Then you didn't get a proper squint of the fellow who—wasn't our own driver?"

"It was too dark. Anyway, I only saw his back."

"But you've some idea who it was?"

She hesitated, then shook her head.

"I want a better answer than that, please!" urged Richard, noting the hesitation.

"What do you mean?"

"You *have* some idea who it was!"

"I haven't *any* idea who it was!"

"Well, then, let me put it another way. You've some idea who it *could* have been?"

"Perhaps."

"I'm simply praying for the moment, Miss Wynne, when you will discard your secretiveness and trust me. Meanwhile, I suppose this means I'm not to know who this—person it *could* have been is?"

"I'm sorry."

"Sorrow shared. But are you *sure* it wasn't the person you have in your mind?"

She looked a little startled at the question, but replied to it, definitely.

"Quite sure."

"Is it a rather stocky person, for instance, age about fifty and dressed like a countryman?"

He expected some sort of an exclamation from her, but none came. Her eyebrows rose, and she regarded him with close interest, but there was no indication from her that she had ever heard of such a person as Richard had described.

"That conveys nothing to you, eh?" he asked, thoroughly perplexed. "You're not being chased by a man of that description?"

She shook her head.

"Then I'm absolutely beaten, Miss Wynne," he told her, "because it was this countryman who tried to kidnap you in this car just now. And the reason we're zigzagging through country lanes instead of going straight back to Bristol is because we're shaking that confounded fellow off our track."

Every now and then Richard gained an impression that Sylvia Wynne was acting. He had no such impression now. She was looking at him in sheer astonishment. She, too, seemed beaten.

"Please tell me," she said, at last. "When did you first come across this—countryman? Was he outside the Carpenter's Arms?"

"I found him near the Carpenter's Arms," responded Richard, "but that wasn't the first time I came across him."

"When was the first time?"

"In the train."

"In the—oh! Do you mean the man who was sitting at a table near us?"

"Yes, that's the chap."

"But—I don't know him!"

"He evidently knows *you*, Miss Wynne."

"It seems like it. But what happened outside the inn? You haven't told me that yet. We may—have to go back."

"You think so?" answered Richard, grimly. "Well, now I'll tell *you* something! We're not *going* back! Not, at any rate, until you convince me of the wisdom of such a mad idea. *Convince* me, Miss Wynne."

"I see. Your—your faith is weakening a bit."

"That's not fair. You know perfectly well it isn't weakening at all. My faith in your—innocence, that is."

"But in my wisdom?"

"Ah, that, perhaps!"

"I'm sorry, because my next move—if we don't go back to Charlton—will seem even madder still. But I'm still waiting for your 'report,' you know," she reminded him.

"So you are. Well, here it is....I say, our driver knows how to twist and turn, doesn't he?"

"And so do you, Mr. Temperley! You keep on twisting and turning from telling me what happened to you! If that's because you've made up your mind that I'm not going back to the inn, you may as well know that *my* mind is made up, too, and if I've got to go back, I'm *going* back."

Her tone was challenging. He postponed the definite encounter and told his story.

At first he told it without full detail. He wanted to save her as much as he could. But she was so quick to perceive when he omitted the details, never failing to take her eyes from his face, and appearing to listen also for each revealing inflection, that he gave way at last, and made his report a full one.

She shivered when he described the incident of the young man with the eye-glass. "Do you know anything about *him*?" asked Richard. "No," she answered, and again he was convinced of her veracity. She had no knowledge of either the countryman or of the young man with the eye-glass, yet both were obviously implicated in the same mosaic. When he had concluded, she sat in thought, and stared out of the window into the darkness.

"And—that's all?" she murmured.

"That's all," replied Richard.

"You saw no one else?"

"I've told you everything."

"Yes, I know you have. Thank you. But—do you think anybody else may have been there without your knowing it?"

"My dear Miss Wynne," said Richard, with a smile, "what I think is being so constantly confounded that I am beginning to wonder whether my thoughts have any value at all. A hundred things have happened to-day that I wouldn't have thought possible! I certainly don't *think* anybody else was in the lane, but whether that opinion is worth half a farthing is for you to decide."

"I agree with the opinion," she responded, "and I was only trying to back up my own."

As she spoke, the taxi slackened speed.

"Well, where does your opinion lead?" inquired Richard. "Back to Charlton?"

"No."

"Thank God for that!" he exclaimed, fervently. "Then where *does* it lead? Our driver is ready for fresh orders—and so am I."

The taxi stopped, and Diggs began to descend from his seat.

"Where shall I tell him?" asked Richard. "Bristol?"

"Yes—I think you'd better tell him that," she replied, her voice suddenly nervous. "Only—"

"Only what?"

"I won't be going back with you."

"Not going back with me?" exclaimed Richard. "What on earth—I say, do you suppose I'm going to dump you down in the middle of Darkest Gloucestershire in the middle of the night."

"I'm afraid there's no alternative," she answered. "You see, there's somewhere else I've got to go."

"I see. The 'even madder move!'"

"Yes."

"But won't to-morrow do?"

"No, to-night."

"Well, I'll take you there."

"It's too far."

"How far?"

"And you've done enough."

"I asked, *how* far?"

"Over a hundred and fifty miles," she said.

"A hundred and—! You know, Miss Wynne, you're getting ridiculous," he declared. "You don't mean to sit there and tell me, in all seriousness, that you intend to travel another hundred and fifty miles before to-morrow morning's breakfast?"

"I'm quite sure I must sound ridiculous," she answered, quietly, "but however ridiculous I sound I'm serious." Her manner bore out her words.

"Well, and where is this place, a hundred and fifty miles away, that you've got to go to?" he demanded.

"I'm afraid I can't tell you that," she responded.

"Why not?"

"Because—you'll be going back to Bristol."

"What difference would that make—if it were true?"

She shot a quick glance at him as he added the last four words, then abruptly shook her head and set her teeth, as though resisting a temptation.

"In Bristol you'll be seeing your detective," she said, "and it will be easier for you to talk to him if you don't know where I've gone."

"But I insist on knowing!"

She made no reply. Of course, he had no right to insist. Abruptly, he gave way. After all, hadn't his heart told him from the start that he would give way?

"Kamerad!" he said. "You can trust me with the name of your next stop."

He thought she was still going to refuse; then he realised that the continuation of her silence was due to another cause. She was struggling with emotion.

"You—mean—?" she stammered, at last.

"Of course, I mean!" he answered. "Mr. Britling can't beat *me* for seeing things through! Now, then, where is this place? I can't take you there unless I know it, can I?"

"It's—Boston," she gulped. "In Lincolnshire."

Chapter XIX

The Beckoning of Boston

Gloucestershire—Lincolnshire! And afterwards?

While Richard was revolving this new move in his mind, Diggs, having waited patiently outside, poked his head in at the window.

"Well, sir, what's it now?" he inquired. "'Ome?"

Richard studied the good-natured, lined face, wondering how much farther the good-nature could be taxed. Diggs had already proved himself better than one had any right to expect, but there must be a limit to his tolerance. Still, no useful purpose would be served by deciding in advance that this limit had been reached; with tact, one must play for an extension.

"Yes, home for you, I expect," he answered, beginning at once to exercise the tact, "but I'm afraid not for us."

His observations produced two effects, and he was conscious of both. Relief on the part of Sylvia Wynne, for the word "us" confirmed his allegiance, and uneasy surprise on the part of Ted Diggs.

"Eh? Not for you?" the driver blinked. Richard shook his head. "Where are you goin', then, if you ain't goin' 'ome—if I may ask?" But before Richard could inform him, Diggs got a brain-wave. "Oh—police station!" he exclaimed. "That's the idea, is it?"

"Not even a police station," replied Richard. "We want you as a final service, to drop us at a garage where they sit up all night."

"What for?" demanded Diggs.

If the question sounded rude, there was no rudeness in the questioner's heart. *He* wanted to get to bed, and he thought it was time these two young people got to bed, too, even if they required a little bullying to drive them there. Unconsciously, Richard replied with an argument that had been used to him by Sylvia only a minute or two earlier.

"That's our business," he remarked, pleasantly, "unless, of course, you care to make it yours."

"Make it mine, eh?"

"No, don't worry," said Richard, recanting subtly. "We really mustn't keep you out any longer."

Diggs thought about it.

"Where do you want to go?" he inquired, cautiously.

Richard felt a sudden nudge at his side. He nudged back, to imply that he had received the signal, and that he hadn't needed it. "Oh, a long way," he said.

"'Ow long?"

"All night session."

"Eh?"

"Session. Meaning, in this case, an all night drive."

"Oh."

"And that's why we want a garage where they sit up all night."

"Oh."

"Do you know of one?"

"Not nearer'n Bristol."

"How far is that?"

"About—twelve mile."

"That's a nuisance," sighed Richard. "By the way, have you any idea what it will cost us to go a hundred and fifty miles?"

"Shilling a mile, that's the rate," answered Diggs, thinking very hard.

"Shilling a mile. Hundred and fifty miles, hundred and fifty shillings. Seven pounds ten. Have to pay both ways, I expect, so twice seven pounds ten makes it fifteen pounds. And an extra fiver for luck makes it twenty. Now, do you suppose, Mr. Diggs, I'll be able to find any one to do this journey for us for twenty pounds?"

Once upon a time, Ted Diggs had had a dog. It had died an unnatural death on the road, and he had always wanted another. In his opinion, a dog was better company than a woman. Just say, "Shut up," and it did. Albert Bowes had a dog that he wanted three pounds ten for, and that Harry Poynter had said could be worked down to three pounds five.

"Where's the place?" asked Diggs.

"Nonsense! You don't mean *you'll* take us there?" exclaimed Richard, feigning incredulity.

It wasn't only the dog. There might be a pound over for his mother. She was worrying over that dentist's bill. Pity she'd been rude to the panel chap.

"Where is it?" he repeated.

Richard turned his head from the window, and glanced at Sylvia. She pursed her lips at him—he could just distinguish them in the dimness, and for an instant he forgot all about Ted Diggs....

"I'll give you the address when I know you're going to take us there," he said.

It wasn't only the dog and the dentist bill. It was these two silly young people themselves, too. Pleasant young feller, for all his nonsense. And, of course, you didn't meet a young lady like this twice a month.

"It's a go," he said. "And *now* let's 'ave it!"

"Good news!" beamed Richard. "I knew you were a sport, from the first moment I clapped eyes on you. And hasn't he proved it?" he added, turning to Sylvia. She nodded confirmation. Then turning back, he asked, "Tell me, do you know Boston?"

Did Diggs know Boston? Once he had been top of his geography class!

"Lummy!" he exclaimed, aghast. "Are you askin' me to drive you to Ameriky?"

Chapter XX

The Individual

It has been mentioned that two remarkable journeys were taken at this time by Bristol drivers. With the most remarkable portion of Ted Diggs's yet to come, let us interrupt his journey and follow the journey of Albert Bowes, who so far has only been introduced as the owner of a dog priced at three pounds ten.

The journey of Albert Bowes commenced, very roughly, about a dozen hours before that of Ted Diggs, and Albert was as crooked as Ted was straight. We will blame him for that or not according to our philosophy. Judged by the usual standard, Albert deserved a good deal of blame. The aforementioned dog, for instance, was not worth more than thirty shillings commercially, despite the friendly way it wagged its tail, and its lack of anger when you pretended to throw a stick and didn't. Then passengers who looked green were induced by Albert to act in accordance with their unintelligent hue, and more than once he had given the wrong change to a foreigner.

But Albert descended crookedly from a crooked ancestry, and of the most recent ancestry, tracing it back merely as far as his eight great-grandparents, only three had been honest out of a total of fourteen. The other eleven had all been as crooked as Albert (and some a great deal crookeder), and their blood flowed crookedly through his veins.

And as we are, so we look to the truly perspective. This may account for the fact that a certain individual, arriving at Bristol on an early morning train, picked Albert out for the remarkable journey about to be described. The individual needed a man like Albert to drive him. Albert, on the other hand, could very happily have done without the individual.

In truth, ugly though Albert was, the sight of the individual nearly frightened him off his seat.

"Do you know Charlton?" inquired the individual.

This was the moment when Albert nearly jumped out of his seat. He had not seen the individual approach. He seemed to have slipped out of a shadow, while his voice seemed to have slipped out of a crack.

"Yes, I do," replied Albert. "It's through Westbury."

"It can be through Hell, for all I mind," said the individual, "Drive me there."

Albert looked at the individual. Then he looked away again. The sight was unpleasant. Even though he could only see the lower portion of the individual's face. The forehead was concealed by a large, well pulled-down hat. He decided to adopt the unusual course of refusing a fare. "Sorry, but I'm engaged," he remarked, staring straight ahead of him.

There was no reply. Albert repeated the information. Then, as there was still no reply, and as the individual had not appeared to be the kind of person to take refusal without a murmur, Albert risked another glance—and found himself staring at space. The individual had vanished. "Good riddance!" muttered Albert.

The next instant, Albert again nearly jumped out of his seat. A soft voice rasped in his ear.

"If you don't start this moment I'll alter the address to a police station. I know the law."

His passenger had got into the car, and was addressing him through the speaking-tube.

Albert knew a bit about the law, also. You have to, to break it. It occurred to him that in this instance he had better not break the law, and the law imposes obligations on a driver whose disengaged car has been entered by a passenger; there was something about this passenger that made you careful. Besides, after all, Charlton was six miles away, and that would be twelve shillings there and back, and if he didn't sell his dog he'd have to raise a bit of extra money somehow to avoid explosions among creditors.

So he started the engine, and let in the clutch. And thus began the most fateful journey of his life.

During this initial stage, Albert tried to forget his passenger, and to concentrate on his driving. He found he could not do so. He had only had one glimpse of the passenger, but that glimpse had stamped a picture on his mind that was not destined to be eradicated during the rest of Albert's life time; and the knowledge that this picture was behind him, in the living flesh, was a constant disconcerting itch. The speaking-tube, too, had become a sinister instrument since the cracked voice had percolated through it. At any moment, that voice might occur again; and something told Albert Bowes that, if the voice did occur again, he would obey whatever it commanded.

The voice did not occur again, however. Although there was no ostensible reason why it should—passengers do not make a habit of keeping up conversations with drivers through speaking-tubes—Albert began to wonder at last whether the car had been vacated as quietly as it had been entered; or whether, as another alternative, the entire episode might not be some hallucination. Albert did not believe in

Prohibition, and this was one reason why he had to sell his dog to meet his creditors.

To settle these conjectures, he turned his head just before they reached Charlton, and thereby participated unconsciously in a moment of queer significance. The significance of this moment was never fully revealed to any of the participators, for unconscious meetings rarely leave their mark afterwards.

The individual leaned, huddled, in a corner. So one might try and fold oneself if one wished to stay undetected. An old woman in the lane stood aside, to let the car pass. Her skin was dark, and she had travelled many miles in her life—but on foot, not in motor cars. She was now travelling her last mile. Overhead, with an insolent hum, an aeroplane soared low, at the bidding of a rather bored flight-officer and a joy-stick....

The moment passed. Another came. The speaking-tube ordered Albert to stop.

"We ain't quite in Charlton yet," said Albert.

"Stop," came the repeated order.

So he stopped. The individual slipped out.

"Wait!" said the individual.

"Wait! Here?" asked Albert, stupidly.

He felt stupid. It was seeing the individual again. Horrible sight! But—where *was* the individual? He had vanished!

Albert need not have waited. Indeed, he was tempted to depart there and then. Two considerations deterred him from that wise course. Firstly, he felt certain that, as soon as he began to move, the individual would hear him and be back again. Secondly, what about his fare?

"Better wait," he thought. "See any one getting off without paying me!"

Thus he attempted to develop his superiority complex and to pretend that his was the stronger will; but all at once he wondered whether his passenger were *really* trying to get off without paying! The superiority complex went up a few points as genuine indignation began to stir within him. He was now almost able to convince himself, while he waited, that commerce was the only reason that held him there.

Two minutes went by. The aeroplane reappeared, making a wide circle. It was still flying low. Br-r-r-r-! Z-z-z-z-z! Round it went, and off again. Another two minutes went by. "Well, I'm blowed!" muttered Albert Bowes, viciously. "Done it on me! Hopped it! If I see that ugly mug again, I'll—"

And at that moment the owner of the ugly mug reappeared. "Now—Boston," came the laconic order. "And don't waste time."

Albert stared. Boston? Why, that was up in Yorkshire somewhere, wasn't it?

"Here, what's the game?" he demanded, angrily.

"That you are to drive me to Boston," said the individual.

Albert continued to stare. Was the individual mad? That seemed the only explanation!

The aeroplane sounded closer again.

"Oh, and how far's Boston?" inquired Albert, with fine sarcasm.

"A hundred and seventy miles, if you go the way I tell you to," answered the individual.

"Hundred and seventy?"

"Didn't you hear me say so?"

The voice was sharp. Albert looked away, to avoid the influence of the speaker's eyes. The aeroplane sounded closer still, although it was out of sight, beyond a low rise.

"And what's it going to cost you, to go a hundred and seventy miles?" demanded Albert, trying hard to keep his end up.

"I expect you'll tell me that when we get there," replied the individual, tartly.

He got into the car. Albert strode to the door, and glared in. The individual was already huddling into the corner.

"I'll tell you *now*!" cried Albert. "Forty pounds!"

"It's fifty if you start this instant!" cried the individual, suddenly moving forward. "But not a ha'penny, if you don't!"

For a second their two faces were so close they almost touched. Albert gasped, then drew back.

The aeroplane sounded louder than ever. Why didn't it come into view? Perhaps it was dropping? The lower they were, the less distance you could see them. Yes, but why should it come down here? The aerodrome at Filton was a couple of miles away....

Fifty pounds! Whew! A bit of money! But—start off at once? That was just nonsense!

Was it? Not so sure! If Albert started at once, he would avoid an interview with his most disturbing creditor, and when he returned he would be able to pay the creditor off and snap his fingers at him....No doubt about it, that aeroplane *was* making a landing over the brow of the hill. It sounded like an angry bee-hive....Fifty pounds...

"Gloucester first," ordered the individual, "then Tewkesbury and Evesham. Start in ten seconds, or the deal's off. *God, man, are you deaf?*"

Sweat appeared on Albert's brow as he climbed galvanically into his seat. All at once the air had become electrical. His mind was swimming. If you'd asked him why he couldn't have told you. Or, if he could have, he wouldn't.

"I'm doing this for fifty pounds, see?" he told himself, as he stepped on the accelerator. "Good enough reason, that, isn't it?" The car started.

"Get a move on!" came the voice through the speaking-tube.

The car lurched.

"Faster! Faster!" came the voice.

"Well, ain't I?" exclaimed Albert, desperately.

As the car went faster, the air grew tighter. Albert's forehead dripped. He felt suddenly as though he had attached himself to the devil.

Perhaps he was not very far wrong.

Chapter XXI

The Power of a Hook

Though the Cotswold Hills rise on your right, the road northwards from Charlton to Gloucester is flat, and assists you if you are in a hurry. Albert was in a hurry. He wanted to put the greatest possible distance between himself and Charlton in the least possible time, and he was urged to this desire by terror and guilt without definitely comprehending either.

The guilt was certainly incomprehensible. This was not the first time Albert had evaded an interview with a creditor. Moreover, in the present case he was earning money with which to pay the creditor. But the terror was hardly easier to understand. (Or so he told himself.) There were plenty of ugly people in the world, and he himself was not exactly beautiful! Why should his passenger have such a chilling effect upon the backbone—and why should his mind be tortured with such horrible curiosity concerning those few minutes when the passenger had slipped from the car, and when the aeroplane had droned so fretfully overhead?

Something had happened during those few minutes. Something that had been reflected in those mirthlessly grinning eyes as their faces had almost touched, and as the unseen aeroplane had descended…Tchar!…

The sign-post on the triangle of green at Charlton said, "Gloucester, 30½ miles." They reached Gloucester in forty-nine minutes. Albert began to slow down.

"What's this for?" inquired the speaking-tube.

Damn the thing!

"What's what for?" replied Albert, gruffly.

"You're slowing."

"Well, I know it!"

"But you don't seem to know that I asked you why!"

"Petrol," muttered Albert.

The speaking-tube was silent for a moment. Then it barked the question:

"Can't you carry on for ten more miles?"

"Just about, I could," answered Albert.

"Then let's see you move again," retorted the speaking-tube, "and fill up at Tewkesbury."

Albert frowned, but obeyed.

On the road to Tewkesbury he did some hard thinking, as well as some hard driving. He wasn't going to give up his fifty pounds. He was quite ready to proceed to Boston for that sum—yes, and to see that he got it! But there would have to be a readjustment on the personal side. This bossing business would have to end.

Thus Tewkesbury, already famous for one battle, was reached by Albert Bowes in a mood for another.

He postponed the second battle until he had drawn sustenance for his car from an ugly yellow petrol pump. (How those who fought the first battle would have rubbed their eyes could they have foreshadowed this queer addition to their picturesque town!) Then, just beyond the final habitations, he stopped.

Rather to his surprise, the speaking-tube made no protest. When he dismounted, and poked his head inside the car, his passenger was sitting silently in the corner with eyes closed. This Albert decided, was a good start. "Here, wake up, you," he said, hectoringly. "I got a word or two to say."

The passenger made no movement.

"Hey, are you deaf?" exclaimed Albert, his courage growing. "I said I wanted to talk to you!"

The passenger still made no movement, and Albert began to lose a little of his courage.

"What's the matter with you?" he asked.

Was his passenger asleep? Or—dead? A sudden fear gripped Albert. Holy smoke! Suppose he *was* dead? Dead in Albert's car. And with money on him!…

A frightful vision of a court flashed into Albert's mind, and a judicial voice droned ominously through the vision:

"I believe you are in financial difficulties, Bowes?"

"Yes, sir."

"And the man found dead in your car had money on him?"

"Yes, sir."

"A good deal of money?"

"Yes, sir."

"And you are telling us, Bowes, that he engaged you to drive him to Boston, in Lincolnshire?"

"Yes, sir."

"Didn't you think that rather strange?"

"Yes, sir."

"Yet it is a fact that you didn't even trouble to ask for an advance?"

"Yes, sir."

"And now you want us to believe that, having driven your passenger as far as Tewkesbury, he conveniently died?"

"Yes, sir."

"Does it occur to you, Bowes, that it is far easier for us to believe that your passenger never asked you to take him to Boston at all? That he was just an ordinary passenger who hired you for just an ordinary journey? That you discovered he had money on him? That you also discovered his—peculiar condition? A condition, Bowes, that would give you a distinct advantage over him in a tussle? That, having engaged in such a tussle, you conveyed the body a long distance—to Tewkesbury, in fact—and then lost your head and reported the matter to the police in the hope that they would accept the interpretation of 'death from natural causes'? You have a bad record, Bowes. Hitherto, you have only just managed to keep on the right side of the law. I am afraid you are no longer on the right side of the law, and the penalty for murder, Bowes, is to be hanged by the neck until..."

Albert swallowed. He found it difficult. Then, in a sudden frenzy, he opened the door of the car, but only to close it again the next instant, and to stand with his back to it. Some one was coming along the middle of the road.

He waited, while the sweat poured down his forehead. The some one reached the car, and paused. It was a grubby tramp.

"Got a match?" asked the tramp.

Albert produced a box, and held it out. He wondered whether the tramp would notice his hand was shaking.

"Thank'ee," said the tramp, and took the box. He studied it carefully, and then inquired, with audacious innocence: "Got a fag?"

Ordinarily, Albert would have sent the tramp about his business, but this was not an ordinary occasion. Still, he hesitated an instant before permitting himself to be victimised so glaringly, and during the instant the tramp winked towards the car and inquired,

"P'r'aps yer fare'll oblidge?"

The tramp winked as he took the cigarette and lit it. Then, with a "Thank'ee," he pocketed the match box absent-mindedly, and continued on his way.

Albert waited till the fellow was round the corner. Then he turned, and again opened the door of the car. Cautiously he leaned forward, till his head was close to the silent figure. The next instant, a hook wound round his sleeve, and held him.

"And, now," inquired the individual with the hook, "is there to be any more nonsense?"

For a complete minute, Albert felt sick. Then, finding himself released, he took out his pocket-handkerchief, and wiped his forehead.

"Ain't you going to tell me the idea?" he muttered.

"Yes, *this* is the idea," answered his passenger, and the cracked voice now had a hiss in it. "If you obey me unquestioningly and unhesitatingly till we get to Boston, you will make fifty pounds. But if you disobey me in any tiny detail, if you make any protest such as you were about to make just now, if you leave me, or go back on me, or double-cross me, you will not only lose your fifty pounds, but you will also lose something else that you probably value far more—though it is doubtful," came the cynical addition, "whether anybody else does. Now, tell me, have you got on to the idea, or haven't you?"

"Yes," growled Albert.

"You're quite sure?"

"Yes."

"Quite, quite certain there's no mistake about it this time, eh?"

"Yes!"

Was he doomed to say "Yes" for the rest of his life, both in reality and imagination? Here he was, answering this freak, just as obediently as he had answered the mythical judge in his mind!

"Very well, then," said his passenger, sinking back into his corner. "Get back into your seat, and carry on to Evesham."

With his spirit broken, Albert Bowes continued with his job. They reached Evesham without incident. A famous battle was also once fought there, but Albert did not contemplate a repetition of history this time. Instead, he obeyed the speaking-tube's command to stop, and waited for the next orders. The next orders were:

"Drive to a quiet street. Then leave the car, and buy a map. Bring it back. If I am not here when you get back, wait for me, and study the route to Boston while you are waiting. I think you will find that the best way is through Stratford and Coventry and Leicester."

"What about something to eat while I'm waiting?" Albert ventured.

"Certainly. Eat a lot. Eating keeps one from talking."

"Thank you for nothing! And how long do I wait—*if* I wait?"

"You will wait just as long as you have to," answered the speaking-tube. "It may be five minutes, or it may be five hours. But however long it is you will wait, and however long I am, I shall return. And if you aren't there when I return, you will be traced. Do you get *that*!"

Albert got it, and nodded. He found a quiet street, and stopped again. "This suits you?" he inquired, as he descended from his seat.

The figure inside the car made no response. Accepting silence as consent, Albert turned away, then, suddenly, turned back again.

"Yes, but how do I know the *car's* going to be here when I get back?" he demanded.

"Could *you* drive a car without any hands?" asked his passenger.

Albert shuddered. The answer was conclusive. Nevertheless, he decided that he would not be away from his car for longer than was necessary.

He soon found a stationer's shop, and possessed himself, for half-a-crown, of a little red-faced copy of Newnes's Tourist Atlas. Then he walked to an inn and had a couple of drinks. He needed them. He also bought some cheese and sandwiches at the inn, but these he slipped into his pocket, for, despite the impossibility of driving a car without hands, his mind was by no means easy, and he wanted to get back to his property as soon as he possibly could.

He got back in twelve minutes from the moment he had started. The car was there. As he had expected, it was empty. "Wonder what he's up to *this* time?" reflected Albert.

But he did not waste any time over the problem. The problem of the route to Boston was both more appealing and practical. He studied the map, and soon the fruits of his study were inscribed on the blank sheet next to the cover:—

Stratford, ...	say,	20
Warwick, ...	,,	8
Kenilworth, ...	,,	6
Coventry, ...	,,	4
Leicester (via Sharnford), ..	,,	22
Melton Mowbray, ...	,,	15
Grantham, ...	,,	15
Boston, ...	,,	25
Total, ...	115 miles	

He went over the list meticulously and checked its figures, while munching his cheese and his sandwiches. The minutes went by. Sixty of them. Then another sixty. He began to grow impatient.

But, though he was impatient, he was not uneasy. He was as certain that his uncouth passenger would return as he was that the sun would set. "I'm beginning to understand that chap," he told himself, for the comfort of assuming himself knowledgable, "and when he says he's going to do a thing, he's going to *do* it. And you're all right with him," he went on, to increase the comfort, "so long as you do what you say *you'll* do! And what I'm going to do is to earn my fifty pounds. And if I drive him to the devil while I'm earning it, well, that's *his* affair!"

Thus fortified, he continued to wait. Five o'clock struck. Six o'clock. A boy strolled along with a bundle of papers. "Here! Let's have one," called Albert.

The boy held one out, and received a penny in exchange. Albert began to read.

His eyes became glued to the page. The page went round. His eyes went round with it. He felt moisture dripping down the inside of his shirt, and the drips seemed to be red. A voice at his elbow inquired,

"Anything interesting?"

His passenger had returned.

Chapter XXII

Nightmare Journey

The silence that followed seemed to Albert Bowes interminable. His head grew light and his legs grew heavy. He wanted to run, but how can you run when your knees won't move and your feet are sewn to the ground? And, even if Albert had possessed the power to run, where would he have run to?

Few of us, whatever our record, lack some form of sanctuary. At first, it is just our mother's knee. Then, perhaps, it becomes a nursery or a house, or a town, or a ship; or, failing these, our thoughts. Albert's sanctuary was an unattractive room in Bristol, where he formed his doubtful policies and sought escape from their consequences. Insecure though it was, it at least provided brief periods of repose and relief, standing between him and immediate retribution.

But now even that unsavoury haven was cut off from him. Should a miracle occur and should he find himself back in Bristol, this hideous monstrosity he had picked up from the road would seek him out and fasten itself upon him. He was certain of it! It was as though the slender rope that had hitherto held Albert to solid ground had been hacked through—by a jagged hook!—leaving him alone in the world with a maniac!

The silence that seemed interminable lasted, actually, only ten seconds. Then Albert's passenger spoke again.

"What's the matter?" he asked.

It was a cynical question. The speaker knew quite well what was the matter, and why Albert's eyes were fixed so vacantly on dancing print. Then, all at once, the dancing print began to dance away from him, and the newspaper slid from his fingers. The passenger was relieving him of it.

This woke Albert up. He leapt into the air, and his back struck the car as he came to the ground again. Meanwhile, the passenger eyed the headlines of the newspaper, and smiled.

"What! Is *this* what has upset you?" he inquired. "Just an old woman being murdered?"

Albert could be callous, but such callousness as this was beyond his experience.

"Come, come, don't lose your nerve," continued the passenger. "These things happen, you know. Why—look at *me!*"

He held up an arm, with its case of flapping sleeve. Albert tried not to look, and failed. His passenger had the power of a snake.

"*I* am quite calm, you see," said the snake. "True, my sleeve flutters, but that is just the breeze. What lies within the sleeve is perfectly, perfectly steady."

He raised the sleeve higher as he spoke, and Albert found it pointing directly at him. "Here—stop that!" the trembling man managed to murmur.

"Stop—what?" inquired the passenger. "First, afraid of a newspaper, and then afraid of a sleeve? Really, my man, you must try and get hold of yourself. We've work ahead of us, don't forget."

Work? What work? Albert fought hard to rediscover that point inside him where his independence resided.

"Look here—I'm not going on!" he muttered.

"Hey? Not going on?" exclaimed his passenger, sardonically. "Of course you are going on! You are going on to Boston, my man—to earn your fifty pounds."

"S'pose I say I'd rather not?"

"It won't make the slightest difference what you say! A bargain is a bargain, and there is a penalty for breaking it." He paused, and, removing his eyes from Albert's, transferred them to the newspaper. How the fellow contrived to retain the newspaper in the flapping folds of sleeve was an uncanny mystery. "Believe me, you'll find it much wiser to keep your bargain," he added, softly. "I've always kept mine."

There was a pause. Albert gulped, and tried a new tack. "Well, this—this work," he said, hoarsely. "Is it—just to drive you to Boston?"

"What else should it be?" answered the passenger.

"I don't know."

"Then why do you ask?"

With unexpected doggedness, Albert floundered on.

"Didn't you say just now that I'd need to keep my nerve?"

"I did."

"Well, then!"

"What, then?"

"Blast it, you don't need nerve just to drive a car!" exploded Albert.

The passenger considered the point for two or three seconds, then stepped a little closer.

"You seem to have something in your mind, my friend," he said. "What is it?"

"Nothing!" replied Albert, quickly, and tried to back away; but when you are already pressing hard against solid substance there is nowhere further to back to. "I told you, didn't I?"

"In that case, please avoid the annoyance of going round and round in a circle," retorted the passenger, now speaking sharply. "You're wasting time, and it's time to move."

Then Albert put up his last fight.

"Is it! All right! I'm *going* to move," he said. "But *you're* not going to move with me!"

He turned towards the driving-seat as he spoke these bold words, and the next moment felt hot breath on his neck. His passenger had slipped up behind him.

"Haven't you learned, *even yet*, what it will cost to double-cross me?" came the hiss in his ear. "No one ever double-crosses me and gets away with it! Do you hear me? *Ever*! EVER!"

The voice began to rise, but suddenly ceased, as though checked by an iron control. Then it continued, more quietly, but no less forcefully, while the speaker's breath burned fiercely on the listener's nape:

"And do you think there's any possibility that you *could* double-cross me, even if you decided to try? Listen, fool! You have no more chance with me than that cat has over there. Watch it!"

The cat had leapt out of a hedge. Now it stood, eyeing some vague object in the distance. An instant later, it rolled over on its side, and lay still.

"And, *now*, will you move?"

There was no more fight in Albert Bowes. He stared horror-stricken at the dead cat, then mechanically mounted to his seat. How his legs, which he had no power to direct, managed to function he could not say. All he knew was that they did function, that they appeared to be directed by some power outside himself, and that here he was, with his right foot touching the accelerator and his left foot touching the clutch.

"One moment, before we start," said the speaking-tube, "so that we may be absolutely and finally clear. From this instant until we reach Boston I shall be behind you. There will not be one instant when I am not behind you. I have slid the glass partition a little to one side, and your back is thus presented to me without any intervening substance. Just to prove this, I will touch it." The voice ceased, and something sharp gently prodded the back of the most terrified man in the kingdom. Then the voice continued, "You felt that? Good! If the necessity arises, you will feel it again. But it may not be quite so gentle, next time. It may be sharper, and hot like a burning furnace. It may even break your back, and you may lie afterwards as quietly as that cat in the road there, and as that old woman you have just read about in the paper, and... But perhaps these are enough to go with, eh! Now, answer me. Did you hear all I said. *And did you understand?*"

Albert tried to answer, but no words came. Something pricked his backbone, and he shrieked hoarsely, "Yes!" Then he let in the clutch, and the car once more moved forward.

His mind became numb. He drove mechanically. Time grew meaningless, and roads merely strips in a nightmare punctuated by sign-posts. He could not have told you during any minute what had happened during the minute before. They might have just left Evesham, or Tewkesbury, or Charlton, or Bristol. All he knew was that the nightmare went on and on and on, while a cold spot in the middle of his back had a large hole in it.

Somewhere in the hole was fifty pounds. It tickled and cracked and burned. Not till the nightmare ended could he turn round and look for it. And the nightmare didn't seem as though it would ever end.

Stratford, Warwick; Warwick, Kenilworth; Kenilworth, Coventry. They meant nothing to him, beyond a temporary change in the nightmare to slow motion. Between Coventry and Leicester they lost their way in the darkening lanes, and did not find the way again for an hour. He did not even remember that; it was his passenger who rediscovered the way and who communicated the necessary instructions to the speaking-tube. The instructions reached the ear of a man stricken through terror with mental paralysis.

Now it was quite dark, and the nightmare was illuminated only by the car's two yellow eyes. The eyes ran into Melton Mowbray. Then they ran up into hills and down into dips.

Beyond Grantham the hills and the dips ceased to exist—if they ever had existed; Albert couldn't tell—and the two yellow eyes ran along the monotonous levels of Lincolnshire. The way was lost again. A tyre got a puncture. The wheel was changed and the way was found, and the nightmare was resumed. Had they lost their way? Did they get a puncture? Albert didn't know...And then, at last, a whiff of sea air, an aroma of salt, a sense of conclusion. Somewhere rose a tall black tower. Somewhere else rose another tower, like the first one's skeleton. Low hedges. Dark buildings...Boston.

But they didn't stop. They went beyond the buildings, and round by a river, and into a new form of flatness beyond. A marshy flatness. You could smell the flatness. And now there were no hedges, and you felt you'd be off the map any minute.

"We'll be in the sea in a minute!" thought Albert.

The thought startled Albert for two reasons. The first was because of its implication. The second was because it *was* a thought! It was the first coherent thought he had had since Evesham!

Others followed, crowding upon him like shrieking, drowning things. Where are we? What time is it? What am I doing? Where's my brain been? What's this thing pressing into my back?

The thing was pressing hard. Ahead loomed a dark embankment. A moment of terrible clarity came to him. Power returned on the wings of frenzied necessity. He stepped on the brake, and leapt.

Chapter XXIII

The Third Murder

He came to earth, unexpectedly, on a soft cushion of grass. If he had descended a yard more to the right he would have been shattered by hard ground, or if he had descended a yard more to the left he would have been impaled on a rusty-toothed farm implement. But, for some reason understood only by the Fates who weave their inscrutable patterns and prolong joy or agony without any interest in either, he descended on softness; and although the breath was nearly knocked out of him, he discovered to his amazement that he was still alive.

He lay very still. Because, after all, he was only just alive, and he could not move until he had got a little of his breath back. Moreover, he did not want to move for a few seconds. Movement would give him away. Before he moved he must try to discover whether movement was also occurring in the vicinity of that large dark monster with bright slanting eyes from which he had leapt.

The monster itself was perfectly still. It had crashed into a post, and was tipping at an angle. It looked like a big black box, or an overturned coffin, and the yellow eyes had been forced round sideways. The light from the eyes streamed over stubble, grotesquely exaggerating its irregularities, and poured itself finally into the embankment that stretched like a vast dark green snake between land and sea.

The embankment had seen many strange sights in its time. It had been raised by Romans, and invaded by Norsemen. Shields and swords had clashed on it, arrows had flown over it, mailed horses had trampled on it and fallen on it, and a German shell had whistled above it. But no queerer battle had ever been staged there than the conflict it was about to witness between a Bristol chauffeur and a man minus hands…

For a few seconds, as he lay with strained ears, Albert wondered whether the man minus hands was also minus life. In that moment of sudden clarity when he had leapt from the car, only one half of his effort had been to save himself. The other half had been to wreck the car and kill its occupant, and besides jamming on the brake he had given a violent twist to the driving-wheel. Thus the car had swung away from him as he had jumped and had struck the post.

Now he listened hard. He listened so hard that he almost burst the veins in his forehead. He heard nothing. Nothing. Suddenly he realised his mistake. He was hearing dozens of things. Little grasses stirring. Little twigs moving. Little breezes blowing. Little drops of water oozing. All around him were minute sound and movement, filling the blackness with a million indecipherable stories. For there is no such thing as utter silence. The ear merely needs to be tuned in.

At first these little sounds terrified Albert. He attributed the stirring grasses and the moving twigs to stealthy human feet, and the oozing to advancing boots. But when his own ear became tuned in, and he heard the sounds repeated in front of him and behind him and on both sides, he interpreted them correctly, and strained his ears afresh so that he might not miss that sound which spelt real Menace.

He looked towards the black car. The Menace would begin from over there, of course. Then a twig snapped abruptly from a spot behind him. He twisted his neck violently. A point touched his face. It was a long grass.

Steadying himself, he twisted his neck back again, and again stared towards the car. In particular he stared towards the two rays of light that slanted off into the embankment. If a figure moved into an edge of either of these two rays, it would be visible, and could be located; and, once located, a policy could be devised. Thus, while one dreaded the moment when a stealthy form would edge into the light, one also wanted it, and became divided against oneself.

No! After all, *did* one want it? The longer this inactivity lasted—the longer this world of little sounds remained unbroken by any big sound—the more possible grew the theory that the man without hands was indeed dead, and that Albert's attempt to kill him by wrecking the car had succeeded. Because what would the man do if he were *not* dead? Why, it was obvious. He would wait a second or two, to collect himself—just as Albert was waiting—and then he would creep out of the car. Then he would creep round the car, searching for Albert. Then he would creep a little farther afield. During these operations, he would be bound to move into one or other of those two thin streets of light, and to reveal himself to the eyes of the man for whom he was searching…

Snap! Again a twig crackled in Albert's rear.

"Not this time!" thought Albert, and kept his eyes on the lights.

Nothing! *Nothing*! NOTHING!

"God, he is dead!" babbled Albert, hysterically.

He rose, tottering, but free! And, as he rose, a cold hook stretched forward from behind and touched the back of his neck.

If life is doubly sweet after thinking you have lost it, death is doubly terrible after believing you have escaped from it. As the cold metal touched Albert's skin, and he visualised Death standing behind him—the Death he himself imagined dead—he endured the worst moment of his existence.

In that moment, while he stood tottering on the edge of Eternity, his past rose from the swaying ground and circled round him. A man he had cheated howled derisively at him. A woman he had cheated clung to him. A dog he had hoped to sell in some far-off life wagged its tail and barked at him, while a piece of curved metal began travelling round his neck.

"*Now* you'll pay!" shrieked the man.

"I forgive you!" wailed the woman.

"Bow-wow!" barked the dog. "Have you forgotten how to kick? Bow-wow!"

Kick? What's that? Kick? Instructed by the ghost of a dog on whom he had practised in that far-off life, Albert swung round and kicked.

His boot met something soft, and the metal vanished. Then Albert turned and ran.

He ran heavily and unscientifically. The ground tried to seize his legs, but he went on kicking. Presently the ground rose, and he fell forward against it. He thought he was lying down, and found he was lying up. He heard panting. Was it his own, or somebody else's? There was no time to stop and inquire. He clambered up the ground that had risen in front of him, clambered with hands as well as feet, and reached the top.

Something clambered up after him.

He was now on the ridge of the embankment, and he had to turn to the right or left to avoid a tumble. For all he knew, the tumble might end in the sea. He chose the right, and ran desperately. It surprised him that he kept on the ridge. He expected to fall over a side of it any moment, for in the darkness he underestimated its width and seemed to be speeding along a tight-rope. Possibly, he was helped, also, by the fact that at this portion of the embankment it took a sweeping curve, and when we cannot see we are apt to move in circles.

Suddenly he became conscious of farm buildings on his left. He did not believe in their reality at first, owing to his misconception that the sea was immediately below him; actually the sea was still some considerable distance away. As he raced by a barn, however, he discovered that it was not an imaginative object but a real one.

He tried to shout. He did not know whether he succeeded or not. No one came to his assistance from the barn, or from any of the other buildings. They were all empty and deserted…

Something obstructed his path. It was a gate. He fell against it, and clung to it. He discovered, to his horror, that he had no strength to open it. He hadn't even the brain to find out how it opened, or at which end of it he was. He turned, like a spent bull at bay, and waited.

Somewhere below him, water gleamed. He wondered vaguely whether there would be any object in reaching it. The fence that ended at the gate took a downward turn towards the water, and if he could climb over the fence he might drop down into some sort of sanctuary while his pursuer passed on through the gate. But was there time? He stared back along the ridge over which he had travelled. There was no sign of his pursuer.

Perhaps his pursuer had stumbled? Perhaps *he* had fallen over a side of the embankment? Or perhaps—and this was more likely—he had decided to take no risks, and was stalking his quarry slowly and cautiously, knowing that the quarry's breath would soon be spent and that ultimate escape was impossible! Well, in any case, the pursuer had not arrived yet, and there might be time to get over the fence and hide before he came.

It was worth trying. The only remaining question was—had one the strength?

Albert took a deep breath, attempting to steady himself, and then proceeded inch by inch along the fence. He had to cling to the fence while he moved, for otherwise he could not have held himself up. When he reached the point immediately above the water, he paused and stared down, trying to estimate how far the water was below him. He thought it was only a very short distance. He judged by a star that gleamed in it. Probably there would be a bank or something which would provide him with cover…Now, then! Be quick!…On to the fence, and over it!…

He managed to get astride of the fence. As he did so, he noticed another farm building. A small shed, near the side of the water. Fool he was! Was he working with a brain or a sieve? He ought to have hidden in one of the farm buildings! They were all empty.…

Hallo! *This* one wasn't! A figure emerged from the shed, and stood regarding him.

"Help!" gasped Albert.

The figure raised a flapping arm and pointed it at him. The next moment Albert toppled from the fence, and reached the water.

The star shivered.

Chapter XXIV

The First Lap

As Albert Bowes's journey to Boston ended, Ted Diggs's began.

Diggs had not been tempted by so large a sum as Albert. Twenty pounds, not fifty, had been offered him for crossing England at a moment's notice, but he was happier in the person who had offered the sum, and stood a likelier chance of getting it. Thus, he set out with a more contented mind.

"Mind you," he told himself, "this is the maddest trip I've ever took, and I don't say I ain't a bit mad myself for takin' it. But, there! We'll all be dead in a 'undred years, won't we? So what's the difference?"

Fortunately he took his work sufficiently seriously to include a map in his outfit. Fortunately, also, he knew the road as far as Gloucester. When they got to Gloucester he'd have a go at the map, and p'r'aps get the young gent to help him. As long as he wasn't asked to cross the Atlantic, he expected he could get to a place called Boston as well as the next man.

Pity there wasn't a moon, though.

Inside the car, his two passengers were also occupied with their thoughts. Each was confused, and each knew of the other's confusion; yet, for some reason known only to the girl—her mind was clearer on that point at least—they could not pool their confusion in the attempt to build something coherent out of it. Darkness lay in their minds as well as on the roads they were travelling through.

But the silence was not entirely uncommunicative! Companionship existed inside the car, and also trust. No words were needed to strengthen these consoling elements; indeed, at this stage, words might have weakened them, implying a leakage in their spiritual armour. The silence was peaceful, too. They could relax into it, and gather strength for what lay ahead.... Yes... what *did* lie ahead?

Richard pondered over this question fruitlessly. Twenty-four hours ago—yes, just twenty-four hours ago!—he had been trying to close his ears to the snoring of John Amble. (How much more appealing was the companion on his present night journey!) Afterwards, John Amble had died at Euston. Was there any connection between Euston and Boston? Via Bristol? And, if so, what?

The crimson Z! Was that the connection? A sentence spoken by Inspector James in the Bristol train came into Richard's mind. Queer how the inspector's words had a habit of reverting to one! "I'm beginning to wonder, Mr. Temperley, how many more of these crimson Z's we are going to find before we've finished the job."

Despite his resolve to form the strength of this little army of two, Richard suddenly shuddered, and the other half of the army, which had been sticking unconsciously close, suddenly spoke.

"What's the matter?" asked Sylvia.

"Nothing," he replied, quickly.

"Just natural St. Vitus's Dance?" she queried.

He smiled, delighted to find that she could jest.

"It was only a thought," he said.

"Let me know it!"

"In return for all the voluminous information you've given me?"

Now she smiled, as though glad that he could jest, too.

"It wasn't important," he went on, to escape gloom. "You know how one's mind goes round and round."

"Yes, I know."

"Well, my mind was going round and round—"

"And it bumped somewhere?"

"That's it. And woke you up. Now try and go to sleep again."

"Where did it bump?"

"Nowhere important. I've told you so already."

"But you do it so badly."

"Do what?"

"Lie."

"Thank you," he laughed. "I'll take that as a compliment."

"You don't even know when you're lying to the wrong people," she observed.

"That's less complimentary," he admitted, and turned his head suddenly to look at her.

The thought that had caused him to turn his head was chased away by another. "Whew, if I were an ordinary young man in a taxi," came the second thought, "what a fool I'd make of myself!" Possibly he was not quite fair to the ordinary young men in taxis. One is apt to lower other people in order to maintain one's own elevation. But there was no time now to reach final conclusions regarding the behaviour of ordinary young men in taxis or how they would behave if seated, after midnight, by such a devastatingly pretty girl as Sylvia Wynne. The devastatingly pretty girl was returning Richard's gaze, and the only way to escape from the danger of the second thought was to swing back to the security of the first…The first thought…What was it?…Oh, yes, the bump in the vicious circle.

"Are you going to tell me?" she asked.

"Well—since it was *only* a thought," he replied.

"Thoughts can be useful."

"And dangerous, if they come from panic."

"I don't associate you with panic, Mr. Temperley."

"I'm glad of that, Miss Wynne. I—do get in a bit of a panic, though, when I think you're in danger."

Something entered her eyes, causing her to remove them quickly from his and to stare into the back of Ted Diggs separated from romance by a sheet of glass. Richard felt cheated of a wonderful moment. Maybe she sensed this. Her next words, coming after a little silence, were compensation.

"I never feel in danger when I'm with you," she said. "And, now, please—the thought?"

"All right! Just this," he said. "I was wondering whether we are going to find any more of those beastly little crimson Z's at Boston?"

She sat very still. Deciding, now the thought had been forced from him, to proceed with it ruthlessly, he inquired. "What's your opinion?"

"I don't know," she murmured.

"Still, you think we *may* find one?"

"Everything's possible, isn't it?"

"Miss Wynne," said Richard, reprovingly, "if I lie badly, you fence badly. And *you* don't know when you're *fencing* with the wrong people!"

"What do you want me to say?" she asked, rather helplessly.

"I asked for an opinion, not a generality."

"But suppose I haven't got an opinion?"

"Nonsense! We've all got opinions. I don't know whether to-morrow's going to be wet or dry, but if I had to bet a shilling one way or the other I'd find that fifty-one per cent. of my opinion regarding the meteorological outlook said, 'Dry.' So I'd bet 'Dry,' without in any sense posing as an expert. Having delivered which little lecture, the annoying but well-intentioned young man repeated, 'What's *your* opinion, Miss Wynne, on the criminalogical outlook in Boston? Wet or dry?'"

"Wet," she replied, giving up.

"That's my opinion, also," he nodded, now becoming sober again, "although I've far less to go upon than you have."

The car slackened speed at a sign-post, then veered round a dark corner and accelerated.

"Do you think I've got a lot to go upon?" she challenged him.

"I don't know," he parried.

"Nonsense! We've all got opinions!" she scored. "What's your fifty-one per cent. on the Sylvia Wynne outlook?"

"A hit, a hit, a palpable hit!" he answered, with a smile. "I'd bet my bob that Sylvia Wynne had a very great deal to go upon."

"Then you'd lose the bob," came the unexpected response. "I *haven't* much to go upon."

He turned and stared at her in genuine surprise.

"What—not much to go upon?" he exclaimed. She shook her head. "Do you mean, you're chasing all over England without knowing exactly why you're doing it?"

"I know why I'm doing it."

"But you're not sure that the reason is a sound one?"

"It might be something like that."

"And you won't even let me help you?"

"But you are helping me—"

"To decide, I mean."

"You'd only see the logic of the case."

"Only the logic!" he echoed. "What else is there?"

"Everything else. Instinct."

"Oh!"

"And I believe in instinct—being a woman, you see."

"Bit dangerous, isn't it?"

"Yes, sometimes. But sometimes instinct brings safety, too."

"I'm afraid that's rather beyond me."

"It shouldn't be, Mr. Temperley. But for my instinct, would I be trusting you like this?"

"By Jove, I expect that's true!" he murmured. "So—I'm the safety, then?"

"The only safety."

"Miss Wynne, I warn you," he said, fighting his pleasure. "When you make remarks like that, I become considerably less safe!"

"I'm not afraid," she answered.

"No, but *I* am!" he retorted. "You don't realise the—the chaos of my mind! Oh, yes, I'm safe enough, I expect! You needn't be afraid, really. Just the same, I demand that you give me a little genuine, human credit for the fact."

"I do," she answered, and unconsciously tested him by moving an inch closer.

"And I demand something else, too," he went on, earnestly. "When we get to Boston, you're going to tell me *everything*!"

"When we get to Boston—you'll be telephoning to Bristol."

"By Jove, you keep your mind pretty clear on details, Miss Wynne," observed Richard, wryly. "Yes, of course, I'll have to get in touch with Inspector James, if I can. That's rather a matter of honour, isn't it?"

"I agree that it is. And it's largely because it is that I can't tell you everything when we get to Boston until—"

she paused, then added, "until *after* you've telephoned to Bristol." His heart leapt.

"Then—*after* I've telephoned to Bristol—?"

"If I am still in trouble," she promised, "I'll tell you everything."

"Thank God!" he murmured, and felt as though a great load had been lifted from him. "Believe me, you won't regret it!"

The car slowed down again. Not far behind, another car also slowed down. Ted had heard the other car for a full minute, but his passengers had been too absorbed in their conversation to notice its approach. But when Ted stopped his car, dismounted, and poked his head in at the window, the sound of the following car was too distinct to be ignored.

"Oi!" called Ted. "Gloucester's jest a'ead. Where's the next stop fer Boston?" But before the reply came, he stood aside briskly. The following car had reached them and came swinging by.

Chapter XXV

The Last Lap

Minds, whether great or small, do not always think alike. The mind that, twelve hours earlier, had planned a previous journey to Boston, had elected to reach Stratford-on-Avon via Tewkesbury and Evesham (it was probably a mere coincidence that these two names are associated historically with bloodshed), but the mind that worked out the present journey favoured Cheltenham and Winchcombe. This route appeared to be shorter, and Diggs's map did not indicate that it was also hillier.

Beyond Stratford, the minds did think alike. Warwick, Kenilworth, Coventry, Leicester via Sharnford, Melton Mowbray, Grantham and Boston—all these names were duly entered in Diggs's note-book, opposite a forecast of next week's washing, in case he should grow sleepy and forget them.

The question of the possible sleepiness was itself touched on. "Are you sure you can keep awake?" inquired Richard.

"You won't be driven into no brick wall," Diggs promised.

"I really think I'll have to make it guineas," said Richard.

"Make it fivers, if you like," suggested Diggs, with a wink. "I ain't one to worry if I'm overpaid!"

Then he returned to his seat, and the journey was resumed.

To Diggs, sitting outside and with all the work to do, the business soon lost the little glamour that had attached to the start of it and became a mere matter of eating up the momentarily illuminated darkness. The illumination travelled along with them, like the illumination of the phosphorescent fish that lives in the black depths and makes its own light; but ahead and behind lay the cloak of night, and there was nothing on which to concentrate beyond the process of getting safely through it.

Small towns were hardly noticed, and large ones were merely milestones. So much nearer Boston. So much nearer twenty guineas. So much nearer the possession of a dog. (Had Diggs known that the owner of the said dog was lying at that moment in a dike near Boston, with unseeing eyes turned upwards to a star, he would have steered a less steady course.) So much nearer a bed, and sleep, and a dream or two.

But to his passengers, leaning back in the cushioned leather on which he rather prided himself, the journey had become more magical. For half-a-dozen hours, they could relax, conscious of each other, safe with each other, and in the quiet enjoyment of each other. There was no need for further conversation. A happy point had been reached in it, and when they arrived at Boston they would together face whatever problem presented itself. If the problem could not be solved with unequally shared knowledge, then Sylvia would yield all the knowledge she possessed to Richard. There would exist no more mystery between them. In its place would be the perfect trust and confidence for which, from the outset, Richard had ached.

So, meanwhile, why worry? Richard decided that he would not worry. And, apparently, the girl at his side made the same decision. She drew a little closer to him—a wonderful acknowledgment, this, of her growing sense of companionship—and presently he found that her head was resting against his shoulder.

At first he hoped she was asleep, so that her head would remain against his shoulder. Then he hoped she was not asleep, for the added significance this would impart to the position. Then he didn't know which he hoped. Then he laughed at himself, and called himself a fool. Then he swore silently at Ted Diggs for failing to avoid a bit of unevenness in the road and causing a bump.

But the head did not stir. It still lay with sweet heaviness against him.

"She *is* asleep," he decided. "Sound!"

Soon, his own eyes began to close. He fought against his drowsiness at first. He was a sort of sentry, and sentries must not sleep at their post. Then, as the drowsiness gained on him, and he knew it would win, he sought some excuse to ease this pleasant drifting into unconsciousness. He found it quite easily. He was going to sleep for her sake! When they arrived at Boston he would need all his senses about him, and all his strength. The previous night had been broken. How could he face Boston if this night were sleepless, also?

So now Richard's head drooped, too. Had Ted Diggs looked back, he would have smiled at the sight. But Ted Diggs did not look back. His job lay ahead of him, and his necessity was "Eyes front!"

The night hours slipped by. The towns on his list were wiped out, one by one. The stars increased. Now the sky above was a black sheet sewn with spangles. Now the spangles grew less bright. The advance rumour of morning depressed their brilliance.

"Lummy, am I still 'ere?" thought Diggs abruptly, with a jerk. He had travelled ten miles without being conscious of any of them!

That wouldn't do. He opened his eyes wide, and as he ran through a sleeping town he wondered why towns didn't have their names written up, like stations…

"'Corse, I'm goin' barmy!" he reflected.

Anyway, he knew the name of the town. It was Grantham. Must be, since the place before had been Melton Mowbray, same as Melton Mowbray must have been Melton Mowbray because the place before it had been whatever it had been. Another twenty-five miles or so, and they'd be there.

"'Ooray," he yawned, to cheer himself.

If you possess a touring map of Lincolnshire, you will see that there are two routes from Grantham to Boston. The northern route goes through Sleaford, and assuming your map knows its business, you will note that the road is level and first-class all the way. The southern route begins by being hillier and ends by being second-class, but it makes up for these deficiencies by being shorter. Which of the two routes, if presented with the problem just before sunrise, would you choose?

That was the problem now before Ted Diggs, and because he felt rather ashamed of his lack of attention just before Grantham he felt that he must equalise matters by additional attention after it. Therefore he stopped the car and consulted his map. It was all he had to consult. His passengers appeared to be fast asleep. "Think I'll go by Sleaford," he decided, utterly unconscious that the decision held any real importance. "Ay, that's what I'll do. Sleaford."

It was a happy decision. Sleaford spelt safety. But man proposes and God disposes, and either through human error or fatalistic design, Diggs missed a turning.

"All right, then," he muttered, finding himself heading for the southern route, "I *won't* go by Sleaford! Wot's it matter, any'ow?"

You cannot put up a fight against Fate in the cold grey hour. And thus Security, which had held out its hands for a moment, slipped back into the shadows, and a grinning, armless spectre slipped into its place.

Grantham, still sleeping, vanished. Up slipped the car into unseen hills, and down it slipped out of them. Now the sea declared itself with a queer, cool tang to the nostrils. It was miles away yet, but only flat land lay between.

"Nearly over!" thought Diggs, gratefully. "That dog's mine!"

Yes, it wasn't far now to Boston, with its tall church tower, and its skeleton standards, and its grassy Roman embankment. Just a few more miles of this flat, almost hedgeless road, with the sea-tang growing stronger and stronger in the faint east wind, and then…

Richard woke up with a jerk. The girl stirred at his side. What was happening?

"Are we there?" murmured the girl.

"I don't think so—don't move yet," Richard murmured back. "We're slowing, though."

He peered out of the window, and his shoulder suddenly felt cold. Sylvia had lifted her head from it.

"We're stopping," she said.

"Yes. P'r'aps he's missed his way or something."

He frowned. It was comfortable in the car. Still, he'd better get out and discover what the trouble was.

The trouble was a man standing in the middle of the road. No, two men. And where was Ted Diggs?…Ah—there he was! He was the second man.

"Anything wrong?" called Richard.

Diggs came ambling back, while the other man vanished.

"Chap in trouble, sir," reported Diggs. "'Is car there in a ditch."

"Where's he gone to?"

"'E's gone back to it. Wants to know if we'll give 'im a 'and."

"Righto!" grunted Richard. "But it's a nuisance." He turned back to Sylvia, who was now sitting bolt upright. "Fellow out there wants us to give his boneshaker a shove. You'll be all right for a minute?"

"Yes, of course," she replied. "But—make it a short minute!"

"You bet, I will!" smiled Richard. "I'll make it the shortest minute that was ever born!"

He opened the door and stepped out on to the road. The salt of the sea met him.

"Where's everybody?" he inquired of the night.

"Over 'ere, sir," came Diggs's voice, through the darkness.

He took a step or two forward. It was confoundedly dark! Where had Diggs shouted from?

"Give us another call!" he cried.

But this time Diggs did not respond.

He took another step or two forward. The stars that had begun to pale became suddenly bright. Something had shaken them violently, with a huge thud…and now they were below him, and he was falling among them. Or was it the sea he was falling into? He certainly smelt something that did not usually reside just outside one's nostrils. Stronger than the sea, though…more like chloroform…more like…

Chapter XXVI

Something Staring Up

The stars vanished, both in the space of Richard's mind and in the vaster space above it. The blackness grew less intense. When Richard opened his eyes, there was grey in the east.

His head was dizzy and throbbing. For a few moments he could not remember where he was. A studio, wasn't it? No, that was last year. Ah—a train! And somebody had just tried to shove him out on the line! No, that was the year before last. Of course—*now* he'd got it! He was in a taxi, travelling to Euston. No, from Euston. Well, one or the other. Or was it Bristol? Something about Bristol. Hold on to Bristol. But how could you hold on to Bristol if the whole blessed city insisted on swaying up and down…

Steady! Take a deep breath. Whew—something a bit wrong with the breathing apparatus! A bit more slowly, this time. Inhale—exhale—that was better. Now one could think, if only that throbbing would stop. What was throbbing? The taxi? And, yes, what *about* that taxi? He was in it, wasn't he? But, if he were in a taxi, why should a prickly branch be sticking into his cheek? He seemed to remember that prickly branches didn't grow in taxis. They grew in the sides of roads…yes, in the sides of roads…

He sat up suddenly and painfully. Recollection swept back, and the abrupt shock of it almost suffocated him. He *was* on the side of a road. The taxi was a thing of the past. When he had left the taxi, somebody had hit him, and had tumbled him into this ditch. Yes, all that was clear now. But—what had happened after he had been tumbled into the ditch?

He put his hand on the ground, with the intention of rising, and it came against a face. The unexpected contact unnerved him for an instant, for he still felt very groggy, and he drew away quickly. But as the face did not rise and thrust itself after him, he bent forward again, and risked an examination.

The face was quite still. The eyes were open, staring upwards. Around the mouth, a coloured handkerchief was tied with cruel tightness.

Gripping on to himself, Richard untied the handkerchief, and the face worked spasmodically. It went through a series of necessary but unpicturesque convulsions. Then slowly, it rose, and Ted Diggs and Richard Temperley stared emotionally at each other.

"Knocked you out, too, eh?" muttered Richard.

"There was two of 'em," Diggs muttered back.

"The taxi—what about the taxi?" asked Richard.

"I feel sick," answered Diggs.

Richard, also, felt sick, but his sickness was in his soul. Struggling to his feet, and leaving Diggs to fend for himself, he turned towards the spot where the taxi had been when he had left it. The next moment he gave an exclamation.

"Thank God! It's still here!" he cried.

He ran forward as he cried, pretending fiercely that all was well. There stood the taxi, and that was all that mattered! Provided, of course…

The door of the taxi was closed. He seized the handle and opened it. No one was inside. "Miss Wynne!" he called, fighting a choking sensation. "Sylvia!" Only his own voice came back to him.

He passed through a period of black agony. He discovered that he was moist with perspiration. Black anger mingled with the black agony, and the blackest recoiled against himself. He had failed. His brain had slept at its post!

When we are angry with ourselves, we try to divert our anger to the nearest thing. The nearest thing to Richard was Ted Diggs. "Diggs! Why don't you come?" he shouted. "She's gone! Where are you?"

"Yer need legs to move with, don't yer?" said Diggs. Diggs's legs were bound, and so were his hands. Informed of the position, Richard returned, and freed the man.

"And, now, after them!" he exclaimed. "Quick! Hurry!"

Diggs did his best, but his legs gave under him. He shook his head miserably. "Don't think I'm much good, fer a bit," he mumbled. "And, any'ow, we don't know which way they went."

"But we can't stay here doing nothing!" retorted Richard. "Keep where you are for a minute, if you're done up, and I'll look for tracks."

He went into the middle of the road and stared at the marks. If any informative marks were there, he could not discern any. The light was too feeble. "Get the lamps on 'em," suggested Diggs, from the roadside.

Richard went to the car. Something in its appearance arrested him. Something he had not noticed before.

"What's up?" called Diggs, apprehensively.

"They've done in two of the tyres," answered Richard. "And—*look!*" Beneath the car was a pool of petrol. He returned to Diggs, who was rubbing his legs to get the circulation back. "You'll be able to move, Diggs, before your car will," he said, desperately. "Two tyres gone west, and all the petrol."

"What—'ave they let out the gas?" gasped Diggs.

"They've made a clean job of it."

"Well, I'm blowed!"

"And we're stranded."

"What's the meanin' of it?"

"Don't let's trouble with the meaning of it for the moment," replied Richard, fighting every moment to regain sufficient calmness for functioning purposes. If he stopped to consider the meaning of it, despair would render him impotent. "Let's just confine ourselves to facts. The first fact is that Miss Wynne—my fellow passenger—is gone."

"Ay. So you said."

"She's been kidnapped!"

"Ay. Looks like it."

"And since we can't chase the kidnappers ourselves, we must report the matter to others who can."

"The police?"

"Yes. How far do you reckon we are from Boston?"

"Two or three miles, sir. But it's a guess."

"Then we'll have to walk there, unless we can get a lift."

"That's right."

"How soon do you think you'll be able to step out?"

"Give me a couple o' minutes."

Richard glanced at his wrist-watch. It was just on six. "Well, if you're longer, I'll have to step out without you," he said. "Meanwhile, here's a cigarette—you look as if you needed one—and use the two minutes by telling me exactly what happened, and what these two men were like."

"There was only one of 'em first," said Diggs, taking the cigarette gratefully. "He stands in the middle of the road—"

"What sort of a man?"

"Biggish. In a rough suit. I see the suit, because there 'e stands, plain as daylight in the lamp, see? Leggings—"

"Appearance of a farmer, in fact?"

"That's right," nodded Diggs. "You've 'it it. 'Oi!' 'e ses, 'my car's in a ditch. Can you give me a 'and to get it out?' Well, you can't pass trouble on the road, no matter what time o' the night, so down I 'ops, and I'm speakin' to 'im when you calls me."

"But you said there were two of them?"

"That's right. The other comes up jest after I answered you, and gives me a crack on the jaw. No, the other one didn't!" he corrected himself. "It was the first one cracked me. The other one—well, I didn't see 'im plain, 'cos 'e keeps in the shadders like, but I'd say 'e was a cripple o' some sort. Nasty looking chap, and no mistake!"

"These descriptions should help," commented Richard. "Have just a puff or two more, and then see if you can manage it. I think I can add a touch or two to your first friend."

"What! D'you know 'im?" exclaimed Diggs, in surprise.

"I believe so."

"What about the other feller?"

"No, I don't know him," replied Richard, thoughtfully, "but I've a feeling I shall, before long."

"Well, you needn't take me with you, sir," observed Diggs, with a grimace, "becos' the very thought of 'im gives me the creeps. Suddenly, there 'e is—then, bing on me nose—and then 'e isn't!"

"What about the car?"

"What about what?"

"The one they said was in the ditch."

"Never saw a sign of it."

"It probably never was in a ditch."

"Couldn't 'ave been, sir, or they wouldn't 'ave got away in it."

"Agreed. Well, ready now?"

"I think I can manage, sir."

"Good. Then, march! And quick as your legs allow."

Diggs rose to his feet, and, as his feet moved, his brain moved, too.

"Yes, but what about my car?" he queried "'Oo's goin' to look after it?"

"A car with no petrol and two of its wheels hors de combat—"

"Horder what?"

"—out of commission—useless—isn't likely to run off," said Richard. "Still, you can stay, if you like."

Did Diggs like? He thought about it. And it occurred to him all at once that he didn't like. He was in a mood for company. "Another reason I'd like you with me," continued Richard, "is that you'll be useful at the police station for identity purposes. *You* saw the men, you know—I didn't."

"That's right," nodded Diggs, with secret gratitude. "I better come along with yer."

And now came the last stage of the journey to Boston. Three began it in a car. Two ended it on foot.

All the way, Richard strove against hideous thoughts and nightmare emotions. Every step seemed to stab his heart. A sense of personal failure was swamped by a sense of personal loss, while the sense of personal loss was swamped by a fear less selfish—a fear for Sylvia herself. Where was she at this moment, and what was happening to her? He tried to make his mind a blank. There was no relief otherwise.

Now the grey became more revealing, and, in the east, was replaced by amber. A point of gold grew up into the amber and expanded. But a perfect morning is fruitless without a perfect mood.

The tall tower of St. Botolph's church stood out like a black silhouette with edges of gold. The roofs of Boston began to waken as they came into view. Which was the roof of the police station? That was the one immediate query in Richard's mind.

A figure came straggling into view. Its head nodded from side to side. The head paused, however, when it was hailed. "Which is the way to the police station?" The head seemed immensely interested in the question. It soon became evident to Richard that it belonged to the village idiot. An expression of profound surprise was followed by another of profound knowledge. The head began wagging again.

"Didn't you hear me?" demanded Richard, sharply.

"Ay," nodded the head. "You've seen it, too, then?"

"Seen what?" asked Richard.

"It," repeated the village idiot.

"If you will explain what you mean by 'it,'" rasped Richard, "I'll tell you whether I've seen it!"

The village idiot looked a little disappointed. He thought he had connected up with somebody of sympathy and understanding. "By the First Pullover," he mumbled. "Tha's where 'tis."

His eyes became distended, and a look of fascinated horror entered into them. "I seen it, as I was comin' by. But I ses, 'I ain't goin' to no police station,' I ses, 'or maybe they'll say I done it!'"

And he laughed slyly at this subtlety.

"Done what?" asked Richard, his heart missing a beat.

"Starin' up, it be!" grinned the village idiot. "Starin' up in the sky. Tha's where we all come from. Tha's where we all go back to. Like a wet dog, it be. Starin' up. But it can't see nothin'. You can't see nothin', no, not when you're dead!"

Chapter XXVII

As Unfolded to Inspector Wetherby

Inspector Wetherby didn't know what to make of it. One thing at a time—that he could grapple with as well as anybody. A row in the Market Place—right. A boat accident in the Witham—right. A burglary—right. A drunk—right. But this queer tangle of things before seven in the morning, when you weren't exactly at your brightest, these disjointed fragments advanced by distracted people—people who seemed to imagine that you only had to say "Boo" to a policeman to set him running off wherever you wanted him to—that wasn't so good! It needed, on your own side, a little caution and thought.

Let's get this straight, now. Just while the police car is being brought round. Two people saying they've been set upon and chloroformed on the road from Grantham. Not the Sleaford road, the Donington road. Right. And a third person who was with them, a girl, was kidnapped. H'm! And the whole lot supposed to have come from Bristol.

Night joy-ride, eh? No? Well, then, might one know the object of the journey? Yes, that's true, of course, plenty of people travelled by car at night, but, in a case like this—an alleged kidnapping case—it helped the police to have precise details. Oh—on business. Just a business trip. H'm. Very informative! Right.

Now, any idea who the kidnappers were? Two of them—right. One large, in a rough suit, and leggings. Sort of farmer. Right. The other—what was this? Deformed, eh? Oh, not deformed. What, then. *Looked* as if he was deformed? Looked deformed, but not deformed. Well, what made him *look* deformed. Can't say, eh? Pity taxi-drivers don't have to pass an intelligence test! Ah, an arm gone. Now we're coming to something. Arm off, and a face like Gawd knows what. Very helpful description, that! Very helpful indeed, Mr. Piggs. Oh, Diggs. Apologies. The full name would be helpful. Ted Diggs, taxi-driver, Bristol. And the taxi standing three miles away by the road-side with two useless wheels and no petrol. Right. That would have to be seen to. Right, right.

And *your* name, sir? Temperley. Richard Temperley. St. John's Wood, London. Right. Yes, sir, certainly. In half a minute. Car being brought right round. But first we must get this other man's story straight, mustn't we? Can't go anywhere before we know just where to go, can we? Right.

Now, you! Your name's Smale, isn't it? And why aren't you in bed, Smale, where all good little boys ought to be at this time of the morning? Couldn't sleep, eh? Right. Often can't sleep? Because of angels ringing bells—quite so, quite so. Right, right. And did the angels wake you this time? Oh, a motor-car. What time? Can't say. Well, *about* what time? Can't say that either., (Yes, yes, sir, I agree, but this fellow isn't over-burdened with brains—they forgot to fill his head when he was born—and we *must* get his story, mustn't we? And the car isn't here yet. Right.)

Now, then, Smale. This car that passed your place. Was it when you went to bed? No. Then was it just after? No. Then was it just before you got up? Yes? Excellent. And how long have you been up. Hour or two. Well, we'll get it presently.

So this motor-car woke you up. Rushed by your cottage. Like what? Like chariots in heaven—yes, yes. And then what did you do? You got up? Yes? And then what did you do? You went out? Yes? And which way did you go? Towards the First Pullover? Right. And why did you go in that direction?

I see. The car had come from that direction? What's that? The *second* time? Was there a *first* time, then? I see. You heard it twice. Why didn't you tell me that before? The first time—that was the time it woke you up—it was going *towards* the sea. And the second time—that was the time you were dressing—it was coming *from* the sea? Right. It had gone towards the sea, and then it had come back again? How long between the times it passed your cottage going and coming? You don't know! Well, then, how long do you take to dress? As long as it takes to boil two hard boiled eggs? Yes, very funny, Smale, very funny. Can't you see, we're all splitting ourselves with laughter? And now the comic turn is over—all right, sir, all right, sir, *I* know how to handle him—we're old friends, you and I, Smale, aren't we?—we'll go to heaven together, won't we?—there you are, you see, sir, all bright and smiling again—well, now that's over, we can put the time down at ten minutes. Right.

Why did you get up, Smale? You always get up when you can't sleep. You like to walk about. Angels calling—right. But what made you go towards the sea? Wanted to find out what the car had been up to. Splendid! We *have* our gleams of intelligence, after all. Now, then, Smale, tell me exactly what you found? Yes, you followed the lane to the First Pullover. Right. You found a car that had run into a post. Yes, but you said...Oh, I see. This was another car—not the car that passed your cottage? H'm.

Well, get on. How did you see the car if it was dark? Were the lights still on? No? Oh, it was getting light. *Now* we can fix the time. Between five and six. (You see, sir, everything comes out after a little patient questioning.) That means that the car went by your cottage, say, round about five o'clock. Well, what next? You went on. You went up the embankment. Why? Something drew you? Not angels this time, perhaps, eh? Never mind what I said—get on with it. You passed the empty farm buildings and sheds—yes, yes, I know them. You reached the gate. Yes. You turned to the left. To the fence. Know why? Quite so, something still drew you, but did you hear any *sound*? A cry or anything? No? You looked over the fence. Looked down into the water. And—yes?

Go on, go on! You're quite safe here! You saw—it? Yes, but what? No, no, tell us exactly, Smale. A body? One of your angels, perhaps? No? Now, listen, Smale, are you quite sure—(Yes, yes, sir, but this man—can't you see? I've had to deal with his illusions before!) *Not* an angel. Just a body. Facing upwards. Can't say whether a man or a woman—right. But—drowned, eh? You're sure of that? You went down to look?

Idiot! Why didn't you? Mind went blank. Oh, well, I see. Wandered about. Yes. And then you met these two men, and you told them your story, and they brought you along here. Right, Smale. Thank you very much.

Yes, yes, don't worry. I'll see the angels don't get you yet awhile. There's plenty of time. Just come along with us for a little ride, and then you can go home again with a nice, large piece of cake. Yes, the same as you had last time. That's right. Pink.

Here's the car, sir. Now, if you please, we'll be getting along.

Chapter XXVIII

The Growing List

While Inspector Wetherby was obtaining his information in his own particular manner, Richard passed through varying emotions.

Smale's news, incoherent though it was when first delivered in the road, had filled him with despair. All that his muddled mind could seize on was the fact that someone had been drowned near by, and since Smale could give no description of the someone—not even, apparently, the gender—the fear that it might be Sylvia bit into his soul. Later, at the police station, the fear had turned into desperate impatience, and the desperate impatience had, in its turn, changed to a revulsion of relief that for a few minutes weakened him even more than his rough handling; for the insistent questions of Inspector Wetherby had elicited details which rendered impossible the theory that the drowned person was Sylvia.

The car had passed Smale's cottage at about five. It was not till well after five that Sylvia had been kidnapped. Whether the kidnappers had been in the car or not, the kidnapping had occurred *after* Smale had made his gruesome discovery. Yes, Inspector Wetherby, for all the impatience he had evoked, had brought out that vital point. Like many another before him, Richard Temperley had not been entirely just to the police force!

Wetherby, in fact, in spite of a certain leisureliness born of false alarms, proved himself well on the job once he had got his teeth into it. He recognised that the two stories he had just listened to might not have any connection with each other, although there was a strong probability that they did; and if they were not connected, then each story would have to be covered by prompt action. Before setting off to investigate Smale's gruesome find, therefore, he passed on the descriptions of the wanted men to his subordinates, and told them to get busy on trying to pick up the trails.

Then, with a sergeant, a police surgeon, and the three men who had routed him too early out of bed, he drove towards the grassy embankment known locally as the First Pullover.

It was a short journey. During the first half, no one spoke. Then the police surgeon, who had learned to accept life and death as a matter of course, and wasn't particularly affected by either, grew a little bored, and asked the inspector if his aunt had written to him yet.

"Had a letter yesterday," replied the inspector.

"Bought that parrot?" inquired the surgeon.

"No, they wanted a pound too much," answered the inspector.

"Well, personally, I can't stand the things," observed the surgeon. "No tact. Had one once that said 'God save the King,' while I was filling in my income-tax form."

Aunts! Parrots! Income-tax forms! While Sylvia Wynne was being spirited away into the unknown…

"Hardly a motoring-road," remarked the surgeon.

"Curly as a pig's tail," replied the inspector.

"Shouldn't care to live at this spot. Too far from neighbours."

"Well, you could always drop in on Smale here," grunted the inspector, dryly. "We're just passing his cottage." Smale grinned sheepishly. No one had called on him for a year.

The road grew lonelier and narrower. It began to give up being a road. Suddenly the inspector gave a sharp exclamation. "There's the car!" he cried.

The sight of it translated theories into facts. Parrots and pigs' tails were forgotten as his own car slowed down and he jumped out.

He examined the car quickly, eyed the ground in the vicinity, and then raised his eyes to the grassy embankment. "Up there, eh?" he inquired, jerking his head towards Smale.

"Ay, and I'm not goin'!" muttered Smale.

"Nonsense, of course you're going!" retorted the inspector. And, to save an argument, added, "There's half-a-crown for you at the end of it."

They climbed on to the ridge. They bore to the right. They passed the first farm buildings on their left. They came to another—a low shed, with a corrugated iron roof. This was also on their left, and it presented its back to them, but the front could be reached by a small path that ran downwards round the end of it.

Ignoring this path and continuing on, they came to a tangle of hedge and a fence. Now, ahead, was a gate.

"There!" whispered Smale, pointing to the fence.

The inspector turned, and walked to the fence. But Richard got there first. He looked down, over the fence, and another face looked up at him.

"Beyond our help," remarked the inspector, at his side.

"Yes—poor fellow!" muttered Richard.

"Recognise him?"

"Never seen him before in my life."

"Not one of the men who attacked you, then?"

"We were attacked *after* this happened."

"Yes, sir, I'm aware of that. According to the times we've been told. But, so far, all these times are circumstantial, if you get me? Stories told at the police station don't always tally with those told in the witness box.... There goes the doctor... down to have a look at him.... Hallo, what's the matter?"

An exclamation had come from behind him. Ted Diggs shoved his head forward.

"Gawd!" he cried. "But—I know 'im!" He stared stupidly, while the inspector swung round.

"What—you *know* him?" exclaimed Wetherby.

"Yes—or I'm dippy!" gasped Diggs. "That's Albert Bowes, that is—another taxi-driver at Bristol!"

Once again Inspector Wetherby proved he was no fool. He recognised genuine amazement when he came across it, and he had never come across more genuine amazement than that depicted on Diggs's face. Unless, perhaps, it was the amazement on Richard's face.

"What! You *know* that man, Diggs?" cried Richard. "And he comes from *Bristol*?"

Diggs nodded. It was all he could do. His mouth was open, and he had forgotten to close it.

Wetherby watched him quietly. Sometimes it is more instructive to watch than to talk. He watched two men stare at each other; and, refusing to bank on his first impression, searched their faces for traces of acting. Suppose—just for the sake of argument—two men had drowned a third man, and had adopted the subtle device of going straight to the police station with some story that would suggest an alibi, and at the same time lay the blame upon other mythical folk invented for the purpose? Then it would be up to them to do a bit of play-acting, wouldn't it? They'd pretend this and they'd pretend that...

Yes, but this wasn't pretence. There wasn't any play-acting here. It was the genuine open-mouthed article. And, that being so, it was of no use wasting time over impossibilities. "You don't know how he came here?" he barked to Diggs.

"Eh?" jerked Diggs.

"You don't know how that fellow came here?"

"'Ow 'e—? Why, 'e was in Bristol yesterday mornin'!" spluttered Diggs. "I know, 'cos I seen 'im."

"Well, *you* were in Bristol yesterday morning," retorted Wetherby, "and you're here now. So, you see, it can be done."

"Eh?"

"If you can pick up a fare, so could he."

"Yes, but—to the same place? To Boston?"

"Why not? If a kidnapping game was on? Well, anyhow, you've identified him. Could you identify his car?"

"'Corse I could."

"I see. Of course you could! Yet it occurs to me that perhaps you *didn't*!"

"Eh?"

"That stranded car we passed just before we came up here. Mightn't that be his car?"

"Well—I'm—! Yes—it was like it," muttered Diggs. "But—nacherly—seein' it then, and not 'avin' 'im in my mind—"

"Yes, naturally, naturally. Tell me, sir," went on the inspector, turning now to Richard, "have you any theory to offer?"

"Absolutely none," answered Richard.

"Quite sure, sir?"

"Quite. Unless—"

"Ah! Unless? Let's have the 'unless.'"

"Unless we were followed, inspector? No, I give it up. This car got here first—"

"But you might have been overtaken and passed," interposed Wetherby, "by some one who had got on to your destination...Hallo!" he broke off. "The doctor seems to be getting excited down there. I must go down and see what the trouble is!"

He clambered down to the water's edge, where the doctor and the sergeant were staring at the sodden body of Albert Bowes. It lay now on the bank to which it had been drawn.
"Not drowned, eh?" inquired the inspector, shrewdly.

"No," answered the police surgeon, with a grimace. "Look at this. Shot!"

Inspector Wetherby looked. If he experienced any surprise, he refused to show it. Surprise is not good form in the police force. It makes you lose your grip.

"Well, I wasn't betting on suicide," he observed, after a pause. "*Or* an accident."

"But were you betting on *this*?" inquired the doctor, and opened his hand.

A little crimson letter lay in the doctor's palm. Now, despite himself, the inspector's eyes gleamed.

"By George!" he muttered tensely. "Another Z murder!"

Chapter XXIX

Boston Rings Up Bristol

At eight o'clock on that same morning, an inspector even more important than Inspector Wetherby, of Boston—to boot, Detective-Inspector James, of Scotland Yard—sat in a room at Bristol Police Station, wondering whether a certain young man of his acquaintance would keep his promise or not.

"Any news of him, Dutton?" he inquired, as a rather tired man entered with a sheaf of papers. He was tired because he had been up half the night preparing the papers; and a bandage round his head added to his somewhat dilapidated appearance.

"Not yet, sir," replied Dutton. "What's the betting?"

"A hundred per cent. on his good faith," answered James unhesitatingly, "but fifty-fifty on his ability to prove the good faith."

"Well, it's a pity some of these nice young chaps with good faith can't trust a bit more in ours, and fall into line," observed Dutton, feelingly.

James glanced at him, and smiled.

"Why, Dutton, that's almost emotional," he said, gentle reproof in his tone. "I didn't know you went in for the passions!"

"Sorry, sir," murmured Dutton, apologetically, "but if Mr. Temperley had given us his co-operation from the start, he might have saved me half *this* trouble!" And he held out the sheaf of papers. "And don't forget, sir, I've had a knock on the head."

"I never forget," answered James, soberly. "That's why I always insist that you work with me on cases that require special skill."

"Thank you, sir. Will you look at these notes now?"

James glanced at the clock. "Two minutes past," he remarked, and sighed. But, as he stretched his hand out for the papers, the telephone rang. "Ah, *now* what's the betting?" he exclaimed, as he lifted the receiver.

"I'll have sixpence on it," responded Dutton.

"Done!" nodded James. A moment later he added, "Afraid I've lost my tanner. It's a call from Boston." But a moment after that, he added again, "No, sir! I've *won*! It's Temperley!"

"Boston! So *that's* where they were all heading for, is it?" muttered Dutton, glancing at his papers. "Damn! Why couldn't I keep on the trail?"

Inspector James held up his hand. "Yes, it's James speaking," he called. "Got any news?"

Then he was silent, and Dutton, watching for signs, realised that big things were happening. The amiability left his superior's face, and the lines around his mouth hardened. For a minute he merely listened. Then he chipped in.

"Hold hard a moment," he said. "I want you to repeat every word you've said, and then to carry on. And speak slowly. I shall repeat after you, so that what you say can be taken down.... Note-book, Dutton. Another Z Murder, and...God, I'm worried!...Ready?"

Dutton nodded. An instant later, his pencil was racing over paper.

It raced for ten minutes. Then there was a short pause. During the pause, Dutton worked his aching knuckles up and down, while, at the other end of the line, Richard Temperley vacated his seat at the telephone, and Inspector Wetherby occupied it.

"Ready again, Dutton?"

Dutton was always ready. When Death itself came, he'd be ready. For another ten minutes the pencil raced. Then James spoke for two minutes, and the pencil rested. Then the receiver was replaced, and James turned to the faithful stenographer.

"Now, you've some additions for your notes, Dutton," he said, gravely.

"Yes, sir," answered Dutton, equally gravely. And all at once added, unexpectedly. "We're up against some pretty damn blackguards, aren't we?"

James nodded. Then asked, "Can you be ready in half-an-hour?"

"With the additions to the reports, sir?"

"Yes."

"That's O.K."

"Good. Do them here. And then we can study them together on the way to Boston."

"Thank you, sir," said Dutton. "I hoped I wasn't going to be left behind. Car or train?"

"What, with an aerodrome round the corner?" replied James. He rose, walked to the door, stopped, and abruptly shot a question. "What's *your* opinion of all this?" he demanded.

Dutton, already seated at his notes, glanced up and shook his head. "I'm on facts, sir, not opinions," he replied. "I'd sooner wait for yours when you've been through these dossiers." Then the inspector left the room, and while he was making final arrangements his subordinate bent over his papers.

There were ten papers. Each was headed with a name, and each bore neat little writing in red and blue ink. The red came out of one end of Dutton's pen, and the blue came out of the other. He often declared that on the day this pen was lost, his career would be over.

Each of the ten papers was now carefully read through, additions were made to some of them, taken from the new shorthand notes of the conversation with Boston. Most of the additions were in blue, and the speed and ease with which they were extracted from the shorthand notes, and added to the longhand notes already existing, formed a further tribute to Dutton's efficiency. While he had taken the shorthand notes he had anticipated the next step, and had appended numbers in the margins. Thus, when he had anything to add to Sheet Seven, he merely had to consult the passages marked "7" in his shorthand to know where to find the required material. Dutton was a detail man. He knew his limitations, and worked meticulously up to them. Presently the inspector returned.

"Aeroplane's O.K.," he announced, "and the car's ready to take us to Filton."

"But I'm not ready," replied Dutton, without looking up. "You gave me half-an-hour, and I've got another minute."

"Well, take your pound of flesh," smiled James, "but not an ounce more. We've got a busy day ahead of us."

"Thanks for reminding me, sir," murmured Dutton, writing hard.

The inspector went to the car and took a back seat. In fifty seconds, Dutton joined him. The car began to move. "You've something interesting in your mind!" challenged James.

"Yes, it is rather interesting, sir," replied Dutton. "Do

you know, this is the fourth journey that has started from Bristol for Boston in the last twenty-four hours?"

When there was a breathing space between one phase of a job and another, Detective-Inspector James liked to smoke a pipe and to think of nothing. He called the process "slipping into neutral." Gradually into the nothingness of his mind returned the salient point of the first phase to be carried on into the second, but the trivial points dropped away like grit off a smoothed surface, and only essential matter remained.

Now James smoked his pipe, and Dutton, aware of his Chief's idiosyncracies, did not disturb him. He watched the progress of the pipe, and, judging the moment to a nicety, held out the notes just before the car reached Filton.

"Thanks, Dutton," said James. "I'll read them in the air. Facts in blue and conjectures in red as usual?"

"Yes, sir," replied Dutton, "and in this case most of the conjectures can be relied on. Mere queries and possibilities, of course, are set down as such."

"And do these reports comprise all the information we have, up to date?" inquired James, as he took them.

"Everything, sir. Right up to the Boston telephone conversations. I have seen or 'phoned every person who, in addition to myself, has contributed information to the reports—and I may say, sir, I am quite satisfied with their work."

"Good," nodded James. "I hope I'll be equally satisfied. Ah, Turndike. Here we are. No low flying *this* trip, please!"

Chapter XXX

Storm Clouds

Flight-Officer Turndike left Filton Aerodrome at a quarter-past nine. He descended at Digby Aerodrome, twenty miles from Boston, at fourteen minutes to twelve. There his two passengers transferred to a waiting car and were raced over the final lap of their journey by road, and during this final lap Detective-Inspector James discussed with Dutton the report he had read above the clouds.

"Excellently concise," he said, approvingly. "These notes set down very clearly all the known facts. Let's go over them, while we've a chance, and see whether we can deduce any further facts. 'John Amble—31b King's Cross—age fifty-two—lived over shop—' Ah! 'No enemies.' Now, can we be sure of that?"

"No, sir," replied Dutton, promptly. "But his aunt, who was interviewed, swears he hadn't any—'"

"The aunt who lived at Preston, and whom he had been visiting—"

"Yes, sir. She seems to have known all about him. Said he was surly, but honest."

"And, like most honest men, found it difficult to make both ends meet!"

"That's right, sir."

"So he may have been in a mood to contemplate suicide."

"No, I think not, sir. Too fond of his skin, she said. And she'd just promised to lend him a hundred pounds."

"I see. Then it comes to this. John Amble died, but he didn't kill himself, and nobody had any motive for killing him, and nobody heard the shot that killed him, or found the weapon from which the shot was fired. He was evidently killed by an inhabitant of the moon whose hobby is potting at planets....Ah, this is interesting, Dutton. Amble left his keys at Preston, and knew he couldn't get into his shop till his assistant turned up with the only other latch-key."

"Yes—makes one think, doesn't it, sir?" murmured Dutton. "If Amble hadn't left his keys behind him, he'd never have entered that smoking-room, and might have been alive at this minute!"

"Quite true," nodded James, gravely. "We never know what's coming to us out of the merest trivialities! If the second victim—'Martha,' I see her name is—hadn't crossed the field at Charlton just when she did, *she* might be alive, too."

"It's only a guess her name's Martha," interposed Dutton. "She may have borrowed somebody else's handkerchief."

"Very probably, since she appears to have been a gipsy, and gipsies aren't always too particular about property. Nothing else known about her, eh?"

"No, sir. But this is worth noting. You'll see she dropped dead at 12.58. It's Turndike's time. That means that the second victim of our Z murders died seven-and-a-half hours after the first, about 125 miles away."

"While the third victim, towards whom we are now going—"

"Albert Bowes, 5 Channel Row, Bristol, age, query—"

"—was found shot—"

"—or drowned, or both—"

"—sixteen hours after the second victim, about 170 miles away."

"*Found* sixteen hours after, yes," agreed Dutton. "But he might have been murdered three or four hours earlier than he was found, according to the police surgeon. No one can say how Albert Bowes came to be in Boston, and he was seen in Bristol round about the time the second victim died. Rather important that, sir, don't you think?"

"Very, Dutton," nodded the inspector. "Almost looks as if Albert Bowes and—our unknown murderer travelled from Bristol to Boston at about the same time. Yes—distinctly important."

He paused and stared ahead of him along the straight flat road. He tried to visualise others who had travelled recently over the road—tried to read the secrets in their eyes and the hidden impulses in their hearts. Soon Boston would appear to him. It would appear out of a grey, cloudy smudge; moistly, for a thin drizzle had now started. How had it appeared in those other, those earlier journeys? Out of what form of light or darkness had it shaped, and with what personal significance?

"Going into dirty weather, sir," observed Dutton.

"It looks like it," answered James, frowning. "Dirty in every sense. This fellow Smale, now, who found Albert Bowes. I should put him down as a semi-imbecile."

"I should delete the 'semi,'" smiled Dutton. "Don't think we need worry about *him*, sir."

"No—nor about Mrs. Mostyn, Gerald Turndike, or Ted Diggs," replied James, glancing at the notes. "You've been very thorough, Dutton, I must say, and don't seem to have left out anybody! While, as for Mr. Richard Temperley, you've written a three-volume novel about him! But we don't suspect him, either, do we?"

"Hardly, sir."

"Nor, any longer, the young lady he is so interested in?"

"Nor any longer, sir. She's a puzzle though. Tied up in the business somehow from the start. Right back as far as Euston. What brought *her* into it? Euston, Bristol, Boston!"

He shook his head, in gloomy impotence.

"For the moment, Dutton, I'm more interested in what has brought the last two individuals on your list into it," responded Inspector James. "It seems to me that the movements of these two really form the key to the whole puzzle. Admire the scenery for a moment, please, while I read through your last two notes again. I want to get them fixed in my mind."

And, while Dutton tried dutifully to discover the beauty of utter flatness, James read:

"'Farmer. Possibly a genuine farmer. Possibly not. Address not known. Age, fifty?

"'Of interest on account of certain incidents obviously implicating him in the business. Big, strong, rough man. Not so simple as he looks.

"'Movements, as far as known. Took the 5.30 p.m. train to Bristol on the day of the first two murders. In train sat opposite Temperley and chatted with him. Later on in the journey, occupied seat at table with myself and two ladies, near table occupied by Temperley and Miss Wynne. Note that, at this point, we did not know the lady was Miss Wynne. Farmer moved over to their table once to ask for the sugar, though our table had plenty. Query, did *he* know the lady was Miss Wynne?

"'Later on still in the journey, he attacked Temperley in his compartment, while Temperley was dozing, and the results might have been fatal if I had not appeared in the corridor. Upon this, the farmer hurriedly left the compartment, and Temperley, meeting me in the corridor, suspected me in my new disguise.'"

James broke off for a moment in his reading, and regarded his faithful second-in-command. Dutton, still dutifully staring at the flatness ahead, stirred slightly.

"Cathedral or something," reported Dutton.

James looked at the tall tower of St. Botolph's Church, then resumed his reading:

"'Freed from the supervision of Temperley, owing to the compact made with him, I was now detailed to watch the farmer, and when we arrived at Bristol my attentions clearly worried him and interfered with his freedom of action. I assumed he was trying to follow Temperley, but now think it more probable he was trying to follow Miss Wynne. He threw me off the scent two or three times, but I stuck to him and discovered, shortly before midnight, that he had a car hidden away near the Carpenter's Arms.

"'Matters came to a head between us a few minutes later. He surprised me round a hedge and laid me out. Fortunately my eye-glass had no glass in it.

"'I adopted the old dodge of feigning insensibility, and while the farmer was bending over me and I was wondering whether the dodge would succeed, Temperley arrived.

"'Farmer made a remark about an accident, then vanished. Temperley started to follow, and then turned back to me. But, by that time, I also had vanished. Felt groggy, but chased the farmer unsuccessfully across several fields. Saw him get into the driver's seat of a waiting car, and then suddenly leap off again.

"'Query: Was this the car subsequently driven by Ted Diggs to Boston, and was Sylvia Wynne inside at the time? If so, this would appear to have been the farmer's first definite attempt to kidnap her.

"'Finally, I lost the farmer in the vicinity of the Carpenter's Arms again. By this time I was feeling very groggy indeed. On reaching the spot where his car had been I discovered that it was gone.

"'It is obvious now, from what we have learned from Boston, that the farmer travelled to Boston. It is also fairly obvious that the farmer's car reached Boston first, either passing Temperley's car on the road, or beating it by taking some alternative route at some point or other. In any case, the farmer succeeded in his second attempt to kidnap Sylvia Wynne a few miles from Boston, and he took her away in his car.

"'Query, where?'"

The drizzle increased. Clouds, flying low, came in from the North Sea, bearing its mood in their frayed edges. The automatic screen-wiper changed from a luxury into a necessity.

"Getting worse, sir," remarked Dutton.

"Damn the North-West of Ireland," grunted James.

"More like the South-East of Finland this time," said Dutton. "Mustn't blame Ireland for everything!"

But James hardly heard him. He was engaged in a battle, unusual for him, against the sinister atmosphere of the elements. They increased a disturbing, gnawing sense of impotence....

"Seems to me, sir, we came down to earth just in time," observed Dutton. "I wouldn't care to be up in the sky just now!"

Yes, one could be pretty helpless up in the sky, if pitched against the fury of the elements. But down below here, when pitched against the simpler mechanisms of mere human beings, no self-respecting detective-inspector should be helpless! Yet there was a human being somewhere who had committed three murders, one after the other, leaving behind him an ironic symbol to identify each as his work, and who was still free to add to his ghastly list of victims...and, unless the detective-inspector dissipated his helplessness and, here in Boston, picked up a definite trail...

"Deformed man," ran the final note in Dutton's report. "Said to have been seen with the farmer, but nothing definite known about him."

"You're wrong in your last note, Dutton," said James. "We do know something definite about the deformed man."

"Yes, sir?"

"We know, I think, that he is Z!"

"And does it help us?" muttered Dutton.

Chapter XXXI

The Z Route

They reached Boston at eighteen minutes past twelve.

It was good going, for the roads were wet and slippery, and during the latter portion of the journey a driving wind had added its inconvenience to the rain; but it was not quite good enough. They missed Richard Temperley by ten minutes, and it was not until some hours later that any news of him reached them. When the news did reach them it was brought by the half-wit, Bob Smale, and for once Detective-Inspector James, who prided himself on his equanimity and had even lectured on the value of composure, forgot himself and swore.

He stared at the note that was handed to him, and his eyes dilated. "But—but this letter was written at 12.45!" he spluttered to the messenger.

"Wer' it?" blinked the messenger.

"Yes—12.45! And look at that clock!"

Bob Smale looked at the clock. It did not seem to make any violent impression on him.

"What have you been doing since this note was given to you?" cried the inspector, angrily. "Watching a dog-fight?"

"There wern't no dog-fight," Bob assured him. "I'd 'a seed it."

"I'm asking you why you didn't come here direct, man!"

"Well, I'm 'ere, ain't I?"

"Yes, you're here!" exclaimed the inspector, already at the telephone. "And probably too late!"

"Ah, now I remember!" ejaculated Bob Smale, suddenly. "Now I do remember. Tha's right. 'Twas a cow. A white cow she was, an' she come round the corner, and I ses to myself, seein' 'er all white, 'You wasn't born on earth,' I ses, 'there ain't no spots on you—'"

"Take him away, Dutton!" shouted James. "How can I telephone while that babble's going on?"

Dutton obeyed. He had not yet seen the letter himself, but he gathered, from his superior's unusual manner, that its contents were disturbing.

Let us return a few hours, and find out how those contents came to be written.

After satisfying the dictates of both conscience and necessity by getting into touch with James over the telephone—and it was merely by the accident of fortune that he was able to fulfil his obligation only a few minutes after the scheduled time—Temperley did not sit down and watch the local police at work. He worked himself, joining one of the hastily improvised search parties, and sharing its failures and its disappointments. For the people for whom they were searching had enjoyed the advantage of a long start, and of commencing their flight in the early hours of the morning when scarcely a soul was about.

Thus, no one could be found who had met the kidnappers on the road, or who could give any clue to their whereabouts. They had vanished into the void.

There was not even any theory to work upon. The murders with which the kidnappers were connected occurred, apparently, at any time and at any place. They appeared to be motiveless and purposeless, and to form no settled scheme. Within thirty hours three tragedies had occurred, known already as "The Z Murders" in thousands of homes, and countless anxious lips were voicing the questions, "How many more?" "Where will the next occur?" and "Who will the next victim be?"

To the first and second of these questions Richard Temperley had no answer, but the answer to the third burned into his brain and sickened his heart. And because he believed he knew the answer without any shadow of doubt, he worked with a desperate calmness that concealed a spirit almost demented.

His faithful ally, Ted Diggs, worked meanwhile on his car. The damage, although rendering his car *hors-de-combat* at the crucial moment when it had been most needed, was not of a permanent description, and the assistance of a local garage soon remedied the petrol trouble and provided new tyres. Then Diggs joined in the search himself, connecting up with Temperley at the Boston police station and participating with him in the hopeless hunt. "Let's get back to the spot where they set on us," said Temperley, after they had made fruitless inquiries at a dozen cottages.

"That ain't likely to 'elp, sir," replied Diggs, gloomily.

"*Nothing's* likely to help!" retorted Temperley. "But we can't stand still, can we?"

"That's right," nodded Diggs. "'Oo minds gettin' wet?"

They returned to the spot. A figure was lurking there. Temperley leapt from the car and dashed at it. The frightened face of Bob Smale stared back at him through the drizzle. "What are *you* doing here?" demanded Temperley, in angry disappointment.

Smale shook his head vaguely. The implication was that he didn't know.

"Well—have you found anything?" asked Temperley, more quietly. Now Smale nodded.

"What?"

"Eh?"

"What? *What?*"

Smale advanced his mouth mysteriously.

"Blue eye!" he whispered. "Angel's, I reckon!"

He unclosed a fist that had been held tight, displaying a small blue button. Temperley recognised it with a pang. "Where did you pick that up?" he demanded, almost fiercely, to hide another emotion.

"Eh?"

"Where did you pick it up?"

"Oh!" Then Smale pointed. "There!"

The spot he pointed to was a little way along the road. Temperley ran to the spot, and searched it.

He found nothing more, but all at once he gave an exclamation. "Diggs!" he cried. "Where was your car, when you stopped?"

Diggs indicated the place.

"And this button was found *behind* it. That is, farther away from Boston. In the direction from which we had come."

"That's right, sir."

"Then—they wouldn't have gone back to Boston, would they?"

"P'r'aps not, sir."

"Why, 'perhaps not?'"

"I mean, sir, that if that there button come off in, well, a struggle like—"

"Yes, yes, I know what you mean!" groaned Temperley. "She might have jumped out of the car, and been caught while trying to run away. And what happened outside the car would be no proof of the direction the car ultimately took."

"Yes, sir."

"I'm just snatching at straws, Diggs. But what else is there to snatch at?" He stared at the button, but its significance almost unnerved him, and he slipped it quickly into his pocket. "Where's your map, Diggs. Let's have another look at it."

"The local map, sir?" asked Diggs, for they had bought one.

"No, no. The one of England. They've gone off the local map by now—damn them!"

Diggs produced the map, and opened it. They gazed at it hopelessly.

"Just look at the route they've travelled!" muttered Temperley. "First, London. That's where the first Z murder took place. Look—just there."

He made a mark with his pencil. A vicious dig. Diggs looked, and thought, "Yus, that's nice for my map, that is!"

"And, second, Charlton. That's where the *second Z* murder took place. See—just there!"

He made another angry jab with his pencil. Diggs thought, "'Corse, wot's a little thing like a map?"

"And then, here's the third place. Boston. London—Charlton—Boston." Another jab. "A Z murder at each spot—a crimson Z left at each spot—London—Charlton... Boston... *God!*"

He became motionless. For a moment, Diggs thought he was going to be sick. "Poor chap!" he muttered, getting ready to catch him. "I thort 'e wouldn't larst!"

But Richard Temperley was not swaying. He was like a statue. Like a statue staring at a map. With eyes galvanised. With mouth apart...

"Gawd, now wot's 'e doin'?" wondered Diggs.

For the statue had sprung into sudden life, and the immobile pencil was now zigzagging across the map. From

London, westwards, to Charlton…from Charlton, north-eastwards, to Boston…

"Well, I can get another for 'arf-a-crown," thought Diggs.

…and from Boston…

"'Ere, where's 'e goin' now?"

…westwards, again, through Notttingham…Derby…

"Whitchurch!" shouted Temperley, in a frenzy. "Whitchurch! The next will be *Whitchurch!*"

Diggs stared, and now *his* mouth opened, too. Across the map of England, in pencil, was a perfect letter Z.

The lead was black, but to the men who stared at it, it looked crimson.

A sudden exclamation from Bob Smale roused them. They had forgotten all about him. He was staring seraphically at a piece of torn paper which he had taken from his pocket. "Angel's feather—*that's* what it is—angel's feather!" he babbled.

He gazed skywards, as though expecting to see another piece of paper come fluttering down. But only rain descended upon his upturned face.

"What's that?" demanded Temperley.

"Angel's feather," repeated Smale. "Down there it was." He pointed towards the spot where he had found the button. "But I kep' it. You took the other thing! That's not fair!"

Temperley snatched it from him. On it was written, in a faint, hardly decipherable scrawl:

"Rose Tree Cott…"

Chapter XXXII

On the Road to Whitchurch

"What are you stopping for?" asked the man without arms.

"Because I want a little chat," answered the countryman who was driving him. "Don't you think it's about time we had one?"

"There will be time enough for our little chat after we have paid our visit to Whitchurch," said the man without arms.

"Yes, but I'm not at all sure that we're going to *pay* that visit to Whitchurch," observed the countryman, while his right foot increased its pressure on the brake.

The man without arms was sitting behind the countryman, and thus the countryman was spared the sight of an expression which the devil himself might have envied. By the time the countryman had brought the car to a standstill and had turned round in his seat, the expression was gone, and in its place was an expressionless blank.

"Do you realise," said the countryman, "that this is the first opportunity we've had for a proper talk since we separated in London yesterday morning?"

"Go on," replied the man without arms.

"I'm going on," nodded the countryman. "I suppose, by the way, there's no chance that our passenger will wake up?"

The man without arms turned his expressionless face for an instant towards the insensible girl at his side. Then he turned back to the countryman, and responded,

"There is not the slightest chance that she will wake up."

"Well, see that she doesn't," frowned the countryman. "*She's* one of the things I want to talk about."

"Oh! You are becoming sentimental?"

"God, no! My sole affection just now is for my own skin, thank you. And I'm not satisfied that this Whitchurch trip is going to be good for it."

"I see. Yet the Whitchurch trip is the only trip of the whole damn lot that really matters!"

"To *you*!"

"Oh! So that's the way of it, eh?"

"Well—I'm interested, too, naturally. I don't want any of your cursed sneers! But there's been too much bungling, and before I decide—"

"Hey? *You* decide?"

"That's what I said! Before I decide what we're going to do, I want to know all that's been *done*? Do you get the idea?" The man without arms did not reply. "Don't make any mistake about it—we're going to have things straight, if we have to stick in this lane all night long. There's been far too much of this Blind Man's Buff!"

"Bungling," murmured the man without arms. "Yes, maybe there has been bungling. There seems to be some of it at this moment."

"Oh, no! *This* ain't bungling! *This* is common sense—reasonable caution. That brain of yours—well, you couldn't run England with it, you know!"

"All you can do with *your* brain is to go round and round in a circle!" rasped the man without arms. "What's this all about? What do you want? Are you *ever* coming to the point?"

"Yes, I'm coming to the point," answered the countryman, calmly, "and this is what I want. There's too many blanks in this business. I'm not going an inch farther without knowing the whole darned mess. Where you've been—"

"And where *you've* been!"

"That's right. We've got to join up our knowledge. And we've got to know who's after us *now*, and what clues and trails they've got. Why, for all we know, there may be somebody waiting for us in Whitchurch at this moment! I'm not going to walk into any booby trap!"

"All right! Go on, go on, go *on*!" suddenly screamed the man without arms. A moment later, however, he was quiet again, and was regarding the countryman with a stony, passionless stare.

"When first we planned this little scheme, a month ago—" began the countryman.

"When first *I* planned this little scheme, twenty years ago," interposed the man without arms.

"Have it your own way!" snapped the countryman. "When first we planned the actual details of it, anyhow—does that satisfy you? When first we planned the details, everything seemed clear sailing. We found out where Ledlow was living—checked the address, rather—"

"And the fact that he had changed his name, to Jones," added the man without arms.

"Yes. And decided on—our little dose of revenge."

"*My* little dose of revenge," said the man without arms.

"Hell, how many more times are you going to interrupt me?" demanded the countryman. "*Your* little scheme—*your* revenge! Have the damn lot! And *your* little hangman's rope at the end of it! I'm not bidding!"

He stared at his companion emotionally, while his companion stared unemotionally back.

"Go on," said the man without arms.

The countryman swallowed slowly, and went on:

"Yes, it *is* your scheme—you're quite right—because, if you'd followed my advice you'd have gone straight to Whitchurch and got the thing over at once. But, instead, when you found out that Ledlow was living paralysed in a lonely cottage with only an old woman to look after him—"

"An old woman who read out all the news to him," the man without arms interrupted again; and, this time, his expressionless face was momentarily illuminated with a faint, sardonic smile.

"—you hatched this roundabout way of working your way towards him so that, as you expressed it, you could pay him in his own coin. I wish to God I'd been a little less conscientious when I was ferreting around for you—or that I'd told you a little less of what I found out. Then you've never have got hold of this mad idea!"

"Mad?" repeated the man without arms. He raised a flapping sleeve. The sleeve flapped towards his head, and a moment later his large hat had been tipped back, revealing the usually covered expanse of forehead. The countryman looked away suddenly. His eyes had seen the sight presented many times before; but, at this moment, it unnerved him. Again he swallowed slowly. Then, angry with himself, he turned his head back to his companion. But the forehead was no longer visible. Those flapping sleeves could work uncannily! "Go on," said the man without arms.

"Yes, but before I go on," replied the countryman, rather hollowly, "I'm going to remind you of something—something even—a madman does not forget."

He laughed mirthlessly at the crude jest. The man without arms did not join in.

"So I really *am* mad, am I?" he said.

"No, of course you're not!" exclaimed the countryman, quickly. "Can't you understand a little joke? What I've got to remind you of is this. All I've *done* for you!"

"What have you done for me?" inquired the man without arms.

"What have I done for you?" repeated the countryman, raising his eyebrows in amazed indignation. "When Ledlow's gang double-crossed ours twenty years ago and left your mutilated body for dead, and—and branded their mark on you, who was it came and carted you off before the police or the crows could get hold of you?"

"You did," said the man without arms.

"Yes, and saved you from the lunatic asylum, as well—because that's all you were fit for at first!—and nursed you back to—"

"Health?"

"Damn it, man I'm not a miracle-worker!" fumed the countryman, fiercely. His memories seemed to be giving him courage. "You can't make a whole man out of half a man! I did what I could, and you'd have been dead or raving if it hadn't been for me. I nursed you and doctored you, and looked after you, and hid you. You've lived in my back room for a third of your life! I even got your damned hook for you and your—your damned other thing—"

"My silent shooter," murmured the man without arms, with a glance towards his right sleeve.

"Yes, your silent shooter," exclaimed the countryman, "that has given you so much fun during the past twenty-four hours—"

"And that is going to give me so much more fun before I've done with it—or with you," said the man without arms.

"Perhaps," retorted the countryman. "And, after all this,

you have the impudence to sit there and ask me what I have done for you!"

The man without arms looked at his right sleeve again. His face remained expressionless, though perhaps there was just a tiny glint in the eyes. But the eyes were concealed under the brim of his hat.

"Then I'll alter my question," he said, after a pause. "*Why* have you done all this for me?"

"Why?"

"Yes. Out of love?"

The countryman frowned. "There's such a thing as sticking together, ain't there?" he demanded.

"Yes, and we're going to *remain* sticking together," replied the man without arms. "But let's hear your other reason?"

"What do you mean?"

"You know what I mean. Ledlow had a reason for double-crossing me twenty years ago—and if you'd been able to find a certain packet of beads when you called at his cottage in the guise of an ex-serviceman and found out what I'd asked you to find out, maybe *you'd* have double-crossed *me*—"

"Oh, so that's what you think, is it?"

"If I thought it, you wouldn't be sitting where you are, talking to me," answered the man without arms. "You'd be talking to your Maker. I'm just reminding *you*, since you've been reminding *me* of things, that I've been double-crossed once in my life, and the man who tries it a second time won't die in his bed. You're interested in that packet of coloured beads, Mr. Kindheart, and that's why you're sticking to me. You think I know something about 'em, or at any rate you need my wits to get 'em back. Well, *that's* as may be. But if we do get 'em back, you can have the lot, because they don't interest *me* any more. I've just one interest in life. Half of it's in this sleeve, and the other half's on my forehead. And we're *going*, Mr. Kindheart, to Whitchurch! See?" And he raised his right sleeve as he spoke, and flapped it towards the countryman. "Or am I wrong?" he asked, with a malicious gleam. "And is it still—perhaps?"

Chapter XXXIII

Writing in Blood

The countryman stared at the sleeve uncomfortably. Then he stared at the insensible girl whose fate, as well as his own, appeared to be at the mercy of that flapping portion of garment. Then he stared back at the man without arms again.

"Are you threatening me?" he asked.

"Yes," replied the man without arms. "If you're not satisfied, no more am I." His tone hardened. "When you called on Ledlow, what did you do—*besides* finding out what I sent you there to find out?"

"Nothing!"

"You *didn't* find that packet of beads?"

"D'you suppose I'd be here, if I had?"

"No, I don't! Thanks for admitting it! We're getting things straight now, aren't we?"

"So much the better!"

"I agree."

"So much the better! Isn't it what I began this conversation for? I didn't do anything when I called on Ledlow but find out what we wanted to find out, and then report to you."

"You needed my brain?"

"Look here, you want it both ways, don't you?" retorted the countryman. "If I work on my own, I'm double-crossing you, and if I don't I'm soft! Your brain, eh? If you call that thing behind your forehead a brain, what's it led us into? It was your brain sent me back to Ledlow a second time, wasn't it, after you'd hatched your insane scheme, and told me to tickle him up by telling him where it was to begin."

"Euston—five a.m.," murmured the man without arms.

"Yes, Euston, five a.m. And it scared him so much that he went off his nut, and babbled, and the old woman who looked after him got scared herself over his delirium, and wrote to—*her*!"

He pointed to the insensible girl.

"Well, we've got her here, haven't we?" answered the man without arms. "*She's* safe not to babble!"

"Yes—*now*! And the devil's own job it's been!" snapped the countryman. "And who carried the job out? You or me?"

"You did, because I was on duty elsewhere," replied the man without arms. "That was your luck. But I'd have enjoyed the job, if I could have done them both. Oh, yes! I'd have enjoyed it! First following her to Euston station, eh, and then on to the hotel—by the way, why did she try the station first? Do you suppose 'Euston' was all she had to go upon. 'Euston—five a.m.,' and the terror of a delirious old man? Anyway, that's what she did, while I was waiting outside the window for some one to occupy that empty chair. Might have been placed for the purpose, eh? Well, I can only wish that other man had sat in it, and then—"

"Yes, then we shouldn't have had *him* on the trail!" interposed the countryman. "Exactly! Your pretty plan brought *two* unwanted people into the business!"

"Unwanted! I don't think so. They've been useful—as I knew they would be when I told you to tail the girl off, and to keep her on the course. Where the girl went, the man would go. Ruth and Lavine, eh? And if they were kept on the course—the police would be kept off it, eh? Don't you realise even yet how prettily we've diverted the police to a couple of red herrings?"

"Damned inconvenient red herrings! What did you want to leave that sign at her studio for before going to Bristol?"

"I thought it might help you, while *you* stayed behind. Yes, and why did you stay behind so long? Why didn't you find some way of bringing the girl after me earlier in the day? It might have saved a gipsy woman's life."

"What do you mean?"

"Why, she would have made an admirable subject for the second fatality—the second point in the letter I am writing—the letter that will be completed at Whitchurch!" A mad leer flashed into his face for an instant, and was gone the next. "But as I couldn't lose her at the second, I wanted her with me at the *third*—"

"And you'd have had her with you," growled the countryman, "if you'd waited at Charlton till I turned up with her, as we'd planned. Why didn't you wait? The car was tucked away near the Carpenter's Arms—"

"Yes, and so were plenty of other people," came the sharp interruption. "That damned aviator raised the hue and cry too soon. You had your instructions to follow, if things went wrong."

"And I did follow—"

"How many hours late?"

"Blast you, that wasn't my fault! Do you think things can only go wrong at your end? I had the devil's time at mine. That girl was dodging all over the place—you scared her properly with that silly sign you slipped through her letter-box—and she wired to Whitchurch. Ah—that interests you! You didn't know that!"

"No, I didn't know that. What did she say in the wire?"

"How do I know?"

"Did she get any reply?"

"She did. And *waited* for it! Now you know why there was no chance of getting her to Bristol in the morning—unless I used force—which we hadn't decided on *then*!" He shot a grim glance at the subject of their conversation. "So I had to use subtlety. Which is more than *you've* ever been capable of!"

"Let's hear your subtlety!"

"That's right! Sneer in advance! But it did the trick. I said to myself, 'She's worried about her grandfather.' I'd worked it out. She hears that Ledlow has been babbling about Euston and 5 a.m., as though the time and place were sending him daft, and she goes off to find out what's the trouble. And some one gets killed. And her grandfather knew that some one was going to get killed. What's the deduction?"

"That an old man, who can't leave his bed, has committed the murder?" inquired the man without arms, sarcastically.

"Murder! You're free with your terms!"

"I'm leaving the subtlety to you."

"It's clear you've got to! No, that wasn't the deduction. Her deduction was that Ledlow had something to *do* with the murder." The countryman paused abruptly. "Of course," he went on, slowly, "a girl in her confused state might make all sorts of deductions. Yes—she might even think that a miracle had happened, and that the old man had managed to leave his bed. Still, after all, that's neither here nor there. The point is—and it's the point I banked on—she was worried stiff about her grandfather, she *was* confused, and she couldn't go for the police."

"Why not?"

"Why not, bonehead? If Ledlow had wanted the police, he'd have babbled for the police, and the old woman would have gone for the police! But *you* know he didn't dare send for the police—that was your whole position, wasn't it?"

The man without arms nodded.

"Well, then! While he's babbling about his Euston and his 5 a.m.—"

"You evidently dinned them into him well," commented the man without arms.

"You told me to," answered the countryman, "and I do everything well. I can even keep to a story when I'm constantly interrupted! While he's babbling he also babbles about his fear of the police. Or maybe the old woman asks him if he wants the police, and he tells her he doesn't. So when the old woman writes in desperation to—to the girl in the corner there—she passes on the injunction that the police mustn't be consulted. That gets it all straight, doesn't it?"

The man without arms nodded again.

"Good. So what I do is this. I slip a note in her letter-box. In the afternoon, when she's gone back to the studio and given those other fools the slip. The note begs her—in printing letters—to be near the Carpenter's Arms at Charlton at midnight. It's written in such a way that it might be from her grandfather or from some one interested in him. It repeats the injunction not to go to the police. It implies that something fatal may happen if she does not go. And so—she goes."

"And you go after her?"

"Yes. And so do some other unwanted people! I tell you, I've had a job! If you'd—delayed your plans a little, you could have had her on the spot when you wanted her."

"You've just implied there were too many other people on the spot for that."

"Quite true. You see, I'm not unreasonable. I can see logic. But why didn't you nip off in the car we'd tucked away for the purpose?"

The man without arms held up his flapping sleeves.

"Who's the intelligent one now?" he asked, cynically.

"Yes, yes, of course!" muttered the countryman, annoyed with himself. "You had to have somebody to drive you."

"Yes. As you weren't there. And I also had to have somebody to—dispose of—as *she* wasn't there!" He flapped a sleeve towards the girl at his side. "The disposal took place in Boston just as you were all leaving Charlton. I seem to have won the race all along the line, don't I?"

"Yes, but now I've caught you up!" grinned the countryman. "Beat the others on the road, and caught you up."

"And *I* guessed you would, and came to meet you."

"That's right."

"And turned you round again."

"That's right."

"And, by a little ruse, caught one of the others!"

"Right beside you!"

"Yes—right beside me," nodded the man without arms. "And now you wonder whether we are going to *finish* the race or not? Whether we're going to fall off the final lap to Whitchurch—"

"And make a bee-line straight for the coast," interposed the countryman, and now his grin vanished, and he looked at the other earnestly. "Yes, that's what I'm wondering, Pretty-mug! This final lap—we may be caught up in it! Who knows? All the runners aren't down. And if we are caught up, there'll be no coast for *us*! It'll be—do you *know* what it'll be?" He banged his fist suddenly on his knee. "Not a piece of plum-cake for being good boys!"

The man without arms shifted his position slightly. His right sleeve lay in his lap, neatly directed towards the driver's seat.

"You have mentioned my plain speaking," he said in his disquieting monotone, and the countryman suddenly became conscious again of the total lack of facial expression. "Here is some more plain speaking. Without fingers, hands, or arms, I am writing a letter across England. The letter Z. The letter on my forehead. The letter that was burned there as a sign that I was finished—the letter I am now writing as a sign that Ledlow is about to be finished. Ledlow knows—Ledlow understands—Ledlow is waiting for the final scratch of the pen." The sleeve moved slightly. "And you suggest that I should leave the letter unfinished—the letter that began at Euston at 5 a.m., and that he has been told to watch?"

He paused, and swallowed softly.

"You are a fool, my friend. You would try and run away from the Universe. You are not even subtle. Those jewels—those coloured beads Ledlow is supposed to have hidden away somewhere—I invented them." The countryman's face twitched. "Yes, invented them, to keep my kind nurse interested all these years. Would you have been quite so devoted without them? Would you have loved me so much if you hadn't believed that, one day, I would point the way to them?"

He raised his sleeve.

"Turn round, please. I am going to finish my letter. The pen has scratched at London and at Bristol and at Boston. It is now going to scratch at Whitchurch—and, this time, with a *double flourish*!"

And the expressionless face turned towards the girl in the corner. But the sleeve remained raised towards the man in the driver's seat.

Chapter XXXIV

Whitchurch

The journey continued. Once more the car travelled towards the west. The sun rose behind it, sending its shadow before like black ink.

But the ink should have been red, for this journey westwards was the final stroke of a crimson brain, a brain that was now tracing its last murderous line across the map of England. The line went through Lincolnshire, Nottinghamshire, Derbyshire, Staffordshire and Cheshire. It would end in Shropshire, in a small cottage tucked away in enfolding hills. There the writing would be completed.

For a long while no further word was spoken. As once before, the man without arms sat behind his driver, dictating with the voiceless gun in his sleeve. The driver himself was not in a mood for conversation.

He thought hard, however. His ego had been insulted and his life was in danger. Despite his unenviable position, he did not admit the theory that he was finished. And indeed, as he thought, a new expression gradually grew in his sullen eyes, and the insulted ego began to feel a little happier. "Not clever enough, aren't I?" he reflected, grimly. "Well, we'll see!"

They ran out of Stafford. A Cheshire labourer winked from his pre-war bicycle as they went past him. Cheshire was soon finished with. They entered Shropshire.

"How much farther?" asked the man without arms.

"Only a few miles now," answered the countryman.

His voice was quite amicable. The man without arms noticed it.

"Feeling better about it?" he inquired, sardonically.

"I'm not worrying," replied the countryman. "You know best."

"Of course I do! Now tell me. What's this Rose-tree Cottage like?"

"Small, and a bit back from the road."

"Front garden?"

"Front weed-dump."

"And at the back?"

"Sort of waste-land. Meadow. Stubble."

"Leading to?"

"A stretch of water."

"River?"

"No, pond. Small lake, rather. Quite a size."

"And the road?"

"What, in front?"

"Is there one at the back?"

"No."

"Then we won't worry about it. Yes, the one in front. Much traffic?"

"Hardly Piccadilly Circus."

"Please be explicit."

"All right. Don't lose your wool. I've never seen any traffic. It's just a lane. This car will be an event."

"Then we must see that the event isn't recorded before we want it recorded. So the road's lonely, eh? No people likely to be about?"

"Probably not a soul."

"Any other cottages?"

"Not one within sight. You can take it from me that the spot was made for you."

"How far is it from the town?"

"Oh—two or three miles. More or less. I don't know, exactly."

"I didn't ask you exactly. Do we have to go through Whitchurch?"

"I think only a part of it. By the station. But we don't touch the chief streets."

"So much the better. Where's this we're coming to?"

"This *is* Whitchurch."

The reply nipped the next question in the bud. The man without arms closed his half-open mouth, and was suddenly silent. His eyes became little black dots.

They ran by the station. They curved into the outskirts of the little low-roofed town. They did not enter the heart of it, and soon its ancient inns, its old-world shops, and the picturesque tower of St. Alkmund's Church fell away on their left, swallowed up by the brooding greyness. They twisted out of one lane into another. Up a steep hill. Down a steeper one. More twists. More hills. The hedges on each side of them grew closer. They did not pass a soul. The car slackened. The countryman half-turned in his seat.

"Almost there," he reported. "Do you know your plan?"

The man without arms did not reply. He was looking at a low wall that replaced the hedges round a curve. Beneath ran a railway track.

They crossed the bridge at a crawling pace.

"Stop," ordered the man without arms.

"I was going to," replied the countryman.

Now the car was still. The countryman descended from his seat, and stood beside the door. "Where's the cottage?" asked the man without arms.

"Round the next bend," answered the countryman. "Just round."

"Then we won't take the car any farther," said the man without arms.

"Not a yard farther," agreed the countryman. The man without arms smiled at him. The countryman smiled back. But, all at once, his expression changed. "Look out!" he cried. "The girl's coming round!"

"That's an old trick," said the man without arms. "I've just given her another dose. Try something else."

The countryman's forehead grew damp. "Damn him!" he thought. It was a bad moment for his ego.

"So you still want to get rid of me, eh?" queried the man without arms.

"What d'you mean?" stammered the countryman. "I thought—"

"No, that's your trouble. You can't think. You need me to think for you. Well, there's a pond over there. How about dropping me in and drowning me? It looks a nice, secluded spot for a body."

"See here!" exploded the countryman. "If you're not careful, I'll *do* it!"

"If I'm not *very* careful, you'll do it," agreed the man without arms. "That's why I've got to be very careful, isn't it? You see—everything would be so nice and easy for you afterwards, wouldn't it?"

"What the hell are you driving at?"

"Why, here's the girl. You've only got to hide her, too, and you can use her as a hostage. For barter."

"Barter? What for?"

"For that little packet of beads you think I lied to you about. You did think I lied to you just now, didn't you? You thought I lied to put you off the scent again. And, thinking that, you went on thinking. You thought you would get rid of me. You thought you would go to Ledlow and say, 'Don't worry about your life, old chap. Worry about your granddaughter's. But you can have *her* life back, too, if you want, for twenty thousand pounds' worth of diamonds. Where are they?' "

"You're a devil, if there ever was one!" blazed the countryman.

"And you're a fool, if there ever was one!" answered the man without arms. "Think I can't see an expression when it's reflected in glass? And read it? You should keep your face better—as I do."

The man without arms presented his expressionless face to the countryman. The countryman saw it through a red haze. In a sudden frenzy of combined anger and fear, he hurled himself upon his tormentor. The next moment, astonishment replaced the anger and the fear.

The man without arms was hanging limply in his own.

"God! I've *got* him!" thought the countryman, holding tight.

The man without arms still hung limply. It was as though the countryman's hugging arms had squeezed the life out of him. He seemed to be dead; to have shrunk out of existence; but whether he were dead or alive made no difference to the immediate position. He was impotent!

The countryman's mind worked swiftly. He noted with satisfaction, and praised himself for his forethought, that he had brought the car to a standstill by a little clump of foliage. He had driven a yard or two off the surface of the lane to secure this sanctuary, and a passer-by, if he noticed the car at all behind its half-screen of overhanging branches, would merely assume it to belong to some picnic party.

The countryman noticed two other things with satisfaction. One was that the large pond was easily accessible from this spot. Just over a bit of broken fence, and then a hundred yards down a gently-sloping field. The other was that the girl in the car was still motionless.

Nevertheless the girl was a grave consideration, and necessitated the quickest action. She might begin to come round at any moment, despite that extra dose she'd just been given, and the countryman would have to be by her when that happened. Yes, and this flabby thing that had once been functioning flesh would have to be *out* of the way. Safely deposited in some place where it would lie snugly for awhile—with no questions asked!

Suddenly the countryman laughed. The wizened creature hugged like a bear's victim against his stomach shook with the movement of the laughter, responding limply to its communicated convulsions. The countryman was a little hysterical.

"'There's a pond over there,' is there?" he quoted deliriously. "'How about dropping me in it and drowning me—it looks a nice secluded spot for a body!' Damned good idea, Mr. Z! Damned good idea!"

He moved to the broken fence as he spoke. Now he was stepping over it, his victim clasped close. He had carried him before, many a time, but never before had he noticed the wasted fellow's lightness!

He continued to laugh, though now more softly.

"Yes, I did think you lied about that packet of beads," he chuckled. "And I do think you lied! And if Ledlow doesn't hand the beads over—or what he has left of 'em—in exchange for the girl's life, or maybe his own life, he's not the worm I take him to be."

The pond grew nearer. As he staggered over the coarse stubble the reeds became more distinct and the tangled, bordering bushes loomed larger.

"Clever, by God, weren't you?" grinned the countryman. He had to keep this up, to fortify him for the horrible moment that was coming. "Clever's not the word! Fancy seeing my expression in the wind-screen, and reading it like that! It was smiling, wasn't it?"

He reached the edge of the pond. No, too open here. Just a bit to the right, through those bushes. No chance of anything being seen there.

"Well, it's *still* smiling!"

A spot of rain descended on his forehead and made a little cold point amid the sweat. Now he was at the water's edge.

"And what's *yours* doing?"

Then a noiseless train passed through his body. He ceased to be a complete piece of flesh, but became, outrageously and illogically, merely edges of solidarity, edges that receded dizzily from the great hole in his middle and could not get back to close the hole up. The world turned round. A thousand suns appeared, fighting madly. The pond rose up, and swallowed him.

On the edge of the pond stood the man without arms.

"I could never have carried you here myself," he said, to the widening circles. "Thank you."

Chapter XXXV

The Silent Cottage

The drizzle had increased to a downpour and the wind to half a gale when, after a dizzy journey through mud-splashed roads, Temperley and Diggs reached Whitchurch.

They found it a depressing and desolate spot. The roads were rivers, and only those who had to be were out on them. Never a centre of liveliest activity, Whitchurch now seemed drowned, and the life it possessed remained, for the most part, unseen beneath sodden roofs. They came upon the town before they realised they had approached it. "'Allo—there's the railway station," said Diggs, as it suddenly loomed on their right. "But it's the police station we want, ain't it?"

"No, it's Rose-tree Cottage we want," answered Temperley. "Keep your eyes skinned for somebody we can ask."

Diggs frowned. He'd missed a night's sleep and driven through a hundred miles of wet roads at a reckless pace, and he wasn't feeling the bravest man on earth. He thought that a bobby ought to do the ringing and the knocking at Rose-tree Cottage. But when he began to point this out he was cut short very definitely.

"The police will already be at Rose-tree Cottage," Temperley told him. "After getting my note Inspector James will have 'phoned through from Boston."

"Then what 'ave we been 'urryin' for?" muttered Diggs.

Diggs was a middle-aged man in the centre of life. He was not a young man at the beginning of it. Youth splashes through mud to reach the youth it loves; it cannot delay its rejoicing or its weeping. With middle-age, comfort supersedes Cupid.

But it is youth that rules—particularly when the middle-age is merely a rather tired taxi-driver—and when a peripatetic sack sprouted two small legs beneath it and turned out to be a diminutive Whitchurchian under an improvised umbrella, Diggs slackened dutifully and growled out: "Oi! Where's Rose-tree Cottage?"

Rather surprisingly, the diminutive Whitchurchian knew it. Once he had been a greengrocer's boy and had delivered potatoes at Rose-tree Cottage, and so he knew the way despite its deviations and its distance; and, since his ambition was to end up as an A. A. man, he explained the route with painstaking and praiseworthy clarity. Diggs, not to be outdone, and also because he wanted to avoid the necessity of stopping again, interpreted the directions with equal skill, and when the boy had finished he declared he could get there blindfold.

"Don't forget the railway bridge," said the boy, earnestly. "It's where it curves and you go over it and then you're nearly there and—"

"And there's some water, but you keep that on your right and the cottage is round the next bend," interposed Diggs. "Yes, I got it, sonny, and thank you very much."

As the car restarted, a shilling sailed out of the window. Diggs had got it. He did not have to inquire again, which was fortunate since, once the small town had been shaken off, they did not encounter a soul. The lanes curled and narrowed. The hedges dripped. The clouds became lower, as though to join in the process of closing them in. "What a spot!" muttered Temperley.

Jolly enough in the sunlight, perhaps, but just now, in these dismal conditions, the last spot on earth!

They began to take an abrupt curve.

"Bridge," reported Diggs.

They crossed the bridge, leaving it with another curve. Like an S. Or a…

"Water," reported Diggs.

He did not refer to the rain. The rain was self-evident. He jerked his head towards his right shoulder as the car swung round to the left. A hundred yards away was the troubled surface of a large pond teased by rain-drops. "Slow down, man—we're there!" ordered Temperley, his heart beating fast.

Diggs was already doing it. They glided along a short stretch, rounded another bend…

There it was! Rose-tree Cottage, with its name faintly showing on its moist little gate. Rose-tree Cottage, the end of a long and tortuous journey that had began before Boston—before Bristol, even. It had began at Euston, some thirty-six hours earlier. And here, in this desolate, insignificant, unpopulated spot, it concluded! But the nature of the conclusion was yet to learn. It would not be learned until that little gate had been passed, and a patch of tangled grass had been traversed, and a weather-stained door had been opened.

"Don't see no rose-trees," grunted Diggs.

It was not the lack of rose-trees that worried Temperley. It was the lack of policemen.

Unlike Diggs, however, he made no comment, but sprang from the car and hurried through the gate. The long neglected grasses clawed at his feet as he squelched through them. "Go away—people don't live here," they seemed to be muttering. The door, when he reached it, was equally unwelcoming. So were the little windows that stared silently at him and gave away no secrets. He found a bell in a tangle of creeper and pulled it. He heard it tinkling inside. No one answered it. He rang again. Again it tinkled uselessly.

"Nobody at 'ome?" asked Diggs, behind him.

"I don't like it!" muttered Temperley.

"I ain't lovin' it meself," replied Diggs. "Try knockin'."

Temperley knocked. His knuckles had never made a more eerie sound. "Well, sir," said Diggs. "If nobody's 'ere, nobody's 'ere."

"What's worrying me, Diggs," answered Temperley, "is that nobody seems to have *been* here."

"'Ow d'you know that, sir?"

"I don't know it. Maybe it's only an idea. Still, there's certainly no sign of it." His eye left the door, and stared at a window. The window was heavily curtained, and there was no sign of light or of life inside.

"Been and gorn, p'r'aps," suggested Diggs.

"Perhaps," nodded Temperley, moving to the window.

"What are you doin', sir?" inquired Diggs, watching him apprehensively. Temperley was peering in at the window; or, rather, trying to. The dim slit between the thick curtains revealed nothing.

"We'd better go," urged Diggs.

A crash of glass answered him. He nearly jumped out of his skin at the sound. Temperley had broken the window.

"'Oi—we can't do that!" gasped Diggs.

"We have done it," answered Temperley, quietly. "Stick outside the door, will you?"

He was climbing through the window as he spoke.

Diggs stuck outside. His heart thumped. What was the use of it? Nobody was in there! That was plain, wasn't it?

If they'd been there they'd have answered the bell, wouldn't they…

And then a queer and horrible vision came into Diggs's mind. A ridiculous, grotesque, outrageous vision. A vision of three people—a man lying crumpled in an arm-chair, a gipsy woman lying silent in a field, and another man—a taxi-driver, like himself—lying face upwards in a dank pool of water. And a bell was ringing through the vision. And none of the three people responded—because they couldn't.

Was a fourth person to be added to the vision? A fourth person somewhere behind this door outside which Diggs waited? A fourth person who, also, couldn't answer a bell…

The door opened suddenly. Diggs nearly fainted. "Come in!" commanded Temperley's voice.

Diggs went in, mechanically. He found his eyes glued on Temperley's wrist. There was blood on it.

"W-what's that?" he stammered.

Temperley looked at his wrist. It was the first time he had noticed the blood.

"Nothing," he answered. "The window, I expect."

Diggs gulped.

"Found anyone?" he asked.

"Not down here. I'm going upstairs now."

He turned and ran up the staircase as he spoke. Diggs hesitated, then abruptly followed him. Diggs needed company. Reaching the upper landing Temperley paused for an instant, and Diggs barged into him.

"What's the matter?" demanded Temperley, sharply.

"Nothing," mumbled Diggs. "I was jest a bit close, like."

Ahead of them were two doors. One was ajar, the other was closed. They tried the door that was ajar first. It opened into a small front bedroom. It was empty. The bed had not been slept in since last being made. Then they tried the other door. It opened into the back bedroom, a rather larger chamber. Through the window across the room was glimpsed the end of a pond some distance off. But the thing that interested Temperley most was the bed. This had not been made since it had last been slept in.

Beneath a counterpane that looked as though it had been hastily replaced were tumbled bedclothes. They made a little mound, and for a second the two men stared at the mound with sickening dread. But when Temperley dashed forward for a closer investigation, he found that the mound sank blessedly beneath his hand. The bed contained no victim.

But a second point of interest lay in the position of the bed. It had been pulled out a little from the wall, and stood at an angle from it. Peering across into the space between it and the wall, Temperley gave an exclamation. Diggs's hand clapped his stomach, where his main emotions resided. "What is it?" he jerked.

"Board up," answered Temperley.

Quickly pulling the bed farther still from the wall, he examined the long, thin gap. The displaced board lay along the wall, and whoever had taken it away had failed to replace it.

"Anything there?" chattered Diggs.

"Nothing," answered Temperley, frowning. "Rather queer—isn't it?" The next instant he had leapt to his feet, and was staring at Diggs.

"Did you close the front door before you came up?" he whispered.

"Eh? No!" Diggs whispered back. "Why?"

Temperley did not reply. It was not necessary. Someone had entered the cottage, and was moving about below.

Chapter XXXVI

In a Back Bedroom

Diggs felt himself going to pieces. He stood by the bed with his mouth open. The sounds below had deprived him of capacity for movement.

Temperley, on the other hand, became more alert. For two or three seconds he stood and listened; then he slipped swiftly towards the door. But as he reached the door he paused abruptly, and stood still again.

"Coming up!" he whispered.

And now he stepped quickly aside, so that he was out of sight of the passage and the doorway.

Then movement returned to Diggs. A sudden realisation of his own necessity—for he was still in full view of the passage and the head of the stairs—gave him back the gift of mobility, and in a flash he was beside Temperley, struggling to pant soundlessly. Meanwhile, the sounds below drew nearer, and reached the stairs.

"When it comes do yer 'it it?" wondered Diggs.

As though divining the thought, Temperley laid his hand on Diggs's wrist. Maybe he had seen a spasmodic movement.

By now the sounds were mounting the stairs; softly, stealthily, with little unnerving pauses.

"You do 'it it," decided Diggs.

The footsteps reached the top of the stairs. There was another little pause. Somebody was wondering which of the two bedrooms to enter—the front one or the back one. The back one was chosen. Temperley steeled himself, while Diggs behind him turned into india-rubber. India-rubber is soft, and ready to bounce away in any direction.

"God! Where's 'e gone?" gulped the india-rubber.

For, just as the unknown individual reached the doorway, Temperley had bounded forward like rubber himself, and a moment later Diggs's eyes beheld the remarkable spectacle of Temperley bearing the half-fainting form of Sylvia Wynne towards the bed.

"Was it 'er?" gasped Diggs, ridiculously, when speech became possible again.

"Close the door," replied Temperley, sharply. "And stand by it."

Diggs obeyed. At that moment he would have done anything anybody had ordered him to do. Happily, this particular instruction did not go against the grain. Closed doors were infinitely preferable to open ones.

"Take it easy," said Temperley, to the girl on the bed.

"How did—you get here?" she answered, faintly.

"It wasn't likely we wouldn't follow, was it?" replied Temperley, patting her shoulder as though she were a little child. "I'll tell you my story later. But just at the moment—when you've got your breath back—I want to hear yours. You're—you're not hurt, are you?"

"No," she murmured. "Just weak."

"Well, rest a bit."

"Is there time?"

"I don't know!" he replied, frankly. "Isn't there? You must tell me that!" He glanced towards the door by which Diggs was standing. "Is—anyone following you?"

"I don't know."

"Don't—? Have you only just got here?"

"Yes."

"But, how—? Who brought you here?"

"Those two men must have."

"The ones who attacked us at Boston?"

"Yes. But I don't remember anything. They—drugged me or something. I'm still muzzy. And when I came to—" She shook her head in confusion.

"You found yourself near here?" he prompted her, encouragingly.

"Yes."

"How far from here?"

"Just round the corner."

"Just round—"

"Yes. In a car. I'll tell you. But, first, are you sure there's nobody about? I'm all to bits!"

"*We're* about," he replied, cheerfully. "Old Ted Diggs and I. So you've no need to worry any more."

"I'm trying not to. But you've not seen anybody else?"

"Not a soul. I don't quite understand, though, Miss Wynne. Those two rascals—weren't *they* in the car when you came to?"

"No."

"Bunked, eh? And you haven't seen any policeman, either?"

"I wish I had!"

"Queer, that, because the moment I got on to it where you were—your bit of paper helped!—I notified Inspector James, and told him to 'phone through to Whitchurch. Meanwhile Diggs drove me here at a thousand miles an hour. We've only just arrived ourselves, you know.... Jove, listen to that wind!…and found this place empty. By the way—who lives here?—when at home?"

"My grandfather," she answered, in a low voice.

"Your grandfather," he repeated, softly. "I see. At least—I think I'm beginning to. Do you—" He paused; then proceeded, very gravely, "Do you know where he is?"

She shook her head.

"Did you expect to find him here?" he went on.

He hated pressing her, in her condition, but there was no time to be lost.

"I don't know what I expected. He was—I mean, he's an invalid." She shuddered as she corrected her tense. "I thought he was helpless. An old woman lived here with him and looked after him. But—when I got anxious yesterday—yesterday, was it?—time's all got mixed up—I sent a telegram here from London, asking if he was all right."

"Yes?"

"The reply came that he had disappeared."

"Who sent the reply?"

"Mrs. Davis. The woman who looked after him. Who looks after him."

"And now—she isn't here, either."

"No."

"Tell me, Miss Wynne. Why didn't you come straight here from London—if you were anxious after receiving the reply?"

"I—I had reason to believe he might be at Bristol. I'd received a queer note, you see. And when I heard he wasn't at Whitchurch, I thought—"

"He might be connected with these Z murders?"

"Yes. I had a reason for that, too. Mrs. Davis had sent me word that he was getting delirious—and something about a mysterious visitor he'd had. He seemed to think that something awful was going to happen at Euston at 5 a.m."

"But why didn't you go straight to the police?"

"He seemed as terrified of the police as of anything else. I didn't have much time to think, you know. And, then—"

"Yes?" he queried, as she paused. "I think you'd better tell me everything?"

"It wasn't that," she answered, quickly. Her eyes were on the door. "I thought I heard something!"

Diggs moved farther away from the door. They listened. All was silent below. "Did you leave the front-door open?" asked Temperley, suddenly.

"I'm afraid I did. I found it open."

"Well, it had better be closed," he said. "I don't know if you feel up to the job, Diggs?"

Diggs didn't. But, with Beauty as audience, he had to put up some sort of a show. So he observed, "Right in my line, that is!" and, after a moment's hesitation, opened the bedroom door, went out into the passage, and half-closed it behind him. They heard him gingerly descending the wooden staircase.

"Now let's finish this quickly," said Temperley, turning to Sylvia again. "You were talking of your grandfather, you know."

"Yes. Will Diggs be all right? There's always been some mystery about my grandfather that I've never found out. I believe it was because of this my parents left England before I was born. They'd found it out, and went to Australia, but they'd never speak about it. But when they died—that was a year ago—I had no relatives left—only grandfather—and he wrote me such a sad letter that I decided to come to England and work here."

"At Whitchurch?"

"No, in London, but I often came to visit grandfather here. He was terribly ill and lonely."

"And he never told you about—his mystery?"

"Never. And so I thought, at first, that he was connected with these horrible murders—though it was all guessing, really."

"And you still think it?"

"Yes. But not that he's responsible for them," she added, quickly.

"No, I agree," answered Temperley. "He fled from this cottage in terror—and a great shock, you know, may temporarily cure a man from paralysis—if that was your uncle's trouble. Now, these two men. They evidently drove you here, and then fled."

"Yes."

"After visiting here first? I doubt it. No window was broken, and if the place was empty, as I found it, they couldn't have got in by any other means...What a time Diggs is!...Did you come straight here from the car?"

"Yes."

"Didn't you hear us come by? We didn't see your car, by the way."

"No. It's hidden, just off the road. Yes, I did hear something going by, I think, but I was too muzzy to know. And then there's the wind, too."

"By Jove, yes! Just listen to it!" It howled round the cottage as he spoke, followed by a fierce rush of rain on the roof and a scrambling flurry of outraged leaves. "But the taxi's outside. You must have seen that?"

"I did. But it might have meant anything. The whole thing was a jumble. I just came in to find—whatever there was to find. And—thank God—found you!"

"I am also thanking God for that, Miss Wynne," he answered, fervently. "Now, just one more question, and then we'll go and find out why the police are so late....Back to your grandfather's mystery again. Look over the other side of the bed. On the floor. Do you think *that* has anything to do with it?"

She turned her head, and stared at the uprooted board. They heard Diggs returning.

"He'd hidden something there!" she exclaimed.

"And has taken it away with him," replied Richard Temperley. "That's as plain as a pikestaff, isn't it? Well, here's Diggs back again, and now for the police, eh?" The door was shoved open. The man without arms stood in the passage.

Chapter XXXVII

The Last Victim

"No, I wouldn't move," said the man without arms. "My sleeve may appear empty, but it can strike."

He raised his right sleeve as he spoke, while Richard Temperley struggled against the temporary paralysis produced by this appalling and unexpected apparition. The man did not merely lack arms. He lacked expression. Beneath the wide rim of an old slouch hat glinted eyes that were as vacant and as cruel as those of an octopus.

"I'm sorry I've had to disappoint you," went on the man without arms, "but Mr. Diggs—I think I heard you describe him by that name as I came up the stairs just now—Mr. Diggs is not fetching the police. He is not in a condition to fetch anything. I have had to give him a little dose—"

"You damned little cur!" cried Temperley, finding his voice at last.

"But it's not such bad stuff, is it?" the man proceeded, turning the expressionless gaze towards Sylvia. "You've tested it, haven't you? It doesn't kill." The expressionless gaze turned back to Temperley. "Not that I would have minded killing Mr. Diggs. One more or less? What would it matter? But—a man without any arms is at a disadvantage." The sleeve flapped slightly. "He cannot strike again and again. The number of his blows is limited. And the few I have left—two, to be exact—must not be wasted on insignificant people like Mr. Diggs."

Temperley's mind raced round and round in a hopeless circle. Madness stood there in the doorway. How did one deal with madness? Before the madness dealt with you? Nothing to appeal to! No spark of ordinary intelligence or sympathy or understanding! All that existed in that miserable, wasted frame, all that signified, was a homicidal lust, that seemed at this moment to be fanned into additional vitality by the outside elements themselves. The rain descended in violent sheets, rapping and squalling against the little window with the view of the troubled lake. The wind howled with venom and shook with laughter, shaking the cottage with it. "Who are you?" Temperley heard himself asking.

He knew the answer, but he had to say something to break up the deadly suspense.

The left sleeve rose in response—the right still remained directed towards them—and brushed off the slouching hat. Above the expressionless eyes was revealed a ragged, zig-zagging scar. It zig-zagged upwards from the top of the nose to the farthest visible extremity of the forehead in the form of a letter Z.

"I see," muttered Temperley.

"Do you?" came the ironical reply.

"Yes," said Temperley. "I see that you are the person who killed—"

"A man in an arm-chair—an old woman in a field—a taximan at Boston? Yes, I am that person. You may like to know that I've added since to the list—"

Sylvia's fingers suddenly clutched Temperley's sleeve.

"—as I have had to dispose of my companion, who grew troublesome."

The fingers relaxed, and became weak.

"He lies dead in the pond out there."

"God!" exclaimed Temperley. "And you think it wise to tell us of these things—"

"I have already warned you once not to move," interrupted the man without arms, sharply. "The next time, she'll get a bullet. And you won't hear it. She'll just sink down on that bed and lie still—as the others have done."

"There must be some way," raced Temperley's mind. "There must be some way! There must be…"

"Wise to tell you of these things?" said the man without arms. "Why not? You won't be able to repeat them?"

"In that case," retorted Temperley, "you might tell us a little more." But his mind was still racing, "There must be some way—there *must* be—!"

"What more?" asked the man without arms.

"Have you been here before to-day?"

"Here?"

"In this cottage?"

"How does one get into a cottage without hands?" inquired the man who lacked them.

"And no one answered the bell, eh?"

"No one."

"You could have broken a window—"

"As you did?"

"Yes."

"And given the alarm? Why? There was no hurry."

"I should have thought there was considerable hurry!" said Temperley.

"Yes, you've thought a lot of things in the last forty-eight hours," replied the man without arms, "and in a minute you will pay for the thinking. I repeat, there was no hurry. If the particular person I wanted to see was in the cottage, he would remain there—provided I did not give him the alarm. And, if he was not—" He shrugged his shoulders. "So I returned to the car—gave the young lady a little more medicine, so that I could rely on her slumber for a few hours longer—and returned to the town."

"What did you do that for?" demanded Temperley, while thinking, "If only he steps a little closer, I might spring on him."

"Just to see whether I could find out anything," answered the man without arms. "And I did find out something." He paused. "In an afternoon local paper. It's on the local placards." And now he did advance a step, and his gaze once more turned on Sylvia.

"An old man has been found, some miles from here, lying by the roadside. A motorist found him and took him to a hospital." The tone of the speaker's voice changed slightly in quality. Unseen emotion was stirring him, but the voice remained steady and slow. "He never recovered."

A gasp came from the bed. Temperley longed to give comfort, but not for an instant could he relax his watch of their tormentor.

"What is the matter?" continued the expressionless voice. "I have not said who he was! He has not yet been identified. All that was found on him was a little bag of precious stones."

"By Jove—two more steps, and I'll have him!" thought Temperley.

"I wonder," said the man without arms, "whether those stones were his own? Or whether they had been stolen—say, twenty years ago? And I wonder whether he has not yet been identified because, since he took his last residence—in such a cottage as this, eh?—he has lived a very retired life? Yes, and whether the silly old woman who has been looking after him, and who is the only local person who can identify him perhaps, has failed to do so because she has rushed off to London—eh?—for advice from *you*, Miss Wynne?" He took another step forward, and his eyes began to glint.

"That's very possible, isn't it?" he went on, his voice now rising slightly. "Yes, I expect that is what has happened. But let others worry about that! Why should *we* three worry? We three in this room? That old man is dead—unfortunately; I had hoped to be in at the kill—and so we only have to think about ourselves now. And it was because of that I returned here, and waited till you came out of the dope. You see, I knew where you'd go as soon as you found yourself free—and alone. And *I* wanted to go there, too."

"Why?" asked Temperley, his blood racing fiercely.

"Why?" repeated the man without arms. His tongue appeared for a second, while they moistened dry lips. "I had to be quite sure—quite sure—that the old man *was* my old friend Ledlow. I had to be quite sure it was no mistake, or trick, and that he wasn't still here. I had to save my—two remaining blows, eh?—till I knew."

He glanced round the room. Temperley suddenly swore at himself for missing the moment. But there was still a considerable space between them.

"Well, now I *do* know," said the man without arms, "*and I can finish the little letter I have been writing!*"

The sleeve shot out.

"You'll hang for it!" cried Temperley.

"What!" shouted Z. "When I've been dead twenty years already?"

He bent forward. Temperley prepared to spring. But, just before he could do so, the madman leapt away, and was in the doorway again. He threw his head back with insane laughter, as his flapping arm stretched out once more. "The end!" he shrieked, and the wind shrieked with him. "The end! The end!"

Temperley stood before Sylvia. It was all he could do. He hoped vaguely that the first bullet would merely wound him, so that he could remain standing just as he was, shielding the girl behind him. But he wished the girl would keep still. She seemed to be objecting to his scheme, and to be struggling convulsively to take a place beside him…

Why didn't the bullet come? Why didn't the outstretched sleeve discharge its death message? All at once Temperley discovered the reason. The sleeve was no longer pointing towards him—it was pointing upwards into the air. Waving, rather…spasmodically…helplessly…

And the head that had been thrown back in mad laughter was no longer visible. It had disappeared, with its grim brand, out of the line of vision. The shrunken, flattening chest looked as though it had been decapitated.

As he had waited hopelessly for the silent bullet Temperley would have sworn that a minute had passed, but actually he waited merely a second, and when he found himself freed from the violence of his whirling emotions and realised what was happening, he hurled himself forward to assist whatever agency lay behind the madman to render him so impotent.

For a few moments he was in the middle of a wild struggle. He became conscious of fiercely-flapping sleeves whirling inadequately against capable hands. There was a pleasant sense of dark blue in the dim little passage, a colour that stood for officialdom and law and order, that might be delayed but that never ceased its effort. Then, all at once, the flapping sleeves ceased to flap, the galvanic form against which law and order were ranged became limp, and an ominous gap appeared in the wasted chest.

"God Almighty, 'oo done that?" panted a policeman, helping two more to lower the lifeless form.

But he would not have understood if he had been told that it was the last scratch of a crimson pen.

◊◊◊

Five minutes later, Richard Temperley returned to the bedroom. "All clear below," he reported, quietly. "And, now, how about you?"

He sat down beside her, and she took his hand.

"I don't know," she murmured. "I don't seem able to feel anything. Is that a good sign?"

"The best," he answered, giving her hand a squeeze. "But you felt that?"

"Yes."

"Then there's hope for the patient! And when the numbness has passed—perhaps we'll be able to save something from the wreck? You and I, Sylvia?"

"Is he dead?"

"Isn't it best? Poor devil! When you've a bruised brain, you're better out of it."

After a silence, during which he felt her fingers clasped tightly round his own, she asked,

"And—my grandfather? Do you think that's best, too?"

"I don't think it's best, my dear—I know it's best. Like the poor lunatic below, he's free now. And so," he added, "are you. What are you going to do?"

"I don't know," she answered. "You see—now, I've no one."

"I was rather hoping you'd say that," replied Temperley. "You see, it gives me such a lovely opportunity to correct you. My dear, you've got *me*. That is, if you want me. By the way, twenty thousand years ago I had a sister living in Richmond. She's heard your voice over the telephone, and she's longing to meet you. What about making her house your headquarters for a bit? You know, till you've got over the shock of all this—and can make up your mind about things?"

"But—I believe I've already made up my mind," she gulped.

"No! Have you?" he exclaimed, happily. "In that case, I've another suggestion to add. After you've stayed at my sister's, what about taking a really long honeymoon in Australia?"

And so life mingled with death, and light threaded its way through the shadows. And so, in this world of strange complexities, it will always be.

To receive a free catalog of Poisoned Pen Press titles, please provide your name and address in one of the following ways:

Phone: 1-800-421-3976
Facsimile: 1-480-949-1707
Email: info@poisonedpenpress.com
Website: www.poisonedpenpress.com

Poisoned Pen Press
6962 E. First Ave. Ste 103
Scottsdale, AZ 85251

CPSIA information can be obtained at www.ICGtesting.com
Printed in the USA
BVOW08s0405201115

427559BV00001B/1/P

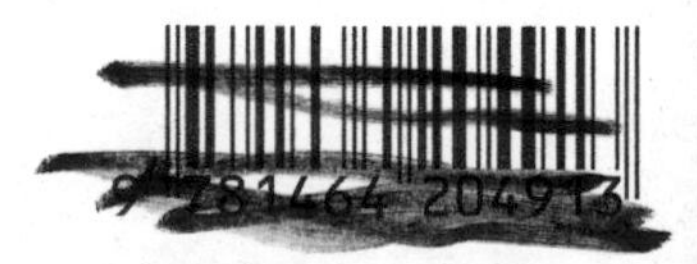